A STORG

When A True Mystery Opens

Paul Underwood

First edition published and printed in the United Kingdom 2023

A CIP catalogue record of this book is available from the British Library.

ISBN (Hardcover): 978-1-7392513-0-7
ISBN (Paperback): 978-1-7392513-1-4
Imprint: Independently published
Editor: Christine Beech
Illustrations: Rebecca Farrell
Typesetting: Matthew J Bird

For further information about this book, please contact the author at: Info@UnderwoodAuthor.com

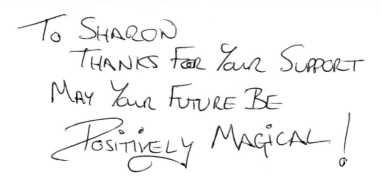

To SHARON
THANKS FOR YOUR SUPPORT
MAY YOUR FUTURE BE
POSITIVELY MAGICAL!

Dedication

To my Mother and Father, Roger and
Barbara Underwood. For their extreme patience and
faith in me and the kind support and encouragement they
gave so that I could get to where I am today.

Also I'd like to dedicate this book to you, the reader of
this book and wish you a positively
magical adventure ahead.

Thank you x

from

CONTENTS

CHAPTER 1

UNEXPLAINED DELIVERIES

Charlie was proud of his mum.

She had successfully given up a habit which brought torment and frustration to their home. She began smoking about a month after her husband, Roger Wafe, disappeared. Her friend from the bingo hall gave her a cigarette to help relieve the stress, which became unbearable. But, far from calming her, it caused a dreadful cough which worsened over the two-year stint, and Charlie was concerned about what the cigarettes were doing to her insides. She stored a multitude of green Mint Imperials around the house and car to compensate. He often wondered if it contributed to her giving up hope of ever seeing his dad again.

There's been weeks of dreary rain over the holidays and school was about to start again. A bored Charlie propped his elbows on the window ledge, sucking on one of those said mints, with his chin nestling in his hands. He was deep in thought as he surveyed the hypnotic stream of water flowing along the street.

His mum pulled up in the car, with their neighbour in the passenger seat. They paused for a brief chat outside, near the front garden gate, keeping dry in the car. A sudden chill and the clatter of the letterbox broke Charlie's trancelike state.

Curious, he moved from his perch to investigate and found a scrunched-up piece of paper lying on the doormat. A quick scan of the floor confirmed it was the only item posted.

He hesitated as he approached the mysterious delivery. He became unnerved when he heard someone, or something, tampering with the lock and the door creaked open. Much to his relief, in stepped his mother, Jennifer, giving her umbrella its ritualistic shake before placing it in the rack. She tutted as she reached down for the screwed-up paper. What had been a dry piece of paper suddenly began to leak a steady stream of water. Startled, she dropped it and it landed in a mushy heap on the mat. She looked angrily at Charlie.

'What's this?'

'I dunno,' Charlie shrugged. 'It just came through the letterbox before you walked in.'

'Have you been playing games, Charlie? What have you been up to this time?'

'Nothing, honest. It literally came through the letterbox just now. I haven't touched it.'

'So, can you explain how this has just 'literally' come through the letterbox when I've been sitting out there for the last few minutes talking to Maureen? I certainly didn't see anyone pass by me. Is this some kind of joke?'

His mother raised her voice as she spoke, a signal to Charlie to acquiesce with a quiet sigh.

'Go to your room now please, Charlie,' she said, sternly.

Charlie turned towards the stairs, ascending silently as his mother gave him a slightly anguished look. But it wasn't long before she screamed for him to come back down as water was rising rapidly and the carpet was soaked.

'Charlie, can you please turn off the water for me? I need to find this leak. Quickly, it's everywhere.'

The water was above their ankles by the time Charlie had reached the bottom of the stairs. He dashed to the kitchen in search of the taps. With water weighing heavily against the cupboard door, he struggled to open it, only to discover that he'd picked the wrong cupboard. No off tap there. By that point, his mother was increasingly upset as the water continued to rise while she struggled to open the front door, hoping to let it out but to no avail.

After frantic attempts to open the cupboards, Charlie reached the final door and gripped it hard, pulling against the weight of the flooding water.

'At last,' he thought with relief, as he exposed the mains taps. He quickly turned them anti-clockwise to close them tightly.

'Got it, Mum!'

There was a momentary pause to check the water level before it became clear that it was still rising.

'Charlie, have you turned the right taps off?'

'Yes, I think so. But not one of the pipes is leaking in the cupboard, so why is the water still rising?'

He splashed through the water over to the kitchen window and, with a swift glance, noted that it was raining softly outside, and the ground was wet but not flooded.

This was getting stranger by the minute.

'Mum, we must try and open the front door. There's no flooding outside so we can at least get the water out that way.'

'Charlie, what do you think I've been trying to do since it started to rise? Come and help me.'

By then, the water was above Charlie's knees as he waded cautiously to the front door, where his mother was waiting. They pulled strenuously, trying to open the door against the weight of the water but, even together, it would not budge.

'Wait, Charlie, let's try the back door. It opens outwards so, hopefully, the water will flow out that way.'

They paddled back to the kitchen, waist-high in water, but the back door was already bowing. They managed to unlock it and began to push down the handle. But the water, all of a sudden, barely covered their feet and was flowing towards the front door.

Charlie and his mother stared at each other, puzzled. Without speaking, Charlie started to walk back towards the front door. As he entered the hall, he saw something that made his hair stand on end. A huge wall of water stretched from floor to ceiling and he couldn't see the front door.

Without hesitation, he turned tail and ran towards his mum who was still at the kitchen door.

'Mum, open that door quickly,' he cried, intent on making a run for it.

A loud crashing and whooshing noise from the hallway became louder as a huge tidal wave headed straight for them. As Jennifer managed to wrench open the door, the wave threw them out into the muddy garden. Smashing windows on either side of the back door, with glass shards spraying dangerously close, the full force of water swept them away and pinned them up against the splintering wood at the back fence.

Charlie and his mother hit the fence with such force that it caused the wood to split. As quickly as the phenomenon began, the water faded away as if it never happened, abandoning them as they sprawled in muddy puddles in the gentle rain. Glass and splintered wood panels were strewn everywhere, and Charlie thought they were lucky not to have been torn to shreds.

He then looked at his mum filled with worry as she was already back up on her feet. He saw she was giddy and woozy, trying to reach out for something to balance herself on before she fell. Charlie quickly got up and grabbed her arm, helping to steady her unstable footing and lurched them both back towards the house. A loud crack, snap and thud filled the air. The large apple tree in the corner of the garden fell where they landed only moments before. Any sooner and they would not have survived.

Charlie and Jennifer spent a day at the hospital and were given the all-clear, bar a couple of bruises, his mum suffering slight concussion but luckily nothing was broken. It took a couple of weeks to fully recover, drain the house and a tree surgeon managed to salvage the apple tree, replanting it with supports back in its sheltered corner of the garden.

The water company finalised their inspection but found no reason for the tsunami-style attack. It was a mystery. The recent downpours had not caused any flooding anywhere else in the town. Everyone was baffled. At least the weather, fortunately, changed to brighter sunshine and the house was moderately dry, although there was still a musty waft of dampness, mixed with the sweeter smell of air freshener dotted around the house. Neither Charlie nor his mum ever mentioned the events of that day again.

The only memento was the crumpled paper that came through the letterbox which started dry, dampened, then miraculously began to leak water from it somehow? Charlie found it in the corner of the garden a few days later by the replanted apple tree. He decided to keep it, hoping to find out how and why the flood happened. He hid it on top of the wardrobe, in a tin foil fortress which he built when he was seven. He has a bed-desk, with his bed on the top bunk and his desk below. He took tin foil from the kitchen cupboard, sneaked it upstairs and stepped from his bed over to the top of the wardrobe in his narrow bedroom. There he would build a fantasy world out of the foil. His parents often wondered why they ran out of tin foil so quickly, with no idea that the answer lay in a make-believe world on top of Charlie's wardrobe.

The following week, Charlie was lying on his bed reading a book when he felt a shiver and shook his cold shoulders. Then he heard the letterbox. He was not normally disturbed by it but this time was different. After whatever was posted landed on the ground inside, the letterbox flapped several times as though someone was tapping at the door for attention. It shouldn't have done this as it was one of those strong spring-close letterboxes.

It continued to flap until Charlie approached the door and it suddenly stopped. He looked cautiously through the spyhole. Nobody there. He was relieved as he didn't like visitors while his mum was shopping, especially unannounced ones. Looking down, he noticed a crumpled piece of paper on the doormat.

'Uh, oh!' he said out loud, with his hand on his forehead. He carefully picked the paper up and uncrumpled it guardedly. It appeared to be an old, dirty, scrunched-up piece of blank paper. 'Who could have stuck this through the door?' he wondered, confused that there was no one there, even though the clattering letterbox silenced as he approached the door.

He was wary after the last time but noted that the paper was dry as he carefully smoothed out the creases. He immediately regretted this when muddy sand started to seep out from one of the creases.

Charlie felt a rising panic. He couldn't seal it back in as the dry soil kept pouring out from the paper, all over the carpet. Charlie quickly attempted to close the paper around it to prevent any more spilling, but there was already a small mound on the carpet below. He just couldn't stop its flow.

Charlie ran to the kitchen door, holding the paper away from himself, with his hands cupped tightly around it. A trail of soil went through the house. He ran into the garden and buried the paper by the back fence.

The catastrophe was averted until Charlie locked the back door and heard the front door opening. His mother entered and froze on the spot as she absorbed the scene, noting his filthy jeans. Not wanting to worry her further after the flooding incident, he decided, perhaps unwisely, to slide the truth, believing it would be alright to tell a fib if it were for her own good.

'Sorry, Mum. My friend dropped off a bag of compost and it split. I've got rid of the bag now and was going to put that pile into my plant upstairs.'

His mother scrutinised him silently as he carefully carried a scoopful of mud from the carpet and headed towards his ill-fated plant upstairs. As he plodded downstairs for another handful, she surveyed the footsteps in the mud trailed hallway. Suspicion nagged her. Firstly, there was the water incident and now this. 'Is it a joke,' she thought, 'or maybe retaliation for something?'. That last thought only came to her because now and then if there's a quarrel between them, Charlie would bring up Roger, his dad and how nobody seems bothered where he is anymore.

'Charlie, you are going to spend the weekend cleaning the whole house from top to bottom. You're not allowed out until it's completely clean. Do you understand me?'

'Yes, Mum. I'm sorr—'

'No, I don't want any apologies. Just get it done. Make sure you give it a good vacuum too. I'll set up the wet vac with the cleaning detergent for where you've trodden some into the carpet. I guess at least it might help get rid of that lingering musty smell.'

Charlie gathered up as much of the soil as possible and his plant pot was overflowing. He felt bad that he hadn't told his mum the truth about how the mud got there.

He managed to remove the remaining mud with the dustpan and brush before using the vacuum. Whilst emptying this for the second time in the garden he spotted that the buried paper had somehow appeared above the ground. He examined the dirty looking, bedraggled piece of paper. Content that it was no longer spurting soil he discreetly popped it into his pocket to study later. Being very domesticated, he returned to his cleaning duties, needing to change the murky shampoo water several times.

Charlie was puzzled. Two unexplained deliveries. Two crumpled pieces of paper with mysterious, supernatural power. He hid the second one, along with the first, in his tin foil fortress on top of the wardrobe. Now and then when he was alone, he'd bring them down and study them but found nothing unusual. One had watermarks and the other was old and dirty, but nothing distinguished them as different or powerful.

***

Two months passed since the second delivery which left Charlie on tenterhooks. He wondered if it was significant that they happened when he was alone. 'Would there have been more,' he brooded, 'if my mother hadn't been keeping a close eye on me?'

Likewise, his mother, who was also unable to forget the strange happenings, concluded that Charlie was the instigator, but she couldn't fathom how he managed it. Worried about him, she made sure she had everything done in order to be at home when Charlie returned from school, even picking him up now and then.

Finally, the weather grew warmer and one day Jennifer ended a lengthy phone call before turning to Charlie with a smile.

'Have I got good news for you? Aunty Kath is coming over and she's bringing your little cousin, Louise, with her. She's always asking after you, Charlie.'

'Yay, that's awesome,' he answered with excitement.

He hadn't seen his cousin in such a long time. He normally took her to his room, brought down his homemade castle and the figures he kept on top of his 'fantasy world' wardrobe and told her stories of princes, princesses and the dragon. He was excited by her visit, as sharing his magical world brought out his artistic nature.

'When are they coming, Mum?'

'This Saturday, so let's make sure the place is tidy, Ok? They'll be coming about lunchtime.'

Saturday soon arrived and the place was spotless. Charlie was up early helping with the housework. His mum, checking the clock on the wall, realised the time.

'Oh my, they'll be here in about an hour. I'm just gonna quickly pop to the shop and get us all pizza for later. You're okay just finishing off, aren't you, Charlie?'

'Yeah, of course, Mum, take your time. I'll entertain them if they get here before you're back,' he laughed.

He was really pleased to see his mum reflect his laughter as she hadn't been happy for a while. Half an hour later, proud of his housework achievement, Charlie fell back on the sofa, resting his feet on the table as he appraised his efforts. He felt a strange coldness go through his body which left as quickly as it came. He spied a lighter on the table next to his foot, probably left there from his mother's old habit and he grabbed it quickly just as he heard the front door. He thoughtfully shoved it into his pocket, out of his cousin's way, as he rose to greet her.

No one entered. Charlie was hit by silence. He checked the door and his heart sank as he saw a crumpled piece of paper, maybe parchment, nestling on the floor as if it had just been dropped through the letterbox.

He didn't hesitate. He quickly opened the door but could see no one. He even walked out to the front gate, scanning left and right down the long but empty street.

'Strange,' he thought, 'please, no weird stuff again, not now.'

Charlie sniffed the tantalising scent of barbecue in the air wishing it was theirs. His mouth-watering envy at the thought of beef burgers, which was his favourite. Then came another smell of a bonfire or something, why not, after all, it was a lovely day. Charlie turned to catch sight of grey smoke billowing from his front door. He was mortified to see that the paper that was delivered has set alight and the doormat was now on fire.

Despite his panic, he sprinted and leapt over the mat, almost catching his socks on the flame. He ran to the garden and grabbed the hose which, luckily, was ready for use. He turned on the tap and ran back through the house. The hallway wallpaper was alight and he sent a spray of water towards the blaze.

Neighbours began gathering outside, crying for Charlie to get out but he refused to leave. He had the fire almost under control as the fire brigade arrived with blue–lights flashing and sirens wailing. Together, they dowsed the fire just as Charlie's mother returned home and his aunt and cousin pulled up in their bright orange car. Jennifer rushed up the path towards the fire crew who were standing in the doorway.

'Charlie, what happened? Are you OK?'

'Your son makes a very good firefighter,' one of the men answered. 'He managed to put the fire out as we arrived. We have stressed the importance of getting out of the house immediately next time, especially with a fire of this size. It may be small but it can spread rapidly. We've checked the house over and it's safe. You're very fortunate to still have your home, Madam.'

'Thank you,' Jennifer replied gratefully.

She was about to hug Charlie when she spotted something glistening from the edge of his trouser pocket.

'What's that?' she asked as she pointed to it.

Charlie had forgotten about the lighter and only remembered as his mother pointed at his pocket.

'Ummm, nothing …'

'What is this then, Charlie?' she interrupted as, in one swift move, she reached into his pocket and pulled out the lighter.

'No, Mum, it's not what it looks like.'

She had no words and just stared at Charlie.

'Now, Madam, we can't always assume …' the firefighter interjected.

He was cut off as she turned towards him in a rage.

'Don't you be telling me what I can and can't say to my son.'

'I'm just advis—'

'No. Are you done here now?'

'Yes, Madam, we are for now. Can we just take your details for our report?'

Jennifer quickly went through her details. When the fire brigade went, Charlie was left to face his mother's anger.

Kath entered, followed by her daughter, as Charlie's mum turned furiously back to him.

'Not another word, Charlie. You go up to your room now and you're grounded for a week. Do you understand? In fact, don't even answer me, just go up out of my sight!'

A tearful Charlie ran silently upstairs to his room. Lying on his bed, he retrieved the remains of the scorched, but intact, paper he rescued from the fire, thankful that he hid it in his other pocket and was therefore undiscovered by his mother.

He flattened it out to inspect and, again, the mystifying pattern of the deliveries was another blank piece of paper. Not one word, symbol or drawing; just burn marks.

'How did they get there? Who posted them?'

No one was seen or heard when they plopped through the letterbox. None of the deliveries, so far, offered Charlie a clue to their origin or meaning.

CHAPTER 2

MYSTERY OF THE BLANK PARCHMENTS

Each time Charlie felt as though he was at fault. Caught in a variety of circumstances that gave the impression he was responsible. He knew he wasn't, but appearances suggested otherwise, leaving him despondent and thinking that he 'didn't have a leg to stand on' when professing his innocence.

He clambered down from his top bunk to study his reflection in the mirror, his messy brown hair almost covering his glazed hazel eyes. It was even more upsetting when he heard the muffled sounds of his mum and aunt chatting downstairs and his little cousin chuckling as she played.

He was still trying to make sense of everything that happened since his father's disappearance two years ago. His mother hadn't been the same since and never once spoke of him. Charlie was constantly standing in his father's shoes to help keep everything together as best as he possibly could. The recent appearance of those three strange deliveries caused increasing tension between him and his mother, and she didn't even know about the last two.

A couple of days after his grounding, when he didn't even get to see his cousin, he could still smell the burning stench despite all the cleaning and the great repainting job his mother did throughout the hallway. Thankfully though, this ensured the musky, damp smell, caused by the mysterious mud a couple of months ago, was finally gone.

Reaching midday, the sky was shrouded in darkness which made the atmosphere even more depressing and was very apt for the way he was feeling. His thoughts moved from his father to the three mysterious deliveries, but he was no closer to knowing who sent them or how they got there. He slumped onto his bed staring at the ceiling, hoping for a solution to present itself. He also wondered how he could prove to his mother that he had nothing to do with them, but he knew that would be impossible.

He began to mentally list the bullies from school as possible culprits, two in particular, but they were soon dismissed. For a start, his mother would have seen them approaching as they were rather big-boned, clumsy and noisy. Secondly, as far as he knew, they had no idea where he lived as he always made a conscious effort to ensure he was not followed and he was intent that it stayed that way. He then realised there's no point listing anyone as potential suspects. Each paper did something miraculous and magical. He knows of no wizard or witch nor anyone that could do magic, let alone whether real magic even existed until these three papers arrived. Charlie was getting frustrated.

He reviewed the situation. The same old parchment-type paper was used each time. All were scrumpled up and blank, yet each had differing distinguishing marks. One was dirty, another had water-stained blotches and the third was scorched.

He suddenly shivered, conscious of his darkening bedroom. He shuddered again, feeling a chill reminiscent of the coldness that had descended upon him before each delivery. Something was trying to get his attention and he nervously directed his gaze towards the window. He froze. Terrified by a shadow which was breathing condensation, he was rendered immobile.

Several items fell from the shelf as his room began to shake, snapping Charlie out of his stupor. The shadow moved stealthily away from the window and the room fell calm. Thumping could be heard outside his room and became louder with every footstep. The bedroom door flung open, making Charlie jump with fright. A very cross-looking mother stood in the doorway.

'Why are you causing such a racket, Charlie? And why are those books all over the floor? What the hell is going on?'

Charlie looked at her mutely, with tears prickling his eyes. His mother's expression suddenly changed to guilt. She approached him and checked his forehead for signs of a high temperature before enveloping him in a spontaneous hug.

'What's wrong with you, sweetness? These last couple of months you've been acting strangely. You seem to have changed. What's up with you, my love? Is it something I've done?'

'Mum, do you think Dad's okay? I mean, do you think about him?'

The loving moment was soon upstaged by the sound of the front door's handle being tried, followed by a knock.

They both looked at each other, a look imbued with wonderment and confusion. His mother sprang to her feet and began to head down the stairs, slowing cautiously as the knocking became louder and more violent, moving from benign to malevolent. She knew something wasn't right.

Halfway down, she halted, with her eyes transfixed on the door. The banging was so ferocious that the hinges were shaking, and the screws were loosening. Another mighty bang forced the door open with a crash and there appeared to be a mini tornado, spinning into the hallway.

Jennifer held the banister tightly and shouted to Charlie to get back into his room and close the door. Wood splintered from the stairs as the gale-force wind mustered impetus, causing the paintings to fly from the walls and the hallway carpet began to curl up.

The fracturing banister caused Jennifer to lose her grip. Charlie, who had disobeyed her command to hide in his bedroom, grabbed her hand and placed it against the top balustrade for support. He then grabbed her other hand by the wrist and began pulling her towards him on the landing. With every effort, Charlie dragged his mother closer as she attempted to lessen the pressure on him by using the miserable remnants of the banister as a stepladder. This was proving increasingly difficult as fragments of handrails, ornaments and artwork were spinning around the outer edges of the hurricane that was increasing in strength and size. At one point she lost her footing as the banister beneath gave way, sending a slipper flying into the tornado's orbit. If it was not for Charlie's quick thinking, by giving her an almighty yank upwards to reach safety, she may well have followed her unfortunate slipper into the eye of the storm.

Diving onto the comparative safety of the landing, they fell in a heap against the back wall as the wind subsided. As the tornado suddenly dispersed, a swirling piece of crumpled paper fluttered to the floor spinning to a halt. They exchanged looks and Charlie hugged his mum in reassurance. They were visibly bewildered by what happened and the resulting devastation.

They hugged as the rain pattered into the hallway until a call, from the gaping hole where the front door used to be, disrupted their embrace.

'Hello, is anyone there? Are you all okay?'

Charlie and his mother quickly stood, brushing off the debris, before Charlie answered.

'Yeah, we're fine thanks.'

From the blue flashing light in the hallway, they quickly realised that the police were at the door, or space, as it now was.

'Mind if I come in and check on you both? Is anyone else here?'

Charlie's mum remained frozen and silent, tears adorning her cheeks. She managed a nod to invite the officer in.

Charlie took the opportunity to carefully pick his way through the rubble, negotiate the loose boards and unobtrusively pick up the scrunched-up paper. As he pocketed it, he recalled the other mysterious deliveries and associated hazards, each so different.

No sooner had the memory started but it was over, and the officer was already next to Charlie and his mother as they walked towards the kitchen.

'Are you okay? You seemed to be in a world of your own just then, shaking. Looking at this place, I can only imagine how you're both feeling. I'll make you a cuppa, shall I? Then you can tell me what happened,' said the police officer.

Memories of the four deliveries were spinning around in Charlie's head.

'I'm okay, thanks. I'm just gonna go and chill in my room for a bit,' he said, as he cautiously picked his way upstairs to his bedroom, hoping to reassure the officer that it was safer than it looked.

In place of the fear, Charlie felt a growing excitement that he needed to figure out the meaning of the deliveries. He knew there had to be something. A clue somewhere on the four pieces of paper he collected. His mind went into overdrive. Puzzles excited him. Was it a clue to his father?

He was drawn to the silver fortress and decided that while his mum was preoccupied with the policeman downstairs, he'd take the opportunity to re-examine the other three pieces of paper. He climbed up to the top bunk and eased himself onto the top of his wardrobe knowing that, if anyone was to walk in, they wouldn't see the papers.

He lifted the fortress. The three pieces of paper were there as if waiting. He proceeded to flatten them as best as he could and pressed the four together so that they made one big square. He studied them keenly but no answers sprang to mind. He turned them around one at a time, but still nothing. He knew which element belonged to which because of their markings. Water stains, earth stains, scorch marks and the last one, which was windblown and misshapen. He rearranged them a little but still nothing made sense.

Charlie almost fell off his wardrobe when a bang against the door made him jump. He carefully hid the four pieces of paper under the fortress and climbed down to see what fell inside the wardrobe. It was just his school bag; a reminder there was homework to do for school, to be handed in the next day. Maybe it was a good thing it fell, as he'd forgotten all about it and he only has that night to complete it. He took out his workbook and began. Luckily it only took him just over an hour to finish; a quick job but passable.

He feared the two bullies in his class at school. They were on his mind constantly, whenever he had school, as he never knew from one day to the next what they were going to do. They were cruel and showed no remorse as they often wound Charlie up about his missing father. He was too afraid to react to them. He would often be sent home when he feigned sickness by wetting his face to give himself a sweaty look, or half chewing a digestive biscuit which looked effective when he threw it up in style.

CHAPTER 3

AN UNORDINARY SCHOOL DAY

Charlie managed to get through the first four days back at school but on Friday there was a sharp sting against his shoulder. He lunged forward, knocking items from his desk. As they scraped noisily across the tiled floor the teacher turned towards Charlie, ominously placing down his marker.

'What's all the commotion about? Charlie, I've already told you once to sit still and copy what I'm writing on the board. Is that too difficult for you to understand?'

Charlie sat speechless, acutely aware of his bullies sitting closely behind him, giggling.

'Charlie, I'm sorry, but this has gone on far too long. I'm going to have to ask you to go and see the headmaster. Now, please.'

'Yes, Sir,' Charlie replied solemnly.

He retrieved the items from the floor and placed them safely inside his desk. He snatched a daring peek at his tormentors, Griff and Dennis. Dennis was still holding the compass and a snigger accompanying his threatening stare was enough to signal Charlie to remain quiet. Charlie went to leave but Griff extended his leg, tripping him up. The class burst into laughter, much to his embarrassment. He picked himself up and speedily exited the classroom. His teacher raised his voice above the raucous noise, demanding the class to be quiet, echoed as Charlie-closed the door behind him.

He walked through several corridors and descended several flights of stairs. The corridors were empty and only the muffled sounds of teaching behind classroom doors signified life. The journey to the headmaster's office seemed to go on forever and Charlie was puzzled by his growing sense of foreboding. When he got that feeling, it always preceded something out of the ordinary. He felt it on the day his father left home and never came back and, more recently, with the mysterious deliveries of screwed-up paper.

A cold shiver settled as he approached the headmaster's door. He paused for a moment before tapping. Despite his gentle knock, the sound reverberated through the stillness of the corridor. A voice from within the office bade him enter. As he reluctantly pushed open the hugely heavy door, the first thing he noticed was that the office appeared so much bigger on the inside, reminding him of the antiquated central library building he used to visit regularly. The library's familiar smell of wood wafting through his nose and the creaks of age teasing his ears were always a delight to his senses.

'Charlie Wafe.'

The sound of his name brought him back to the situation at hand, snapping him into reality. A tall elderly gentleman, holding open a seemingly antique book, appeared from behind a bookcase. His gaze was transfixed on the pages for some time until he finally slammed the book closed, spraying ancient dust into the air, as he looked sternly at Charlie.

'Charlie Wafe. I might have guessed you'd be the first visitor to my new, well old, temporary office. I have to say that I rather like it and I may even request to stay here permanently.'

Mr Grimauld, the headmaster, grinned proudly whilst surveying the room and relished the opportunity to share his satisfaction. He sniffed the air as he stretched out his arms graciously, almost flamboyantly, turning ninety degrees towards his desk before sitting. His hand gestured to the vacant chair on the opposite side.

'Take a seat.'

He dropped the heavy book on the table with a thud, unsettling dust and causing Charlie to jump with fright before reluctantly obeying. Charlie was taken aback by a design that he recognised on its front cover. He was mesmerised by it but couldn't understand why. It was a large black book which once had beautiful navy and gold embossed writing on the front cover, but some of the lettering was now worn and illegible. He was fascinated by the book and wanted to borrow it but it wasn't the time to ask, and the headmaster broke his thoughts when he smacked his hand on top of it.

'What brings you here, Charlie? What have you done this time?'

Charlie was about to speak when storm clouds began to cover the outside of the windows. He thought he could hear the faint rolling of thunder. The office darkened quickly. The automatic switch on the desk lamp clicked on in response and vapour from Charlie's every breath was suddenly tracked by the light. He began to shiver as he noticed a familiar dark shadow at the window. It seemed to evaporate as the window slid open and closed itself.

Charlie's attention was brought back to Mr Grimauld who remained still. In the lamplight, he noticed the headmaster's eyes widen with the shiny blackness of an onyx stone. He suddenly jerked awkwardly, with his head looking uncomfortably rigid as he gazed up at the ceiling. He let out a painful moan as his eyes closed. Slowly his head levelled and his eyes snapped open to stare directly at Charlie. A flame-like redness shone in them and he began to speak in a deep echoey voice.

'Deliver.'

Paralysed with fear, Charlie yearned to run from the petrifying situation but couldn't make himself move. Confused and afraid, he clung tightly to the sides of his chair with his nails digging into the wood. Trembling, he could barely speak.

'W…what, Sir?' he asked in a squeaky voice.

The headmaster leaned forward, a dark frown deepening, as he chanted:

'Elements foretold to one so bold

Will take you forth to the cave so old.

The courage of a lion leads to the Father of Zion

But a choice will unfold for you to behold.'

The lamp bulb shattered and darkness shrouded the room. Charlie jumped. Realising he could feel his limbs once more, he rose slowly from his chair, hoping that his movements were unnoticed. Bolting for the exit, he fumbled for the door handle in panic. Books started flying ferociously around the room, hitting the door and walls around him with force. The headmaster laughed. A maniacal, possessed laugh. Charlie managed with difficulty to start pulling the door. A heavy book narrowly missed his head, breaking against the frame next to him as he managed to duck in time. Prising open the door was a battle, as there was a wilful force working against him keeping it shut. With fear-mustering strength, he managed to pull it open wide enough to squeeze through despite an unidentifiable pressure trying to pin him against the doorframe. He slithered through the narrowing gap in the doorway just as the door slammed shut in apparent eagerness at the opportunity to crush his foot.

Leaning back, Charlie stood momentarily to catch his breath until a sudden blow to the office door, the resulting shudder shaking it to its hinges, propelled him into the hallway. Dashing down the corridor, he launched himself through unlocked doors, relieved that he was on the ground floor as the doors obligingly led him across the school grounds. Ignoring the sound of his name being called, he sped along a shortcut over the playing field towards prickly hedging at the edge of it. He clambered through the bush where the students had made lots of tunnels towards the hole in the fence leading into the field next to the school. They had made the hole for easy truanting and getting out without the hassle of queuing at the secure entrance, without security knowing. He darted out through the wire fence and away from the school premises to freedom. He continued crossing the field to the pathway and sprinted down the street to the right, running onwards a few hundred yards, before reaching the bottom of the steep hill which led to his home.

Charlie stopped. His breathing was laboured as he crouched in pain. He clutched his side where a stitch began nagging him halfway through his desperate escape. He risked a glance back for the first time since running away from the school. It looked clear. Charlie noticed the dark clouds had dispersed and it was like a dry and normal summer's day. There was nothing but a gentle breeze, giving relief to the heat.

He scanned the hill. Not far now. Composing himself, he walked slowly up the hill, glancing behind now and then to check if he was being followed. Although there was nothing behind him, and despite the steepness of the hill, he hastened his pace and forced himself to stop looking back. After seven minutes into a journey which normally took about fifteen, he reached the Pastures. This was a small park at the top of the hill that he crossed daily, and his house was located on the far side of it.

He couldn't make sense of what he just experienced. Doubting the wisdom of crossing a wide open space after what happened, he decided to walk around the park, believing the streets to be safer. He couldn't get that book out of his mind or the look on the headmaster as he chanted those words in that strange voice. Fortunately, nothing more eventful occurred and Charlie, at last, reached home.

He saw his mother looking out the window with the phone to her ear. She didn't look in the best of moods as she put the phone down and scuttled to the front door.

'Charlie, what's going on? I've just had the school on the phone.'

Charlie clammed up and didn't answer. It was a trait of his whenever he was in trouble, even if he could defend himself, that he'd just stay quiet and take what was coming. He knew it would be pointless to try and explain to his mum what happened. It was way too out of the ordinary to be believed.

'Well don't just stand there, Charlie Wafe, get in here,' she beckoned vigorously.

Charlie entered the house quickly to avoid a scene in the street, knowing there would be trouble as his mum used his full name. She grabbed his arm and pulled him towards the sofa. He sat down meekly as she continued.

'I've just had your teacher on the phone, very concerned about your behaviour and safety. I heard what you've done to the headmaster's office too. You'd better have a good explanation for why you trashed it.'

Charlie sat silently in frustrated disbelief, knowing that he had done nothing wrong throughout the whole ordeal and was now facing his mother's wrath because of his school's blatant lie. He could feel the heat of his cheeks as they flushed. He wanted to tell her how he was being bullied at school and what happened in the headmaster's office but he just couldn't. His mum had been through so much since the disappearance of her husband, Roger. She'd become very fragile and had lost hope of ever seeing him again.

Charlie lowered his head, shaking it to confirm his lack of explanation. He decided to apologise as a tear dripped down his cheek. His demeanour changed his mother's emotion and she sat next to him on the sofa, placing her arm around him.

'Charlie, you're only twelve, coming up to thirteen; your teen years already. You've been through so much, Babe. We've not seen your father for the last couple of years, and it's bound to affect you, Love. Honestly, we'll get through this together, I promise. And in answer to your question last week; yes, I do think about your father, every day. Not a day goes by that I don't hope he would walk back through that front door.'

She hugged her son tightly as he broke down in sobs and her tears flowed too.

***

At this point, Charlie had a flashback to a day in the hills with his father a few years ago. It was his first time riding his bike, as he started much later than the other boys and went straight onto two wheels without stabilisers for assistance. It was tough at first but Charlie's confidence started to grow as, after several attempts, he managed to stay on and balance. Until he rode too close to the edge of the hill where the bike set its journey downwards. Losing control, Charlie fought to keep his balance but, with gripping fear, he wobbled towards some bushes. When he tried frantically to apply the brakes it felt as if he was about to be thrown over the handlebars. He changed tactics and attempted to turn the bike instead.

It was too late as the bike continued to pick up speed. He screamed out for his dad and was too scared to look around in case he fell. There was nothing more Charlie could do as his bike came to a complete stop and catapulted him over the handlebars to land smack in the middle of a thorny bush.

His dad tousled with the bush to get to Charlie and lift him out. He placed him on the grass next to the fallen bike. The bike was not in bad condition, considering, apart from the chain coming off. But Charlie wasn't so lucky. Bruises on his wrist were already developing and small cuts to his skin appeared where the thorny bush had scraped him. His father tended to his scratches.

'Are you okay, Son?'

'Yeah, just hurts a bit … ouch,' Charlie answered, trying to hide how much he was hurting while his dad plucked at the loose thorns.

'That was quite a spectacular fall there, Charlie. I'm proud of you, Son. You did very well on your first attempt. It's not something to feel embarrassed about. Come on, let's head home. You can try riding your bike again when I get that chain back on.'

'No, it's okay, Dad. I'd rather not thanks. I don't think I want to ride that thing anytime soon.'

Charlie was afraid. Roger sat down in front of him. He stretched out his arms, placed a hand on each of Charlie's shoulders and looked him straight in the eye before giving this advice.

'Look, Son, that may have scared you right now and understandably so. You're probably thinking you don't even wanna go near that bike again. But let me tell you now, you need to beat this thought, fight it as soon as you can. Let me tell you why, Charlie. To conquer and defeat this fear you're feeling, you need to get up and face the cause of it immediately. Think of your achievement already. You got up, you balanced and you rode, within a day. That's special as there aren't many that can say that.'

They looked towards the bike and back at each other before his dad continued, 'Don't pause, don't wait and never give up. While you can still walk, you can still ride. You're to get on that bike once we get it back up there and then you can ride it next to me carefully, at a walking pace. If you falter, make excuses and walk away from this, the fear that you feel now will fester and grow. It may affect you so much that you might be too frightened to ride that bike ever again. You'll develop a phobia of it. You may miss an opportunity for a wonderful adventure and a world of discovery because of it. Would you want that?'

'No, of course not,' he answered immediately.

His father stood, straightened the bike and held his hand out to Charlie.

'So come on, Son, are you ready to try again?'

Charlie felt strength and confidence, understanding exactly what his father said. He beamed an understanding smile and nodded. His father grabbed his hand to help him up and then showed him how to fix the chain. They walked together, wheeling the bike back to the top of the hill. After Charlie had mounted, his father adjusted the handlebars slightly as they'd slipped out of alignment with the wheel. They then took a slow journey home and Charlie felt proud of himself for managing to keep his balance all the way.

***

The memory faded as Charlie refocused his thoughts back on the room, prompting him to hug his mother tighter. He idolised his father. Any mention of him upset Charlie deeply, rendering him unable to formulate thoughts about him. No one knew what had become of his dad. Roger Wafe left home one day to attend an exhibition, having discovered something so significant that it could change the world's history. Mysteriously since that day, almost three years ago, he had not been seen or heard from.

Charlie didn't mention what happened at school. His mother showed strength for his benefit but he was fully aware of her fragility. To tell her what happened would surely push her over the edge. He could never lie to his mother. He knew when to stay quiet and it was usually for a good reason.

Or so he thought.

CHAPTER 4

OPERATION RETRIEVAL

It turned noon, lunchtime, affording him time to head back to school. But he was afraid. As though reading his mind, his mum stood her ground.

'Right, Love, I'm gonna make you a bit of lunch. See if you wanna go back in this afternoon now, okay? I'll let your teacher know we're coming back in and see if he wants a chat with us.'

Charlie knew he had to go back at some point. Why not now? He remembered his dad saying he needed to conquer his fear and take it head-on. His mother and teacher would be there. If anything happened, at least it would be witnessed. He still had the image of that book in his mind and if he could get it, he would. One thing about Charlie is that he's a very quick logical thinker and can find a way around a situation no matter how scary it is. He knew he had to hold it together for his mum's sake.

Charlie nodded agreement, with a slight smile.

'There you are then, my lovely,' said his mother, ruffling his medium-length brown hair.

Soon enough, Charlie ate his corned beef sandwiches and a pack of leek and ham-flavoured crisps, washed down with a glass of Dandelion & Burdock before he was ready to brave school.

His mum was already waiting in the car when Charlie locked up the house and clambered into the passenger seat. Ensuring his seatbelt was safely on, Jennifer turned the key in the ignition. Nothing. She tried again. Still nothing.

'That's strange,' she tutted. 'I only just got it back from the garage this morning, it was perfectly fine then. What's wrong with it now?'

After trying the ignition several times and pulling the key out and putting it back in again, still nothing. Charlie looked towards the bus stop where a few people had gathered.

'Mum, I think the bus is due if you want to try that.'

'Nice one, Charlie.'

On vacating the car, as his mother was locking the car door, they heard the faint sound of a bus engine in the distance. They sprinted towards the bus stop as the bus was appearing from around the corner. The driver seemed well-known in the area and the passengers took time to chitchat before taking their seats.

Charlie's school was the fourth bus stop from his home, but it's generally overlooked by the bus driver. If he ever stopped at the third stop and reminded them that they needed to get off, they'd just disembark there as it was only a five-minute walk up the hill, so Charlie's mum asked, 'Can I have two 3-stop hop tickets, please?'

They took a seat as the driver set the bus in gear, the door closed with a hiss and the engine started to sputter noisily.

The bus jerked forward. All the lights flickered and then went out, along with the engine. The passengers heard the driver's frustration, muttering under his breath at the faint sound of ticking as he repeatedly turned the key in the ignition. The engine didn't even want to try and kick back into life. The passengers' suspicions were confirmed after hearing snatches of the driver's annoyed conversation on his radio. He left his cabin to speak to them directly, calling for quiet.

'Sorry about this everyone. The bus has broken down. The office is aware and will be sending a replacement shortly. If you'd like to remain seated, we'll get you on the other bus when it arrives shortly.'

The annoyance of some passengers bristled the air as Charlie and his mother decided they may as well sit and wait it out. Jennifer took a pack of green Mint Imperials from her bag, offering one to her son. Ten minutes went by before a vehicle carrying some engineers stopped behind the bus. One opened something at the side rear of the bus, possibly to get access to the engine. The other, covered in oil stains, boarded the bus to talk to the driver. They switched places.

'You'll not have got much further anyway,' the engineer informed the driver, 'as the traffic is horrendous down the road. One of the large oak trees on the embankment fell into the road about five minutes ago.'

Charlie and his mum instantly looked at each other, knowing intuitively what the other was thinking. They could easily have been under that felled tree if they'd journeyed by car or if the bus hadn't broken down. Jennifer was visibly shaken by this news.

'Come on, Charlie, let's go home. I'll call the school.'

'Mum, we can walk. It isn't far,' Charlie beamed.

His mind had diverted to the book that the headmaster slammed onto his desk, and he desperately wanted to find it, or borrow it, although he doubted borrowing was an option. He'd have to find a way to take it for now, then, maybe return it … somehow … later.

They disembarked from the bus and started the walk. Dark rainclouds swamped the sky. Only moments earlier it was blue and sunny. The weather, as always, was unpredictable. A flash, causing them to jump, was followed by a loud roll of thunder. The rain was pouring but they were already halfway to school and had reached the huge stricken tree which caused horrendous traffic problems. Flashing yellow lights indicated that a heavy goods vehicle was already at the scene to lift the tree. Flashing blue lights warned of the hazard ahead as the emergency team attempted to control the traffic congestion.

Luckily, the umbrella Jennifer always packed in her bag was accomplishing a sterling job against the heavy downpour, managing to keep Charlie and at least half of her, dry. Before entering the main entrance of the school through the security gate, and after a quick phone call, they continued into the main school building. She shook the rainwater, which was dripping from her umbrella, onto the threshold. Once inside, she placed the umbrella against the glass so that it could dry while they were in the school.

'Right, where do we go, Charlie? You can lead the way. I was told to pop by the headmaster's office.'

Smiling, Charlie guided his mum along the winding corridors. She was understandably lost in the labyrinth and trusted that his sense of direction would lead them to the headmaster's office. Turning a corner, Charlie could see the door at the end of the hallway. He wasn't feeling the same emotion that he felt earlier, maybe because his mum was with him. He reached the door.

'Hang on a sec, Mum,' he said, knocking on the door.

There was no answer. Nonetheless, he rotated the doorknob, slowly pushing the heavy door inwards. Again, it struck Charlie that he wasn't feeling as afraid as he was previously. He peered into the office.

'Sir?'

Still no answer. Turning, Charlie held his hand up toward his mum and signalled her to wait while he went into the office. He approached the desk cautiously, noting the shards of broken glass from the lamp's lightbulb. There, still sitting in the middle of the desk was the very book he wanted. He remembered being captivated by it when Mr Grimauld first appeared, clutching it firmly in his hands. Charlie was fascinated by the huge navy blue and gold gilt lettering adorning the front cover. Feeling odd again, he knew instinctively that he had to move quickly. The compelling feeling of being drawn towards the book intensified. Not hesitating, he whipped off his backpack, unzipped it and shoved the book inside just as he heard his mother talking to someone in the corridor.

Hastily zipping up his backpack and wriggling his arms through the straps to secure it on his back, he ran to the chair opposite the desk and sat, rather breathlessly feigning innocence, as the headmaster and his mother entered the room.

'Sorry, Reginald,' his mother said to Mr Grimauld, 'I was under the impression you were already in here by the way my son asked me to wait a moment. I was waiting for him to call me in.' She scowled at Charlie and asked him, 'What are you up to?'

The headmaster's first name, Reginald, was rarely used. They had obviously made their introductions in the corridor before entering the office.

'Nothing. I thought I'd sit and wait for Mr Grimauld first, especially as there's only one chair.'

He patted the wooden arms of his chair. Jauntily swinging his legs, he grinned cheekily at them as he spoke. His smile slowly waned. The realisation of something weird, bad even, dawned on him as he noticed the cracks and dents in the office door behind where his mother was standing. Mr Grimauld grabbed another chair and placed it next to Charlie.

'Please take a seat, Mrs Wafe.'

'Oh, please just call me Jenny, honestly.'

The headmaster moved across to sit behind his desk, looking more pleasant this time. Charlie was feeling nerves kick in, knowing he had the book; the book that seemed to have started everything, in his bag right now, as he sat opposite the headmaster. He tried desperately to look casual and not give anything away.

'Are you okay, Charlie?' asked Mr Grimauld, noticing his flushed cheeks.

'Yes thanks, just feeling a little under the weather, that's all.'

'I think the weather's affecting all of us, to be honest, Charlie. First sun, then a storm. But I'd like to hear your side of the story of what happened. I remember seeing you come into my office but from thereon I only know that I woke with such a headache and my office looked like a bomb hit it. I had a few bruises on my arm but there was no sign of you, and it concerns me what happened.'

Mr Grimauld rolled his sleeve up to show dark bruising along his arm, precisely where he'd held the book. Charlie decided to explain as close to the truth as possible while making it believable.–He knew nobody would understand what happened and he'd be in so much more trouble.

'Well … you came from over there,' Charlie said, pointing to the gap between the bookshelves. 'You asked me to sit down, then you looked very wobbly and knocked several books from the shelves before you fell onto your chair and started mumbling things I couldn't understand. Your face looked very strange and it scared me. I decided to run. You just weren't making sense and it was like I wasn't here. I'm sorry, I didn't mean to run.'

'I can understand how it may have come across as scary, but next time, I urge you, Charlie, to please call for an ambulance. If you don't have a phone, pop into the staff office along the corridor and use one there. Don't worry, you're not in trouble. There was a pile of books against the door inside the office which was enough to tell me you hadn't caused this mess. They were all piled up enough that if someone had opened the door to get in or out they'd have been clear of the door. I can only assume that I'd knocked them over, or something. Again, I'm sorry if I frightened you, Charlie.'

Studying his face keenly, the headmaster paused for a moment, rubbing his head a little in thought, then continued.

'I'm going to let go of the fact that you were sent to me by your teacher. But please, no more disruptions in class. We do have a nurse in the school if you need to talk about anything. It's the weekend tomorrow, so I suggest that you go home with your mum and dry yourself off for a start. Try to relax and enjoy the weekend. Come back refreshed on Monday morning. Now, if you'd like to wait outside, Charlie, I'd like to have a quick chat with your mum if that's okay.'

Charlie nodded silently, leaving the room with a sigh of relief. It could have gone so much worse but it left him wondering what Mr Grimauld and his mother were discussing. He strained to make sense of the subdued mutterings coming from the other side of the door. It felt like forever, but it was only around five minutes before the office door opened and his mother was thanking Mr Grimauld for holding it ajar for her to leave.

'No problem, Jenny,' Mr Grimauld said. 'It was nice meeting you. Have a good weekend, Charlie, and stay out of trouble.'

He gave Charlie a reassuring wink and a smile.

'I'll update your tutor, so don't worry. Get yourself home now.'

That was it then. All seemed settled. Charlie felt slightly reassured but continued to wonder what his mum and the headmaster had talked about. She seemed quieter than her usual self on the journey home. It was nice getting back to their cosy dry house out of the rain. As they entered, through the front door, a faint smell of roses from the air fresheners that were almost ready for replacement tickled his nose.

'Right, Charlie, pop up and have a quick shower and change those damp clothes. I'll have one after you. We'll have a chat before tea tonight.'

'Okay, Mum.'

He gave a cheeky smile again, one he hoped would calm any potentially hostile situation ahead. He turned and headed upstairs, relieved that school was over for a couple of days. Racing to his bedroom, he threw his bag into the corner, grabbed a towel, undressed and headed to the shower, unaware that his schoolbag had started to shine a golden glow through an opening in its zip.

CHAPTER 5

SINISTRE WREAKS HAVOC

Elsewhere in a mysterious cavern, darkness reigned. Only a gentle breeze and the rhythmic sound of dripping water echoing throughout signalled life. A new presence, heralded by pattering feet, broke the calm as it stumbled over scattered rocks, sending them tumbling onto the rocky ground.

Two slits of light appeared in the darkness, widening to show a pair of eyes, glowing red. The dilated pupils, shrinking to elliptical gashes, narrowed at the centre to an hourglass shape as scampering feet approached before coming to an abrupt halt. Beneath the eyes of the waiting one, a chilling baritone voice began speaking.

'I hope you bring me good news, Sinistre. You've successfully brought me the book of the prophecy, no doubt.'

Sinistre fumbled a little as he attempted to release his words, still breathless and trembling.

'Uhhhhh, ummmmm …'

'Get to the point, I'm waiting. Give me the book NOW and don't say you haven't got it.'

A sudden bang echoed through the dark cavern, followed by rubble falling from the impact of the creature's fist.

Sinistre shrieked, recoiling into the safety of his lizard shape, resembling a dishevelled chameleon but larger, standing on two of his four feet when still. On this occasion, hunched on four feet, he quivered. His natural colour was a dirty green with patches of brown shedding skin dangling loosely in places. He wore an old waistcoat to help maintain his body temperature. Unnoticed in this dark place, he turned a shade of red when the voice from the darkness shouted.

The silence felt eternal as the voice from the darkness, in a moment's flash, came nose to nose with Sinistre. The stench of rotting meat accompanied his cold breath.

'Where is it? You've failed me again haven't you?' it shouted, coating Sinistre in spittle with each word, forcing him backwards.

'Not exssssactly, sire … I've located the book and I've made very good planssss to retrieve it.'

The ground shook as huge claws thudded hard, one by one, onto the ground on either side of Sinistre. The creature pushed hard against Sinistre's nose.

'DO NOT let me down or I'll close the door myself to that despicable world out there, while you're still in it.'

Sinistre knew that would be fatal to him. Creatures from this realm were unable to cross the threshold in their physical forms, so became spectres when passing through. Without getting back through the gate, within a certain time, the spectre would evaporate and die, taking its physical form with it as it disintegrated.

'Pleasssse, massster. Don't lock me out … you know what that will do to me.'

The creature, still shrouded in darkness, screamed out his command.

'GET OUT OF MY SIGHT. GET THE BOOK NOW AND DON'T RETURN UNTIL YOU HAVE IT.'

Sinistre was already scurrying away at great speed before the creature even finished his sentence, stumbling on rocks in his haste to escape the roar that shook the cavern.

***

Back in his bedroom, Charlie was ready for his first day at the local wrestling club. He loved watching wrestling on the television at the weekend and, after a little push from Mum, he decided it would be a great idea to give it a go. He was a little hesitant but knew it could benefit him as he'd contemplated using wrestling to stand up against the bullies, Griff and Dennis. He imagined slam-dunking them through the school tables with their workbooks flying everywhere and the cheer he'd get from the other students. They put so much pressure on Charlie that it was starting to take its toll.

He changed into his shorts and slid on the old green loose T-shirt he kept scrunched up in the bottom corner of his wardrobe. It wouldn't bother him if it was torn while he performed. He didn't want to destroy his favourite T-shirts when there was a possibility that they could tear during a wrestling match; that is if he was to have a match, of course. He'd only just started so it was unlikely.

He almost skipped down the stairs excitedly but felt a little nervous too as he called out for his mum.

'I'm ready,' he smiled.

'Awww, good for you, Charlie. I'm glad you're giving this a go. I think it'll help you loads. Just be careful now that you don't get hurt.'

'I know, Mum. Thanks,' he said, smiling again.

Jennifer grabbed the car keys from the hook and they left.

***

At the school, even though it was closed for the weekend break, Mr Grimauld was busy tidying his office. In just a few weeks, he'd grown to love his occupation and had applied to the board to make it a permanent arrangement.

While he was dusting down the paintings on the office wall, he felt a coldness on the back of his neck causing his hair follicles to stand on end. It had gotten very dark outside through the window. He paused for a moment before heading back to his desk and opening a drawer to retrieve his office door key, preparing to leave. He'd decided to call it a day as something just didn't feel right. He'd felt this before when Charlie was in the office and, even now, he didn't know what happened that day as the whole experience was blanked from his memory.

The ground began to rock. He reached for his desk to steady himself as the room began to darken and blur. From the corner of his eye, he could see a slightly dark mist moving on its own and edging towards him. He ventured closer but the mist moved quickly and was soon directly behind him. He had no chance as the entity floated over the top of his head and in through his wide, frightened eyes. He fell back into his chair. Becoming rigid in his seat with his eyes tightly closed, he surrendered to the pain and writhed in agony before relief came and the ground corrected itself.

He snapped to attention and, once again, amidst his lifeless eyes of darkness, glowed a red centre. Sinistre had taken control. He gave a deep dark frown as he scanned the desk and then surveyed the office. He was looking for something. His eyes diverted to the drawers on the desk. He held his hand out and, without touching them, each drawer shook for a moment then slid out from its housing, floating for a second until he put his hand down and let them collapse to the floor one at a time. He then leapt from his chair to the first cluttered drawer that was on the ground and scratched through the contents, having them fly erratically around the office in a clumsy mess. Whatever he was looking for wasn't there. He continued to the next drawer and finally the third drawer, before grabbing each of them, hurling them across the room with his newfound strength and smashing them against the wall.

He looked at the bookcases filled with dusty old books. It had to be there. He stood but instead of walking towards them, he bent his elbows, opened his arms then gracefully floated high enough to grab each of the books on the topmost shelf without the need for the stepladder. He glided along the shelf with his hand raised and, as he scanned over each spine, the book slid out of its housing and dropped to the ground. This continued until all the books on the top row of the library lay strewn around the office floor leaving the top row empty. He then repeated the process until the books, once nestling comfortably on the shelves, now carpeted the office floor.

The headmaster's face contorted in pain as he opened his mouth wide in rage. He floated with his arms still outstretched. He let out the loudest roar, shaking the entire room, as the books were hurled from the ground, hitting every wall and breaking to pieces. Some of the heavier books shot at the bookshelf like bullets, destroying the ancient wooden shelves. Sliced into splinters, they fell into a pile of wood on the ground. The desk slid backwards, hard against the wall below, breaking apart as the window shattered outwards.

By now, the school alarm started ringing, causing the staff members in the school to evacuate. A couple of heavy books flew through the opening, where a window once was, and scattered in the field outside the office with a thud, alerting the small crowd gathering at the evacuation point.

'Wait, Reginald's in there,' said Mr Smith clearly worried, as he watched the commotion.

As he spoke, distant sirens were closing in. The school alarm, linked directly to the fire station and police headquarters, triggered their immediate dispatch. They raced into the school car park and screeched to a stop. The fire officer, first at the scene, approached the group gathered on the school grounds.

'Who's in charge here?' he enquired, needing to be advised where the safety zone boards were and the location of a potential fire.

As the firefighter gathered vital information, a police officer approached. Books launched through the window, like projectiles, heading straight towards the crowd. The officer was quick to leap forward, bringing several people down with him to avoid injury as the books whistled past their ears. They hit the ground just a few inches away, with the force impaling the lawn, leaving them buried in deep holes in the ground.

In the ensuing panic, the officer led them from the school grounds and out to safety through the gates leading out of the premises. Whilst doing this, he radioed dispatch for urgent backup. A teacher moved forwards with his clipboard and advised the police officer that everyone was accounted for, apart from the headmaster, Reginald Grimauld.

The officer returned to the firefighters advising them to retreat to their vehicle for their own safety as a precaution. By now, they'd established that there was no smell of fire but there was obvious danger as more objects, including parts of a wooden chair, flew from the smashed window, with sharp ends skewering the grounds.

There was now a new urgency that became a matter of high priority. It was to try establishing the whereabouts of Mr Grimauld and if he was safe. Another two police vehicles arrived. A sergeant approached the officer covering the gates, to give a briefing.

Back inside the office, Mr Grimauld remained floating about a foot above the ground with his arms outstretched. His eyes, now jet black and glowing red in the centre, were scanning everywhere. He let out another roar, sending a whirlwind of debris through the hole where the destroyed window used to be. The stonework in the office began to erode and give way. Papers, wood, books and debris were flying around him with great speed. Mr Grimauld, distracted by the commotion outside, placed his hands back to his side to lower himself. Everything spinning around him suddenly stopped in motion, dropping straight to the ground. He closed his eyes tightly in a deep frown, thinking hard about where his prize might be. It was clear that it was no longer in the office.

In that meditative state, an image of a boy flashed into his mind. Then something very strange happened. Sinistre, losing control of the headmaster's mind, began to shake so violently that his host body collapsed with flailing limbs. Sinistre was left as a misty spectre hovering in the air in momentary distortion.

Who was it? There was a flash of recognition but the image faded too quickly to be sure of who he thought he saw.

Mr Grimauld, although shaken, was starting to recover consciousness. Regaining his composure, Sinistre took back control of his host. Suddenly he snapped up straight and opened his black lifeless eyes. His thoughts were now on the boy who had been in his host's office … and to his location.

Sinistre was attempting to probe the headmaster's mind for information but he wasn't strong enough to gain access. Sensing a barrier, as though something was personally blocking him, in his frustration he decided to question the crowd outside, in the hope that they might know this boy.

His control took pace as Mr Grimauld threw his arms forwards. The wall leading outside crumbled outwards, dispersing into dust. He walked through the debris to view the carnage before approaching the police officers and the crowd of onlookers who were gathering.

'Where is the boy?' Mr Grimauld shouted to the crowd. The sound coming from his mouth was dark and echoey; it was not his voice. His stare caused unease amongst the crowd as they edged toward the exit of the school field. He cast a piercing glare at the teachers.

'I said, where is the boy?'

A police officer moved forwards, advising the headmaster to calm himself so they could discuss the boy for whom he searched. Mr Grimauld did not divert his attention and raised his right hand towards the officer. Like a rag doll, the officer was hurled with force against his patrol car, causing a deep dent in the side panel of the door before collapsing unconscious to the ground. The other officers were starting to react against Mr Grimauld but the headmaster raised his hand in warning. They decided to stand back.

CHAPTER
6

RELENTLESS

Focused on the teachers, he bellowed again, menacingly, as though it would be the last time he would ask them.

'NOW, WHERE IS THE BOY?'

Clearly afraid, the teachers trembled and were confused about who Reginald was referring to. The sergeant moved forwards raising a taser device at the headmaster.

'Now calm down, Mr Grimauld. I need you to come with us.'

The headmaster simply pointed a finger at the device before it exploded in the sergeant's hand. Bolts of electricity sent him flying to the ground, shaking uncontrollably, incapable of speech as his body vibrated.

The headmaster then raised both hands towards the group of teachers, and they started to quake in fear. Their feet left the ground, dangling helplessly a couple of feet in the air. By now several more police cars had arrived at the scene.

Officers were piling out and shielding behind the cars as they aimed their tasers at the headmaster.

Mr Grimauld ignored them, maintaining eye contact with the trembling floating teachers.

'THE BOY,' he roared impatiently.

At this same moment, an officer jumped, accidentally firing his taser at the headmaster. This set off the rest of the officers firing their tasers straight at him. He did not flinch but his face began to show great anger as he closed his eyes and absorbed the electricity bolts, relishing the power coursing through his body. He released his hold on the teachers, dropping them into a heap on the ground then raised his hands in the air. As he thrust both arms outstretched toward the firing officers, huge electrical bolts zapped through his fingers towards each of them holding a taser, engulfing them in electrical charges as they flew backwards a fair distance to the ground, in agony.

His eyes opened again, looking towards the huge crowd, but he'd lost sight of the teachers. His attention was diverted to the fire engine still parked in the car park. The firefighter had managed to turn the hosepipe very slowly towards the headmaster until it clunked to a stop. He only had to press a button and it would send a jet of water at him to force him off balance.

A teacher realised what the firefighter was about to do and called out to the headmaster to try and attract his attention. It was Charlie's teacher, Mr Smith, and he decided to pretend to know the boy for whom the headmaster searched.

'The boy. You saw him a couple of weeks ago in your office, didn't you?' he cried out.

The headmaster turned to Mr Smith and started to walk slowly towards him.

'He was the one I'd sent to you. You remember who it was, don't you?' the teacher continued, as he vaguely remembered sending a boy to the headmaster and was using that as an idea to deflect him long enough for the fire brigade to act.

As the headmaster started to raise his hand to Mr Smith, Grimauld was suddenly grounded as a jet stream from the hose unexpectedly hit full on, sliding him across the grassy field.

The crowd accumulating outside the gates ran in terror. The headmaster regained his standing position and put his hand out, creating a forcefield around himself so that the jetting water no longer hit him. Gritting his teeth in a deep frowning grimace he started to walk towards the fire engine, pulling his hand back, then in a quick motion pushed forward. The jet of water doubled up on itself, heading back to the hose nozzle, which caused it to explode and rip the tank open. Water poured out, flooding the entire car park and field. The headmaster raised his other hand and spun a circular pattern in the air, lifting the engine from the ground and launching it across the field, rolling and breaking apart in the process, leaving a couple of the firefighters sitting in random areas of the field.

The teachers, including Mr Smith, took this opportunity to head away at speed. The headmaster shook his head as he turned giddily. He looked towards the crowd, noticing it had dispersed, including the teacher who had addressed him. Sinistre slid himself out of the headmaster's eyes and let him fall in a crumpled heap to the ground. The dark, shadowy mist seemed to be much more translucent. He'd lost track of time and, depleted of energy, he needed to reclaim himself by heading back to his realm as quickly as possible.

The entity flew at speed away from the carnage, over the hills, houses, waters, and headed back to the opening of his realm, leaving the rumpled awkward shape of the headmaster unconscious in the field. The team of ambulance and police, taking advantage of his incapacitation, moved the unconscious headmaster onto a stretcher, handcuffs in place, to where they were tending the injured.

Fading fast, Sinistre only just made it to the opening. With great relief, he managed to cross the threshold before turning back into the frail lizard-type creature of before. He decided not to report the latest fiasco to his master as he knew the news, that he hadn't found the book, would possibly lead to his execution. He sat, meditating, unaware of the book's whereabouts. He tried to visualise the boy in the office at the time the book was last seen. Sinistre was frustrated and confused because, as much as tried to remember, he just couldn't access certain parts of his memory. His mind was blank, as though something was preventing him from retrieving the information. He knew it had to be important, which frustrated him even more.

Who was this boy?

It would only be a matter of time before he discovered the boy's identity and location.

***

Meanwhile, Charlie was making himself fall backwards onto a mat and slapping his hands flatly on impact. The wrestling instructor approached him as the lesson was coming to an end.

'Charlie, you're doing very well for your first session. But remember, you need to keep as flat as you can when you fall. Slapping your hands on the ground will take the impact and disperse it, so you don't hurt yourself. It's much better than letting your backside hit the mat first. I bet you're feeling it there right now, aren't you?'

Charlie laughed a little and nodded in agreement. He could feel the ache in his lower back when his bottom tried to break his backwards fall first.

'Honestly, Charlie. Really well done on your first day. Loads don't even attempt the fall on the first day and I was pleased to see you were very involved. That's what we like to see. I think you'll make a fine wrestler. Keep it up, Charlie. You should be proud of him, Mum,' the instructor said, as he smiled towards Charlie's mum who was approaching, having watched the session.

'He's my champ. We'll have to see how it goes,' Jennifer smiled, ruffling Charlie's hair.

Charlie smiled back with confidence. They left the gym to begin the ride home and Charlie was buzzing with excitement.

'Did you see that, Mum? It felt amazing. Can't wait until next week.'

'I saw it, Charlie, you were really good. Looked painful though, are you okay with that?'

'Yeah ... feels achy on my bum, but all good,' he smiled.

They drove by Charlie's school on the way home and noticed that there were blue and white strips across the entrance and police were standing guard.

'I wonder what happened there, Mum.'

'I'm not sure, Charlie. Hope everyone's okay.'

'Yeah, me too ...'

They both felt a little unsettled and remained silent for the rest of the journey home.

The moment they arrived home, Charlie popped upstairs to his bedroom and pulled out his tablet. His mum went into the living room and started to boot up the PC she had on a desk in the corner of the living room. Charlie searched the internet for anything about his school. Then the headlines started to roll.

"Headmaster's Insanity Leaves Several People Seriously Injured and a School in Devastation."

"Seven emergency force team members in Critical Condition, a school in ruins after Headmaster's Rampage."

"Crazy headmaster still unconscious as emergency forces suffer and a school is left in ruins."

Charlie was shocked.

His mother called from downstairs. He ran down, leaping the last three steps at the bottom and raced into the living room. His mum was sitting at the computer screen. Charlie could see the school and the huge hole left in the wall with rubble everywhere. The school didn't look as bad as suggested by the headlines he just read, but he knew that the hole was where the headmaster's office was. It all started to make sense. Charlie knew that the headmaster would not have done this knowingly. He remembered the day when he went into the office and the headmaster was clearly not himself, as though controlled by something, or someone, like a puppet. He couldn't mention this at the time because it would have sounded ridiculous. Who would believe him?

Charlie returned to his room where from the bottom of his wardrobe he lifted the base panel to pull out the dusty old book he'd acquired from the headmaster's office that day. He wondered whether it might be what the headmaster was searching for. It made sense. As those thoughts were circulating his head, the book began to sparkle, intensifying into an emanating glow. Charlie felt the book was calling out to him.

'Read me,' it enticed.

He quickly put the heavy book under his quilt in preparation. He knew his mum would be heading to her therapy shortly for a couple of hours. He needed to be sure that he wouldn't be disturbed. He went through his schoolbag, pulling out his pencil case and grabbing a notebook from the shelf. He looked up toward his tin foil kingdom on top of his wardrobe, thinking that the four parchments he hid there might be connected to the book. He decided to leave them, for now, in their secret place.

There was an unexpected knock at the front door. His mother opened it to a familiar voice and his immediate suspicions were confirmed when she called him down. Charlie left the room and saw his teacher, Mr Smith, standing in the hallway, smiling up at him.

'Hi, Charlie. I was hoping you have a minute to talk, please.'

Charlie nodded in agreement, following his mother as she led Mr Smith into the kitchen and invited him to sit at the table.

'Would you like tea, or coffee, maybe?' Jennifer offered.

'Ah, no thanks, I won't take up much of your time.'

The three sat at the table and Mr Smith began.

'I'm sure you're aware by now but, if not, Mr Grimauld has been hospitalised. He seemed to be insane and not himself. I'd never seen him like that before and I admit that it was frightening. I can't explain what I witnessed but it was shocking, to say the least. He seemed … like someone else, it just wasn't him.'

Charlie and his mother shared a worried glance, then returned their attention to Mr Smith as he continued.

'Basically, Charlie, the reason I'm here is … there's something that hasn't been mentioned in the news stories and articles that are out there.'

He paused before saying, 'I think he was looking for you, Charlie. I can't be sure but he was asking for 'the boy' constantly and the only person I could think he meant was you. I haven't told anyone about this but my immediate thought was to let you both know.'

Jennifer interrupted, 'But why do you think he's referring to my son? Is he in any danger?'

'I don't think you've anything to worry about, at this point,' he answered. 'Whatever was happening stopped before he could get any information. I only think it might be Charlie because Mr Grimauld's office has been demolished. Books, wood and stone were everywhere, similar to what had happened when Charlie was in his office, except that day it was only the books in disarray, not the whole office wrecked. I'm only guessing, and he hasn't, as yet, picked up on a name but when he kept shouting, "Where is the boy?" Charlie here popped into my mind. That's partly why I don't think that *thing* we witnessed was the headmaster. He'd have known straight away that it was Charlie.'

The kitchen fell silent and all that could be heard was the ticking of a large clock on the kitchen wall. The scraping of the chair legs woke everyone from their thoughts as Mr Smith stood to leave.

'I'd best go now, Charlie. I don't want to arouse suspicion by being here. I hope you both stay safe. I'm sorry but I felt compelled to let you know my thoughts.'

Charlie's mum assured him that she was very grateful as she led him out of the house via the front door. She returned to the kitchen, but her demeanour was solemn and her complexion was ashen.

'Charlie, what's happening to us? There have been so many things happening lately, it can't be a coincidence. Do you know anything about this?'

Charlie remained quiet, not wanting to worry his mum.

'I'm not sure whether I'll be going to that thing tonight, Charlie.'

'No, Mum, you must go. It helps you so much. I'll be okay, honestly. I've always got the neighbours if I need something or feel unsafe. You love that group, and it helps you. It'll be awful if you miss it. Plus, we don't exactly know if it was anything to do with me. You heard what Mr Smith said, he doesn't know either.'

'I dunno …'

'Please, Mum. Ultimately, we don't know and we're only guessing. I'm feeling fine and would feel much better if you keep going to your therapy, Mum.'

'Okay … but I'll let Maureen next door know to keep an eye on you. As long as you're sure now, Charlie.'

'Absolutely, Mum.'

They hugged each other before Jennifer grabbed her coat.

'Right, Charlie. There's a micro meal in the fridge if you get hungry. I'm just gonna pop to the neighbour quickly and then I'll be off. Anything you might need, Love?'

'Nah, I'm fine thanks, Mum. Hope you have a good session tonight. See you when you're back. Safe journey.'

They gave each other a big hug once more, and then Jennifer dropped a quick kiss on her son's forehead and left, locking the door on the way.

This was it. Charlie felt quite apprehensive but was determined that he might find answers to what was happening with that book. He knew what he had to do.

He sat on the bottom stair, staring at the front door for several minutes until he heard the car door close and saw his mum driving away. He stood, then bounded up the stairs to his bedroom and the mysterious book hidden under his quilt.

***

Back at the hospital, the headmaster lay unconscious with his wrists handcuffed to the bed railing and a guard waiting on a seat by the door. The guard didn't notice the dark entity slink into the room through a small gap in the window. He just felt a chill, shuddered and stood up to close the window. By this time the entity, with renewed energy, had travelled across the room and gained access to Mr Grimauld's body, easing through his lips which remained slightly parted by an inserted tube. It all happened so quickly that it passed unnoticed.

A new officer entered the room and, after a brief handover, was alone with the patient and took the warmed seat. He began to involuntarily jiggle his legs, wishing he'd at least used the toilet before starting his shift. It was too much, he had to go. He checked the motionless Mr Grimauld who was secured in handcuffs and connected to wires and tubes.

'There's no way he'll be going anywhere anytime soon,' said the officer to himself, leaving Mr Grimauld unattended as he raced for the nearest toilet, located on the corridor just beyond the private room.

From the cubicle, he heard a loud bang and smash followed by a piercing scream. Realising the source, he quickly composed himself and ran back to the patient's room to see a nurse in such shock that she was being physically supported by a doctor. There was a huge hole in the outside wall. Tubes and wires were dangling next to the now-empty, hospital bed.

The headmaster had escaped.

CHAPTER 7

THE SACRED BOOK OF TALLEMSEEN

Charlie was on his bed where the book was hidden under the quilt. He felt a slight warmth flow through him as a soothing glow emanated from underneath the quilt. He pulled back the cover, ready for his first thorough look inside the book. A brilliant golden circle glowed around an ornate design of an island with slightly leaning trees on a sunny day. It was this design that attracted Charlie and made him determined to have the book, whatever the cost. He was still wondering why it affected him so much.

He sat on the bed with his legs crossed. He reached for the book and lifted it onto his legs. It felt heavier than he'd remembered and the glow seemed to diminish as he placed it in a comfortable position. The black cover was solid, possibly made of wood, and had an ancient design embossed around the golden circle and the beautiful island design within.

Charlie felt comfortable. It was as though the book has been calling him, and,- now they were together, they felt like one. He quickly flicked through from the back. The edges of the pages flickered a golden light which reflected the sun from Charlie's window. Faded designs surrounded the words that were central on the pages which were aged with a tint of beige. The words did not make any sense as they were in a mixed bundle, maybe even in another language. However, when Charlie reached the first page of the book, it was different as it was written in English and easy to read.

He paused for a moment, confused why only the first page was in a language he knew. He started to read.

'Welcome to the Tallemseen. If you are reading these pages, the book has found its way to you. Please understand that what you are about to read will change your life. You have a choice. Close this book and never return, in which case you must destroy it. Or continue to read and embrace what is within.

It will not be easy. If you have chosen not to read this book, there is only one way you can destroy it. You must set it in flame, then scatter the ashes in the wind where the earth meets the water. By reading these words, you have opened the enchanted gateway so this book must not end up in the wrong hands. If you decide to read on, then embrace it and take very seriously what you read and learn within these pages. It will be your teaching, your growth and your origin. Please be warned, you must never abuse your gift.'

Charlie closed the book firmly. This was strange. He felt something open inside himself and strongly believed that the book had something to do with it. Throughout his life, he often felt things, especially if there was a warning or possible danger. This new feeling within him was amazing.

He decided that the bedroom was not an ideal place to read the book, so he quickly popped it back under the quilt and leapt from the bunk. He knew the perfect location to read it in safety but he had to prepare first.

He headed to the kitchen and mashed up a banana before spreading it between two slices of bread. He then picked up a Pink Lady apple, pulled a packet of leek and potato crisps from the cupboard and a strawberry Ribena carton from the fridge, and then placed them all neatly into his lunchbox. He went back upstairs and emptied his school bag. He put his lunchbox into it and grabbed a towel from the airing cupboard which he used to wrap the book carefully before placing it into his bag. He then popped back downstairs to the lounge, grabbed a cushion that wouldn't be missed from the sofa as there were so many, and managed to squeeze it into his bag. Finally, he went to the front door to wait for the right opportunity.

He wrote a message on the notepad near the front door explaining to his mum that he'd decided to go on a nature walk as the weather was good. Charlie was interested in nature so that wouldn't surprise his mum. He unlocked the front door and was careful to lock it behind him before heading for the woods. They were close, literally just across the Pastures, in the opposite direction to his school.

Charlie often explored the densely populated wood. It had all manner of wildlife, and he would log his findings in detail, along with drawings of an array of interesting foliage, birds, animals and insects, in the numerous notebooks he kept.

A few months ago, he started making a treehouse and got as far as creating the floor and basic framework in the lower part of an old tree which was hidden between a thicket of bushes. It was surrounded by a cluster of trees deep in the centre of the wood. It was Charlie's secret hiding place where he felt safe. He clambered through the circle of trees and pulled back the loose part of the bush that he used to cover the entrance to his private area. He scrambled through the small hole in the bush and covered his tracks before pulling it back into place.

He then climbed the tree and perched on the wooden flooring which was low enough to be hidden from the view of any passers-by. He pulled the cushion from his bag, placed it on the slightly uneven wooden floor and made himself comfortable. With his lunchbox next to him, he finally unwrapped the towel, folded it neatly to provide a cushion and laid the book on it, in front of him. He sat back with a reassuring smile, mesmerised by the intricate design and admiring the work that someone put into it.

It was too late to turn back now. Charlie decided to read it and continue the secret journey the book mentioned. He was conscious of how much time he would have to read, as he wanted to get home before his mum returned, despite having left her a message. More because he didn't want to answer questions on something he'd not done. Then he recalled that only the first page was in English, and the rest was gibberish, so maybe he didn't have to worry too much about time. Regardless, he felt strongly there was something more to it, perhaps a code or secret he could recover, decipher or solve.

He opened the book and began to read from where he'd read previously at home. Whilst reading each word, he felt a warmth flow within him...? By the time he'd reached the bottom line of the first page, he felt confident with a particular strength that he'd not felt before. He felt slightly hesitant when he read …

'If you feel ready to continue, please turn the page. If not, please put the book in a safe place until you are ready. If you do not wish to be part o7f this great journey with its dangers, you must destroy this book so that it never falls into the wrong hands.'

Charlie sat back and thought very hard about whether he was ready. This was something very big and he could feel the pressure of it starting to spin through his mind. He closed his eyes and breathed in the fresh air through his nose, listening to the sounds of different birds chirping their songs around the trees. He breathed out through his mouth, releasing the tension. He repeated this a few times as it relieved him of stress and helped him relax, compose himself and make the decision with the right frame of mind. He decided now was the best time to open his lunch box and he took a sip from the juice carton. It was a warm day and through the thick branches and leaves above, the sky was cloudless and a beautiful blue. He looked at the book and decided it was time. He had to turn the page.

He took his fingertips to the edge of the page and began to turn it. At that moment, a warm breeze encircled him and the scent of pine became more prominent as he inhaled a deep breath with his eyes closing into a trance. Charlie slowly opened his eyes while exhaling and he suddenly gasped as he was taken by surprise but confused at the same time. The writing which had been a jumbled mix of unknown words, that he was about to try and decode as he had his notebook primed and ready, was now written in English text that could easily be read by anyone. He was astounded and it took a moment to take the reality of this on board. He tried to remember if he had previously checked the second page because he felt sure that only the front page was legible. He was certain that the second page and onwards was unreadable yet here were words written in the English language. He started to flick through the pages after this one and all the words were still gibberish and unreadable. Maybe this page had been stuck to the first one.

He felt no danger but a certain intrigue and strength were building inside him as he decided to continue. He began to read the second page, and as he got down to the end, he read the words, 'You'll soon begin to unlock a newfound magic that has always existed within you.'

Charlie felt a strange tingle and shook his shoulders, feeling a chill like goosebumps. He was curious and wondered who the person of magic might be that the book was meant for.

He continued to read and, without thinking, flicked to the next page before realising it too, had become legible. He couldn't understand what was happening and how it was possible. He blew on the book in case dust or something had obscured the words, but soon realised that was useless as nothing changed. He decided to carry on regardless. By the time he reached the fifth page, the words only became legible when he read through the pages in order. He then read some words that he would never forget. They etched into his mind and made him feel uneasy. The words read …

'The prophecy will begin when the four deliveries of blank parchment are made. One of water, one of air, another of fire and one of earth.'

Charlie slammed the book closed.

'This isn't possible,' he thought.

He realised it had become silent in the surrounding woods, with no sound from the chirping wrens and swallows. There wasn't even the odd 'caw' from the crows. Even though he felt safe, he began to feel isolated and uneasy, as though suddenly the world didn't exist around him.

The familiar words he just read struck a chord. Charlie was sure the parchments mentioned in the book were the same as those delivered to him, now hidden securely in the tin foil castle in his secretly-created world on top of the wardrobe. He started to make excuses that the book had to be referring to something different, but then asked himself quietly, 'This book can't possibly mean those pieces that were delivered to me, can it?'

He wasn't sure if he should continue reading. It had become personal and too close to home. It didn't make sense that the book described exactly what had already happened to him. Could it be a coincidence? He wasn't sure.

He sat back on his cushion and took another drop of juice. He decided to eat one-half of the banana sandwich as it was already slightly brown by this point. He ate his apple and placed the core in his lunchbox. He then looked towards the book and hesitantly continued to read …

'The parchments alone hold their secrets but the only way to unveil them is to undergo the four trials. One for each element of the earthen realm. A trial by water, by air, by fire and by earth.'

Charlie now understood why there was nothing on the parchments, as he read on about the four trials. 'After completing each trial, part of a message will reveal itself within the page. This will continue until the four trials are completed, and the answer will be revealed as a secret prophecy. Until such time, you'll not be able to read on here.'

When he turned the page this time, the words were unreadable. It was obvious the only way to continue was if he was willing to take on the four challenges of the elements.

This scared him a little, as he now believed the book was referring to him and that he was meant to read it. But how and when would these trials start? Lots of questions raced through his mind.

He took out his notebook and started to make a few notes so he wouldn't forget. To be extra safe, he wrote cryptically in a code he learned from a children's spy book that he and his friend had when they were younger. They loved all that James Bond stuff even then and would often send each other secret messages written in lemon juice which could only be seen when held close to a flame. Charlie ate the other half of his sandwich before the banana turned black. It was sweet and he enjoyed it.

CHAPTER 8

WHISPERING BREEZE

Charlie turned his attention back to the book to continue, but he couldn't. At this point, the words were obscure, illegible and certainly not in a language he understood. How was he to find out more about the challenges? It didn't say.

What did the trials mean? Were they to be completed before the book revealed its prophecy? Or so he could read more of the book? He used all kinds of tactics in his notebook to decipher the scrambled text, but he couldn't.

Charlie reluctantly closed the book and wondered if there would be any clues for the trials ahead. Where are they? When? How would he know?

He continued scribbling in his notepad to tease a clue out of the words. He wrote 'Tallemseen' at the top of a new page and started to create a list of words from the title until he eventually found a ten-letter word which made perfect sense. 'Elementals.'

He wrote down the elements: water, air, fire and earth. His head was going into a spin now. He couldn't help feeling that the book and he were meant to find each other. He continued trying to decipher the elements until he saw something, as clear as day, that made him drop his notebook. He had to get off the tree for a moment and pace back and forth around its base. He was freaked out as he realised that the first letter of each of the elements made up his name. Water, Air, Fire and Earth spelt WAFE.

Charlie's thoughts were racing with so many more questions. 'Could this be pure coincidence? What does it mean? Was this book meant for me all along? Was this why I was drawn to it? Could this be a clue about my dad, who's a Wafe too?'

Charlie climbed back up to the platform and checked the book again. He could read up to the trials but the writing was obscure after that point. He closed the book and checked it carefully from all angles. That was it. No further clues.

He slowly finished the remainder of his lunch, in deep thought. So much started to make sense now but he felt the answer was further from his reach.

He packed the box, book and cushion back into his bag and was about to climb down, but something prevented him from going any further. He felt apprehensive and a little nauseous, the feeling he got when there was possible danger.

It seemed to have gotten darker, but when Charlie checked his watch, it was only just past two o'clock in the afternoon. He remained silent, as he lay on the wooden flooring, keeping as still as possible. There was no sound from the birds that normally adorned the wood.

Then Charlie heard it. Someone or something was close to the bush that hid his sanctuary. He heard steps encircling where he was lying. It stopped, then walked around the other way, and then stopped again. Charlie could hear deep intakes of air through its nostrils as though it was sniffing the surroundings. It sounded like a hound, sniffing about the bush, looking for a place to mark as his own. Charlie became tense and afraid as it seemed to get closer. He could hear scratching on the ground around the bush, but it was difficult to tell where it was coming from.

Any minute now and Charlie thought it, whatever it was, was about to uncover his secret den but then something strange happened. A seed appeared, one of those seeds that you're told to release into the open if you see them trapped, as they are hidden fairies and will bring you good luck. The round fluffy ones with a tiny seed in the centre.

It was floating for a moment, as they usually do, but this one had a glow to it and started to move irregularly. There was no breeze, just a certain coldness, but the fluffy seedling remained in the air just above Charlie, while moving in all directions.

Suddenly, he became conscious of the bush. Whatever was out there began to pull at it. At that point, the seedling moved at speed away from Charlie into the woods and a huge crack sounded in the far distance in that direction.

Whatever was trying to get through the bush had suddenly stopped with this disturbance. Charlie heard sniffing, then the sound of feet or hooves scuttling at speed, away from the bush, towards where the crack came from.

Charlie took that opportunity to climb down and escape. He scrambled to the moveable bush and pushed it. He was careful to check around and saw feet and handprints on the ground surrounding the bush. The handprints seemed to scrape at the ground in several places and then rest. He noticed a couple of crimson droplets by a part of the bush which the creature must have recklessly grabbed, trying to pull it apart. Charlie's adrenaline began to pump, and he made a bolt for it.

He ran as fast as he'd ever run before. He seemed to leap huge clumps and tree stumps with ease as the adrenaline kicked in. It wasn't long before he was out of the woods and back in the pastures. He continued to run across the pastures, back to his street, to his front door. He fumbled nervously for his keys, then managed to unlock the door, get in fast and close the door before securing it. It was only at that moment that Charlie could relax. With his back to the front door, he slid down in a slump on the floor, with his elbows resting on his knees, and placed his head into his hands in relief.

It was lighter again outside but Charlie remained where he was for what seemed like an age. He managed to compose himself, relieved that he hadn't been followed and headed upstairs to his bedroom. He took out the contents of his bag and stared at the book. He wondered whether he should keep it and go on, or get rid of it and forget everything. Too many weird things happened, ever since those deliveries arrived and the book came into his life.

He needed to talk to someone about what was going on, as he was starting to feel insane and alone. He decided to keep hold of the book for now and hid it back in the base of his wardrobe. He put his schoolbooks back into his bag and slung them into his wardrobe. He popped the cushion back onto the sofa in the living room en route to the kitchen, where he threw the crisp packet and empty carton into the recycling bin and rinsed out his lunch box.

He then returned to the living room and slumped onto the sofa. His heart had calmed down to a much better pace. He pondered about who he could talk to about what was happening. He didn't want to worry his mum but he knew he needed to tell someone because his experiences were starting to drive him mad.

The phone rang at that point, snapping Charlie out of his thoughts. He went over to the phone and lifted the handset.

'Hi, Charlie here.'

'Charlieeeeeee, haha, just the guy I'm after,' said a familiar voice.

'Kevin, wow I haven't heard from you in a while. How're things?'

Charlie beamed when he realised, from the voice, that it was his best friend whom he'd not heard from in a couple of years. He had to move to another town as his dad had got a new job in the city.

'Yeah, not so bad thanks, Cha. Sorry I haven't called for a while. Luckily, you've not changed your number. How've you been?'

'Yeah, not too bad thanks. Strange things happening but other than that, all good.'

'Hahaha, things never change with you, Cha. Always strange things going on. I'm just calling as my parents are planning to head back up there for a few days to stay with Aunty Lou, and I wondered if you were about so maybe we can meet up like the good ole times.'

Charlie couldn't contain his excitement.

'Wow, that'd be amazing. That's fantastic news. I'd be more than happy to catch up with you, Kev. I'm super made-up now.'

'Hey, easy Cha, haha. We'll take it a step at a time, not too fast now,' Kevin laughed.

'Haha, you know what I mean, Kev. Honestly, it'll be amazing to see you. I've missed you loads. I think we still had a wee spy mission we were in the middle of too, haha.'

'I thought it was a UFO mission we had when we found that Pufo egg from space.' They chuckled.

Kevin was referring to a large broken ping-pong ball, but they had decided it was an alien egg from a race called The Pufo. They had hunted for UFOs and found marks in the ground left by a hedge trimmer vehicle that they used to pretend were UFO landing marks.

'Yeah, I remember. We'll have to continue the search.'

'Yeah, definitely. Awww, Charlie, it's great to be in touch with you again. I miss you, to be honest, so when my parents said we were heading your way to stay at my Aunt's, I just had to call.'

'Yay, thanks. I'm soooo glad you did. I have so much to talk to you about. When are you coming?'

'In a couple of weeks, on a Friday evening.'

'That's great, Kev. I'll just check my diary. Haha, just kidding. I'm free as always.'

'Haha, I was gonna say the day you have a diary, I'd eat my cap. Well, I best be off now. Really looking forward to catching up with you.'

'Awww, me too and thanks again for calling. Will see you soon. Bye, for now, Kev.'

'Bye, Cha, and try and get your mum to make those Chocolate Krispie cakes she used to make us for when I get there. They were out of this world, haha.'

'Will do, Kev. See you soon.'

'Cool, see you soon.'

The phone clicked off and Charlie replaced the handset, realising he was beaming which he hadn't done for a while. He felt relieved and thought it was coincidental that he needed to tell someone about his crazy experiences and his best pal got in touch. It had to be a sign that he could trust Kevin with anything.

The phone rang again. It was his mum, just checking that he was okay. He took the opportunity to tell her that Kevin was coming up in a couple of weeks and mentioned the Krispie Cakes too. She was happy to hear that his friend was coming and, more so, to hear Charlie's excitement.

Whilst they were talking, a gentle breeze crossed his other ear and seemed to whisper, 'Charlieeeeeee.'

His mum realised that he had stopped listening for a moment and asked, 'Charlie, are you still there? Is everything okay?'

'Yeah. Sorry, Mum. I thought I heard something. Anyways, I best go. I'll see you soon. Love you, Mum.'

'No problem, Charlie. I shouldn't be much longer, but call if you need me, okay? Bye for now and I love you too, Babe.'

The handsets were replaced. Charlie hadn't felt afraid, but he had been caught by surprise and wasn't sure what he heard. Then a warm breeze seemed to wind itself, almost like a python, up his body and when it reached his ear, he heard another whisper.

'Chaaaaaarlie.'

He looked around the room but could see nothing out of place. He knew he'd felt a breeze but, strangely, he was not afraid. He wondered if he had heard his name or whether the quietness of his home was playing tricks on him.

He checked the window and saw that no one was there. He would have died of embarrassment if anyone saw him parading around, talking to himself when he asked, 'Hello, is anyone there? Can you hear me? If you can, please say my name again.'

Another warm breeze spun around his legs, spiralled upwards towards his left ear and whispered.

'Charlieeeeeeee.'

It then circled to his right ear and continued, 'It's time.'

'Wait. Time for what?'

The living room door was slowly pushed open by the breeze as if it was signalling Charlie to follow. This was confirmed when it came behind him, circled his head and felt like it was heading towards the door whispering, 'Folloooooooooow' as it trailed off into the hallway.

Charlie wondered whether he should follow, but instinctively knew he must. It felt right so there was only one choice he could make.

He went through the door.

CHAPTER 9

A PREPARATION OF ANCIENT POWER

Charlie followed the breeze whispering in his ears, beckoning him to follow. It seemed to lead him into the kitchen towards the back door.

He looked out of the door and saw a low mist over the grassy area. It didn't make him feel uneasy but it did feel a bit strange. He reluctantly went out into the garden, having locked the back door, and stood in the centre of the mist. It was different to what he expected, as though he was walking on water with the waves of mist lifting and lowering him. It was as though he wasn't touching the grass but floating.

Charlie then heard the same voice in the breeze, 'Quickly Charlie, si-i-i-t.'

As he sat in the mist, he had the strangely familiar feeling that something was about to happen. A feeling of dread struck him as the mist started to rise around him. Although he couldn't hear anything, he knew that something was banging the back gate ferociously from the other side, as the large black ring handle was pulsating. He saw the gate's hinge screws being forcibly pushed away from the post with every pounding. Just as the mist rose thick and fast, he could see the gate being smashed open. For a moment, before he was engulfed in the fog, he thought he saw his headmaster.

With a sudden intake of breath, Charlie thought that he was rocking slightly on the mist and that the fog around him was starting to thin. He felt as though he was floating forwards and could just about make out a large river, in the centre of which was an island with a huge tree in the middle. He had to squint to see this before the mist thickened again.

He was frozen to the spot. He dared not move for fear of falling.

He could smell wet grass and then heather before he felt a wave across his body as though he had gone through a curtain and then there were sweet scents he'd never smelt before. The mist around him started to clear, apart from the area he was sitting which, when he touched it, felt like cotton wool balls.

As the fog cleared, it seemed to be carrying him to a completely different place, where below him there seemed to be some kind of sandy desert, but the colour was a mixture of turquoise, purple and pink. He could see a settlement in the desert and then the cloud seemed to pick up pace as mountains appeared ahead. Charlie tried to find something to hold onto as he was perspiring and starting to panic, feeling very woozy.

'I'm sitting on a cushion on the ground. I'm sitting on a cushion on the ground,' he was saying, over and over in his head, trying to convince himself that he was not in the air.

Charlie started to rise higher towards sparkling clouds. He felt slight tickles as he went through them and, eventually, he could see mountain peaks above them. He was grateful to no longer be floating as he glided along some sparkling snow toward a mountain peak ahead.

This was confirmed as his misty carpet began to descend, then disappeared when Charlie was gently lowered to the ground, much to his relief. It appeared to be a grassy area but it was a light golden-sand colour and very soft to the touch, with a slightly furry texture. He plucked at it and managed to pull some out to examine it closely. He was fascinated as he had never seen anything like it. When he released it, it seemed to straighten before nestling back in its original location, as though nothing happened.

'That's strange,' thought Charlie.

When he eventually got up, he needed to sit down again quickly as he was unsteady on his feet. He had no idea where he was or what was happening to him. He plucked more tufts of the grass and again, as he let them fall, they seemed to split apart and fall exactly in the places he picked them from.

He lay back on the grass. It felt soft below him and very comfortable, but he was feeling more light-headed. Before he knew it, he closed his eyes, subdued to unconsciousness.

He wasn't certain how long he was out, but he woke to the aroma of hot milk. His blurred vision was starting to clear, and he realised that he was lying on a cloth in some sort of hut. In the centre of the room was a cooking pot, being heated over an open fire, with a type of chimney above it to let out the steam. Whatever was bubbling in the pot smelt of hot milk.

Charlie jumped when he heard the voice of an elderly lady, 'Ahhhh, he's awake, he is.'

His vision was still blurred but he could make out someone hobbling towards him, carrying a ladle. She was small, about half his height, with a friendly smile. The milky substance was steaming as she pushed the ladle towards his lips, and his vision cleared a bit more.

'Come on now, Child. You must drink this. Make you feel better.'

Charlie wouldn't normally trust an offer from someone he didn't know but he felt that he could trust her. He sipped from the ladle and the taste was amazing. Hot milk with a hint of cinnamon and maple syrup. It made him feel warm inside and he sipped more.

The elderly lady continued, 'There, there, my boy. You'll feel as good as new soon. You were very lucky.'

Charlie's vision started to blur again but he managed a smile before he lay down and drifted off into a deep sleep. The elderly lady smiled to herself and whispered, as she stroked his forehead, 'That's it, my boy. You sleep well. It'll help you recover and become stronger.'

She tasted some of the drink from the ladle and frowned slightly before heading back towards the cooking pot. She plucked what looked like a mint leaf from a plant growing close by and added it to the pot. It flashed with a soft bang and a waft of thick steam headed up the chimney.

'Yes, that's much better,' she said as she tasted it and gave a satisfied smile.

She hobbled back to Charlie and poured a small amount through his lips, after raising his head a little. He swallowed the elixir and smiled slightly as his head was lowered onto a pile of old clothes serving as his pillow.

A little time passed and he opened his eyes. He wasn't sure if he was in bed, after a dream, and felt disorientated. His eyes began to focus, and he sat up with difficulty as his head was still spinning. He was still dressed and lying on the floor, on a thick pile of blankets which seemed to act as a mattress. He could see a cooking pot in the middle of the room and steam going upwards through a chimney.

He was in an igloo-shaped hut with old clothes piled up as makeshift stools. At one end of the room, there was an area jutting out from the main hut, with glass to allow the sun through. It had a greenhouse appearance with lots of herbs and plants.

There was no one there in the hut.

Charlie slowly managed to get up and stretched. He could smell a lot of unique herbs and spices. He couldn't raise his arms as the ceiling was very low and he had to sit down again as he felt the floor move under his feet.

'Where am I?' he wondered, as his mind started to focus.

He could hear someone attempting to hum a tune near the opening of the hut. A blanket over the entrance was pulled to one side and Charlie remembered the lady he saw before drifting off to sleep.

'Ahhhhhh, my child. Good to see you awake at last. It's been a couple of days now,' said the stranger.

Charlie was confused. He rubbed his head as it was spinning a little. He needed clarification and asked, 'A couple of days?'

'Yes. Well, two and a half days. You were very lucky, to be honest, Dearie. We found you in the middle of some wolf fur grass. Very toxic indeed. Its spores emit a poison that kills anything venturing into it. Its roots then feed on the rotting flesh as they decay. Anyway, enough of that now. You're safe. It's good to see that you managed to make it through my child. I was quite worried to begin with if I'm honest.'

'Wow. Thank you. I'm Charlie, by the way. Charlie Wafe. One minute, I was in my garden and, somehow, I made it to here.' He had to lie down again as his head was throbbing.

'Ooh, you're not quite there yet, Dearie. Lie down and I'll fetch you something that will help.'

The old lady hobbled across to the herbs and plucked a few leaves. At the sink, she poured water over them in a sieve-style bowl before soaking a torn piece of cloth. There was no conventional tap. She opened a cover at the end of a pipe to allow the water to pour. Then she pulled a thick leaf from a plant sitting on a window by the pipe, snapped it in half and squeezed it. She kneaded the slimy white goo until the cloth was saturated, then she wrung it and hobbled back to Charlie. She carefully folded it and placed it across his forehead. He immediately felt its effects.

The scent was like lavender mixed with pine and the cloth felt cool. He closed his eyes as the tingling seemed to seep into his mind. The dizziness began to stabilise and the throbbing eased. He opened his eyes and saw the lady bringing a bowl on a small flat wooden board, with what looked like a couple of small buns on it and a roughly-made varnished wooden spoon.

'There now, Charlie. Try this. It's very good for you and you haven't eaten, which doesn't help. I'm Janairealonova, by the way, but you can call me Jan if you like. It's probably easier for you to say and remember.'

Charlie smiled and sat up, leaning against the wall. Jan placed the wooden tray on his lap.

'Thanks, Jan, for taking care of me too.'

Jan smiled at him.

'There, there, my child. It's the least I could do. You can rest a little more to build up your strength. But don't go wandering about out there, Charlie. There are huge drops on all sides up here and you might fall off the edge. You're safe in here though and in the small area around my home. I'm sure that Griflon will land at some point, so you can carry on doing what it was you were doing.'

She ruffled his hair and said, 'Now eat and build up your strength, Dearie.'

A lot of questions came to mind, but Charlie realised that he was famished, so he picked up his spoon and stirred what was like vegetable soup. He took one of the buns and dipped it into the bowl before tasting it. It was amazing. If you mix minestrone and chicken soup, then add a couple of herbs, that would be as close to the flavour as he could describe. The warm roll was soft and springy, with a nutty taste, and went well with the soup. He felt stronger with each mouthful.

Jan removed the cloth from Charlie's head before she went to the sink, unfastened the nozzle at the end of the pipe and repeated the earlier process. By the time she returned, he had finished his soup.

'Thanks, Jan. That was delicious. I needed that.'

'Ah, no bother at all, my child. Now lie back again and I'll pop this on your head. It shouldn't be too long before you feel much better.'

Charlie lay down slowly. When Jan placed the cloth over his head and forehead, the healing tingles felt amazing.

It gave him time to reflect on everything that had happened and he had a lot of questions.

He suddenly sat bolt upright with a look of horror and exclaimed, 'Wait, I have to get home. My mum is in danger. Something broke through the back fence …'

Jan placed her hand on his lips to calm him and answered, 'Dearie, when you get home, you'll return to the same time and place, so no time will have passed. Granted, it means you will face something then but, at least, you'll be prepared. I'll explain later.'

She removed her hand and he seemed more relaxed.

Jan advised, 'Now rest a little longer, Charlie. There'll be enough time later to answer questions that I know you have.'

She smiled. Charlie nodded and wondered if Jan could hear his thoughts. He tried to blank his mind and relax just in case she could. It wasn't long before he drifted off again.

Jan turned a tap on the side of the pot to empty its contents into large cauldrons, which differed slightly in style and colour and dragged them across the floor and through the door. She poured a few pots of water into her huge empty cauldron and swirled it, to clean out the remaining contents, and poured this through a pipe system that was below the tap. 'Tsangali will enjoy that,' she muttered to herself.

She went to a shelf and brought down an old dusty tan-coloured book. She looked towards a sleeping Charlie.

'Can he truly be "The One"?' she wondered, smiling hopefully.

She blew on the front of the book and a lot of dust went through the air, revealing a shining golden symbol, like a monolith sitting on clouds.

A few hours passed before Charlie stirred. He felt much better when he sat up. He decided to stand but felt uneasy with Vertigo, as the ground felt like it was rocking. Apart from that, he felt fine and carefully made his way over to Jan who was sitting at a makeshift table.

She hadn't noticed him as she had been staring at the book and her spectacles had slid down her nose, ready to fall off at any moment. She was starting to nod off so Charlie gave a purposeful cough to gently get her attention. She jumped and turned towards him.

'Oooooh, Charlie. Come and sit here with me.'

She patted a makeshift stool of blankets and dust flew from them.

'How do you feel?'

'Feeling much better, thanks,' he smiled. 'Still not used to walking much yet.'

'Ahhhhh, don't you worry, Dearie. That's not you, that would be Tsangali.'

'Tsangali?'

'Yes, my child. I'll explain a little later but, now, I need to get you ready.'

'Ready? Ready for what?'

She stared quizzically at Charlie before asking, 'Have you ever done anything like this before?'

Charlie wondered what she meant and then answered, 'No, I don't think I have.'

'Oooh, it's an honour that I must be the first and, hopefully not the last, Charlie.'

Charlie didn't like the words Jan used as they didn't sit well with him.

'What do you mean by "Hopefully not the last"?'

'Wait and I'll explain.'

She hobbled over to some bottles, poured a purple liquid into two glasses and brought them back to the table.

'Drink up, Charlie. I think you might need this for what I'm about to tell you.'

He took a sip. It was tasty, like violets mixed with a little mango. It warmed him inside and he felt confident. Jan then diverted his attention to the book and said, 'Charlie, I want you to take the time to read this book very carefully. You'll need to learn everything within its pages as you can't take it with you. It is the sacred book of Air and is the only one in existence. Tsangali and I have guarded it for centuries.

That's half the reason I never stay in one place for longer than necessary.'

'You keep mentioning Tsangali? Who is it?'

'Come, my child. It's about time I showed you.'

She held onto his hand and led him out of the hut. Charlie squinted as the glare of the purple sunlight almost dazzled him. He quickly adjusted and felt the ground move a little and a breeze flow over him. Jan gently took him further where the soft ground was royal blue with sky-blue intermittent strips. He thought he was standing on thick, soft grass, until Jan called out, 'Tsangali, I'd like you to meet Charlie, the destined one we have been waiting for, for so long.'

Charlie felt as though a hill was being created below his feet, as a giant tiger-like face turned towards them, with the biggest smile, showing a long fang on one side and a half-broken fang on the other. It spoke in a deep baritone and slow voice.

'Charlieee is it? We are truly grateful you've arrived, Sire. I feel humbled to have you travel on my back. Pleased to meet you. Have you met the others yet?'

In fright, Charlie fell on his backside but composed himself and was grateful for a soft landing.

'Ummmm, hello. No, you're the first I've met, to be honest.'

'Hmmmm, you'll do well, Charlie. You'll be fine.'

Tsangali smiled and lowered his head as they continued to travel forwards. Jan took Charlie by the hand and led him back to the hut. He had a slight problem walking, not only because of the ground movement but due to what he just witnessed.

'That was Tsangali. He is a dragon of the Air Elementals, from a group of Air Dragons known as the Griflon. There are many types of dragons in this realm. I live on his back as he flies, to keep us and this book safe.'

She tapped the book on the table and continued, 'This must only be seen by the Chosen One from the prophecy. You, Charlie, are obviously the One. I felt it the moment I saw you innocently lying on the toxic grass.'

Charlie was finding it hard to speak. He was still in shock after meeting the dragon face to face and realising that the ground was continually moving because they were riding on a dragon's back.

ELEMENTAL MAGIC

Jan put her hands reassuringly around Charlie's hand.
'Now listen, Charlie. You have a challenge ahead that only you can do. It will be a dangerous task but, once you've completed it, you'll receive the first of the four Elemental Wands. Now don't worry, magic doesn't need a wand, although it does enhance the magic you learn. The more of the wand you put together, the greater the level and the greater the magic you'll be able to achieve. This book will teach you some of the basic magic of air that may help you when you do not need a wand.'

Charlie remained silent, still shocked about what was happening. The kindly dragon he just met was a first for him. He had met many creatures but never a dragon.

Jan continued, 'You have time to rest as we travel to where you need to be. We have another day but, as I'm the first, then there's something you might need to know.'

She paused and debated whether she should tell Charlie or not. She decided to wait until the time was right and diverted the conversation swiftly so that he raised no question.

'My child, you have a grave challenge ahead. We are travelling towards the Kingdom of the Airithria which exists in the skies above our world. There you'll face a puzzle. If you choose incorrectly, you'll fall to your doom, so you must listen and prepare.'

Charlie sat up, horrified at the thought of what was coming. He was fine going up a flight of stairs but would often freeze at the top when he looked down. Once, a fire service had been called out to get him off the roof of his home after he went up a stepladder to get his kite. He had become nauseous and insecure when he looked down.

He was fine knowing he was on a dragon, but he hadn't gone to the edge and looked down yet. Jan could see his fear as the colour faded from his face. She held his hand reassuringly.

'Now, Charlie, you're from that human world, aren't you? I guess they have steppingstones on rivers in your world.'

'Human world?'

'Now's not the time, Charlie, but yes. You will be dropped at a sacred temple. If you are the Chosen One, the temple doors in the sky will open and allow you access. Getting across the clouds is like crossing a river on steppingstones.'

'And if I'm not this Chosen One you keep talking about?'

'Then the temple doors simply will not open. Now listen. You'll see several large cloud clusters that will get smaller as you get closer to the podium. On this podium, there is a wand known as the Sacred Wand of Air. You need to retrieve it and it will get you home.'

'But why me? Can't someone just fly to it and pick it up?'

'No, Charlie. There is a barrier that surrounds this temple, and no one can enter while the floating doors remain closed. They will only open for the Chosen One.'

Charlie started to feel deflated and admitted, 'I'm petrified. I've never been one for heights.'

'Oh, my child. You'll be fine. We have one day so I'll teach you a few things before we arrive, and you can rest well tonight. So come on now, Child. No dawdling. Let's start training. We will start with something simple. I'll show you first, so you know what you're about to do.'

Jan brought one of her water jars to the table and then hobbled back to fetch a plant, which she placed next to the jar. She stared hard at the plant and the jar, then closed her eyes and muttered a few words. When she opened them, they were still transfixed on the plant and jar that were on the table. She raised her hands.

Charlie jumped and backed away as the jar began to rise. It floated towards the plant, tilted and poured its water contents gently onto the soil in the pot. The plant pot then rose and started to spin slowly as Jan raised her left hand and slowly spun her pointed finger in a clockwise direction. Her right hand was forward as though she was holding something and tilting it, yet was nowhere near the jar or pot. She continued this miming action in the air until the pot had completed a full turn and was watered.

She then slowly lowered her right hand to the table, and the jar, with a little water left, settled on the table. She then pointed to the plant and gently directed it as it floated and settled on the shelf it came from.

'Now then, Charlie. I'll teach you this simple magic from the book.'

'That was incredible. Do you think you can teach me that, with no wand needed as you said?' he nervously laughed.

'You just saw that I did that with no wand at all, Charlie. As I have mentioned, not all magic needs a wand, as you'll soon find out. It's only the most powerful magic that needs a wand's enhancement. Now, please come and sit down. There's no need to feel nervous.'

Charlie hesitantly sat down.

'Wait. Do I need to fill the jar up again and bring over a plant?'

'No, no, not yet,' she laughed. 'Patience, Charlie. We are going to begin by testing your imagination and belief in what you're imagining. So, to start with, I want you to feel the air around you, encircling your body from your toes to the top of your head. Close your eyes and feel the tingle of the breeze around your feet, Charlie, and relax.'

He closed his eyes and readjusted his feet, as he smiled reassuringly.

'Now feel it circle around your feet, up your ankles and legs, to the bottom of your stomach.'

Still with his eyes closed, Charlie imagined this as he repositioned his legs and relaxed before settling.

'Now feel this feeling climb up your tummy and encircle you. Let it circle your neck, run down your arms then your hands and fingers. Allow the breeze to be a barrier surrounding you.'

The painting on the wall next to Charlie shook a little, then dislodged itself and fell to the floor, snapping him out of his meditation. A breeze waved gently away from him across the tablecloth, causing a light wave, but luckily not spilling the jar. He felt frustrated and angry.

'I can't do this. Why am I even trying? It's impossible.'

'You can, Charlie. Have faith in yourself. I am impressed that you managed as much as you have for the first time. You were doing great. The power is very strong in you and seems to flow naturally. No air creature has ever summoned a breeze in their first few attempts, but you did, right up to your neck. The only reason you snapped out of it was that you were distracted when you caused that painting to fall. Did you notice that no one was anywhere near it?'

He looked at the painting on the ground and realised that it was further than his arm's length away.

'Come on, Charlie. Let's carry on. You've got this.'

He took a deep breath and closed his eyes, imagining a swirl of breeze climbing up his body, reaching up to his neck and climbing up his chin, his cheeks, mouth, nose and eyes, and eventually climbing and swirling to his forehead and hair, then to the top of his head. He felt strange but concentrated hard, not allowing this to distract him. He had no idea what was happening or how he was doing it, as the hairs over his body stood on end as the gentle breeze entwined him.

'That's it, Charlie,' Jan whispered. 'Now, slowly open your eyes and keep concentrating.'

He slowly opened his eyes as Jan continued to instruct him.

'Now, slowly reach forward to the jar on the table with the hand you use to write. But don't physically touch the jar. Let your breeze be your hand to hold the glass, then raise it slowly. Try to move it to the left, to the right, forwards, backwards, up and down very gently and carefully. But you must stay in the meditative state that you are in now.'

Charlie very gently raised his left hand towards the glass. Nothing happened but he did not want to give up. His hand was open, as though his fingers were around a mug. The glass tilted on the table away from him and fell back into position. The movement surprised him and he almost lost his concentration. Jan continued to encourage him.

'Charlie, that's it. That's very good. That was you tilting the glass. You didn't allow it to break your concentration. You've almost got this now, so push yourself and imagine that you are holding the glass now. Imagine your arm is extending to reach it. Mime it in the air.'

His concentration was obvious as he frowned at the jar with a piercing hypnotic stare and stretched his hand towards it. It began to shake a little and, as he began to raise his hand, it started to float upwards.

'That's it, Charlie. Slowly to the left now and then slowly back to the right. Pull it near you, then further away again.'

As Jan was speaking, Charlie was doing it. His hand was nowhere near the jar but it floated to the left, then the right, then floated closer toward him, then back again. He then aimed it towards the window and the jar floated towards the plant there. When it was above the plant, he tilted his hand gently and the floating jar leaned until it spilt the remaining contents of water over the plant. He slowly returned the jar to the table, and it gently settled itself.

Jan cried, 'WAIT!'

But it was too late, as Charlie let out a sigh of relief and suddenly relaxed, thinking he'd done it. A sonic wave emanated from him and the table flew away, smashing the jar and knocking Jan to the floor. The plants behind him flew out through the windows, shattering the glass. The huge cauldron, in the middle of the room, dismantled itself from the stand and rolled towards the sink, crushing the pipe on the wall which leaked a spray of water around the hut.

Jan managed to get up and readjust herself. She hurried to the sink and quickly wrapped the pipe with waterproof cloths. Charlie suddenly felt deflated and could hardly move with exhaustion. Jan returned to him as he muttered, 'I'm so sorry, I'm really sorry.'

Jan felt his forehead and reassured him. 'My child, this is my fault, not yours. There's no need to apologise. I should have told you how to relieve yourself of the power. You must be exhausted. That was impressive control you had there, Charlie. Honestly, don't worry yourself. I need to redecorate anyway.' She said this as the only painting left hanging dropped to the ground.

Charlie hugged Jan and she felt motherly for a moment as she hugged him back, giving his hair a gentle stroke and reassuring him that everything was fine.

'Charlie. You have exceeded my expectations beyond belief. You really have. You should be proud of yourself. Don't you worry, we will just have to work on the last part so that this doesn't happen in future.'

'What do you mean? Are we doing it again?' asked Charlie.

'Yes, Charlie. We must. You'll be at the temple doors tomorrow and there's still much to learn from the book.'

He understood and managed enough energy to get up and tidy. He even managed, with Jan's help, to roll the giant heavy cauldron back onto its stand in the centre of the room. All the pictures were put back in place and everything was in order, apart from the water pipe with a hole, which was bandaged for now.

'Okay, Charlie. Let's do this one more time but just raise the jar, move it a little and place it back down. Then you need to reverse the concentration. Imagine the breeze as a long creature which has wrapped you inside itself. Let it unwind from your head down to your toes and let it slide away gently. Do you understand?'

'Yes. Like a snake has wrapped around me and it's uncoiling itself, releasing me and sliding away.'

'I'm not sure what a snake is, Charlie, but yes, it sounds like you understand what I mean.'

Charlie was taken aback that she had no idea what a snake was but didn't want to question it, in fear of insulting her. He closed his eyes and repeated everything, only this time as he placed the jar back on the table, he put his hands gently by his side, closed his eyes and imagined that a snake was slithering away from him, releasing its hold by uncovering his head, then slowly down his neck, tummy, hands, arms, legs and eventually releasing his feet before sliding away.

He opened his eyes and still felt the energy. He wasn't exhausted this time. Jan cheered out loudly, 'Yayyyyyyy, Charlie, that's it. You did it. You did it on your third attempt, which is unheard of.'

Jan gave Charlie's cheek a gentle pat or two and he felt super proud of himself. The celebration was kept short as he still had a lot to learn from the book before the following day's trial.

CHAPTER 11

THE TRIALS BEGIN

Before they embarked on the next practice, Charlie took a short break with a refreshing herbal milk drink that Jan made.

'Charlie, you did amazingly well for your first bit of magic. Now it's time to go outside. We'll take this broom as there are two things we are going to learn out there.'

Charlie didn't have to be told twice. He had grabbed the broom and was already at the door before Jan had finished her sentence. She laughed and they headed out of the hut together. They were only a few metres from the entrance when Jan continued.

'Here will do, Charlie. Now, this time I'm going to lay this broom here. Firstly, you are to try and surround the broom in a vortex. This is very useful if a dangerous beast is coming and you just want to trap or disorientate it. I'll show you first.'

Jan closed her eyes for a moment before opening them and pointing both arms forwards at the motionless broom. A moment later, she placed her hands on her heart, spun around and thrust them forwards again towards the broom. A mini tornado began to form and headed towards the broom which rose and started to spin in an irregular pattern. Jan snapped her fingers on both hands and the tornado dispersed, leaving the broom to fall to the furry ground. It continued to spin for a moment before coming to a stop.

Jan didn't stop there. She put her arms straight down by her sides, then spread her hands open with the palms facing the ground. There seemed to be a jet stream coming from her hands as she lifted herself and floated a few feet above the ground, arching her hands a little as though she was using them to steer towards Charlie. She slowly straightened them when she reached him. Very slowly, she closed them and was lowered in front of Charlie. His mouth was wide open, mesmerised by what he just saw.

Jan pushed his chin up to close his mouth.

'Now, Charlie, your turn. That was two pieces of magic there in one.'

He couldn't get his words out. He just stuttered, 'B-b-but how? What did I just see? That's incredible. Can I do that?'

'Charlie, you have too many questions but, alas, we don't have much time. I'll show you these two basic things from the book to keep you right.'

'Basic things?'

'For someone like you, Charlie, yes. One day, you'll think back on today and laugh. If you get through these imminent trials, my child. Now, if you were watching me carefully, you'll be able to practise this. Remember, you always begin by entwining the air around you like a 'snake',

I think you called it. That is crucial to the start of any of this magic. The calling, we say.

Once you have conjured up the breeze, send it away from you by holding your hands at your chest. Then spin carefully, with your arms close to your sides, before raising them and aiming your spin towards what you want to cover in the vortex. You will feel the cocoon of breeze move forwards and it will feel strange, like a wave through your body.

Now stay focused and aim at the broom. You'll see where the vortex is by the dust being kicked up en route. Just keep focused as you will want to stop at the broom so that it is taken in. When you want to stop, just snap your fingers and it'll disperse gently and release the broom. It's a bit like what you did with the jar in there, but this one's useful if there's a threat and you need to throw it off-guard, giving you a chance to escape to safety.'

Charlie understood. He took a few steps forwards and did the motion exactly as Jan showed him, although he almost fell over during his first spin. This was reflected in the tornado as it dispersed before it even moved forwards one foot. After a couple of tries, he had the broom spinning in the vortex he created. His grin said it all, but the smile disappeared when he realised that he had never snapped his fingers before and was unable to. He panicked.

'Don't worry, Charlie. Don't panic. Just clap your hands instead but brace yourself.'

With that, Jan was about to get on the ground but, before she could, Charlie clapped his hands and the air dispersed with the strength of a sonic boom. Jan was knocked off her feet and stumbled but, luckily, she landed on the soft fur so wasn't hurt. She picked herself up.

'Now don't worry. I'm okay. Charlie, that was very impressive. You picked that up quickly. We can practise finger-snapping but, for now, just clap and remember to brace yourself. Now it's time to fly.'

Charlie stood motionless.

'Don't worry, Dearie. Just a foot from the ground is all you need. Not far at all.'

With those words, his shoulders relaxed a little.

'Now, exactly like I said before, it all starts with wrapping yourself in the breeze through meditation. This time, place your hands straight down by your sides and use them as an energy stream to lift you. Be careful as you need to concentrate or you will catapult yourself and you don't want that. Concentrate gently and imagine the air emanating from your hands. The softer the lower and the harder the higher. Keep your palms flat towards the ground to stay still. Experiment steering yourself forwards by tilting your hands gently in the opposite direction of where you want to go. Okay?'

'Okay, thanks. I think I got this one.'

Charlie closed his eyes for a moment as the breeze entwined him. He then did as he was told but, as soon as he had lifted slightly off the ground, he couldn't contain his excitement and instinctively closed his hands. He fell to the ground. He knew that he must resist the urge to get excited. The next time, he lifted and stayed steady. He couldn't believe the feeling and the tingling inside as he steered himself, haphazardly to begin with, but soon was able to go where he wanted. He shouted a loud 'Wahaaaaay' as he felt the breeze against his face, flying slightly off the ground.

'Okay, Charlie, come on down now. You got that one extremely quickly. Well done,' said Jan, very proud of him.

He flew towards her and gently closed his hands to lower himself to the ground.

'Oh, my goodness. That was amazing. It felt so good.'

Jan looked up at the sky and could see it was starting to get dark. She smiled proudly at Charlie and took him into the hut to prepare supper, as it would soon be time for his first trial.

After they had eaten, she passed the sacred book to him to continue reading. It was small with, luckily, not too many pages, and they'd already gone through most of it. There was no writing on its cover, just the symbol.

'This book is a part of the Tallemseen which you're already aware of, Charlie. The prophecy was given in fragments, in the form of small sacred books like this one, to worthy members of the elementals. They were to be looked after and cherished, and only revealed to a Chosen One. Once read, the book will fade away. It is only short but it is powerful and I think you should read the rest of it before you sleep. If you must, just finish it as soon as you wake as it will soon be time for the trial.'

She slid the book towards Charlie and hobbled to a rocking chair, covered herself with a chequered red and black sheet, and closed her eyes. He readied himself by lying on a mound of blankets and began to read.

It gave him a brief history of a realm that exists only for the elemental masters and its people. There was a lot of information about the power of the air, the control of winds and skies, atmospheres and pressures. One part particularly stood out as it was an ancient casting spell that should only be used in the darkest hour and not everyone can conjure this from within. He read the instructions carefully, taking a mental note, not that he wanted to try it, ever, but you never know. Charlie took all the information in with great interest.

He read a lot before his eyes started to close and he realised how tired he was. He set the book to one side and went to sleep.

He slept undisturbed for about five hours, which was a luxury lately. He stretched, went to get a jar of water, and then sat back on his makeshift bed, quietly so as not to disturb Jan, who was still resting soundly in her rocking chair.

He continued to read the book and, as he neared the end, he inhaled a gentle breeze through his mouth. It filled him with a strangely positive, uplifting energy. He looked back at the book and read the words, "It is done."

As the book began to float and fade, it shot towards Charlie. He noticed something appearing on his chest. It didn't hurt or tingle, it just began to appear. He couldn't bend his head far enough to see it so he went to a nearby mirror. There was a circular pattern on his upper chest which looked like an artistic painting of a summer sky but in black ink. He was confused and rubbed it, but it wouldn't smudge or fade. He licked his fingers and tried harder, but it stayed as it was.

A voice behind him made him jump. He hadn't noticed that Jan had awoken, coming to see what was wrong.

'Ahhhhh, Charlie. It has confirmed that you are indeed the Chosen One. You must have read the book as you now have the mark. You won't be able to remove it.'

'Oh no, but I have to somehow get it off. My mum's gonna kill me!'

'I'm afraid, Charlie, that's there permanently. It may be better to be honest with her. I think she will understand this more than you know.'

'I know my mum and she's usually calm, but I just know I'm gonna be in serious trouble with this.'

'You could conceal it but that will not have a positive impact on you. You'll be worrying every day about the possibility of her seeing it and you will be stressed. Try and see the positive side to this. It's a symbol of nobility and hope. It's a privilege. Wear it well, just as your father did.'

Jan realised that she said out loud this time what she managed to keep quiet earlier.

'My dad? How do you know my dad?'

There was a roar from outside as the flight was slowing.

'Charlie, get ready quickly. There's no time to lose. We are approaching the gates and we don't have much time before they fade. There'll be time to talk more again soon, okay?'

He quickly prepared. He practised for a moment by closing his eyes, bringing in the circling breeze and then he floated through the door to join Jan. Looking up at the sky, there were two floating golden door posts with a solid golden door between them which was closed.

'Well, that's silly,' said Charlie. 'Luckily, it's not too high. I'll just fly around the door.'

But as he was about to fly, Jan stopped him by holding his foot before he was out of reach. He lifted her a little, before floating slowly down so that they were back on the ground.

'Never be deceived, Charlie. Nothing's ever as easy as it looks. There'll be an invisibility field around it. You might smash into it, render yourself unconscious in your haste and the doors will have faded. You must go through the door. Just place your hand against the hand impression in the centre of it and it will open. Good luck, Charlie. Tsangali will stay close below you so that you don't feel afraid.'

With that, she gave him a bit of a smile and hugged him tightly.

'You'll do this. I know you will.'

She released her hold and ushered him to hurry.

Tsangali raised his head and, in his warm deep voice, said, 'Go now, Warrior, and may the guardians of the air keep you safe.' He gave his reassuring smile which instilled calmness.

Concentrating, Charlie looked at the door and floated up so that he was level with it. He looked down, pleased to see that he wasn't too high and wouldn't get hurt if he fell. On the door, he saw a small hand impression surrounded by a slightly larger one. He smiled proudly, wondering if his dad had put his hand there, from what Jan mentioned. Charlie placed his left hand against the impression. He was careful to keep his right hand central to his body, pointing downwards to keep a floating balance with his flight magic.

There was a loud click and the door slowly began to open. He quickly regained his balance with both hands and looked back at Jan and Tsangali. He smiled and gave them a reassuring nod. Jan waved and Tsangali returned a nod with a broad smile and a sparkle in his eye. Charlie entered the open door and vanished from their view. The door closed and faded away.

'Fear not, Janairealonova. I feel there's much more to him than you can imagine,' Tsangali reassured her.

She smiled back, then silently returned to her hut as they continued their journey.

CHAPTER 12

ACROPHOBIA

The doors closed and Charlie found himself standing on what seemed to be a cloud. Ahead of him other clouds, like steppingstones, led towards a tall pedestal, above which a glass rod was floating and spinning slightly. Charlie dared not look down. He was in a predicament as he knew if he looked down, the height would be obvious. He hoped that Tsangali was still just below him in case he fell. The cloud felt soft but it was secure. He realised that he must jump onto each cloud, like steppingstones, to get to the rod.

He closed his eyes and concentrated to start the magic, but he couldn't feel a breeze. Nothing. Despite this, he tested it again by putting his hands into position and attempted to float. Nothing. It was no good. He realised that the trial must be enchanted and would try to prevent him from using powers to get where he needed to be. It annoyed him and he felt stupid for not realising the obvious.

He then stepped towards the edge of the cloud and dared to look over the edge. Suddenly, he felt sick and dizzy when he saw that Tsangali was no longer there, and mountain peaks were passing at speed below him. He slowly knelt on the cloud, nauseous and petrified. He lay on it to secure himself, trying to imagine that he was lying on the ground and not high up at all.

He knew he needed to do this challenge and tried to persuade himself that it was just a river below with steppingstones. He eventually got onto his knees and edged back towards the door, but when he tried to open it, it would not budge. His fate was sealed. He would either starve on the cloud and eventually die, get to the rod on the other side, or fall thousands of feet to his death.

Charlie knew he must get across, as it was the only way. After kneeling for several minutes, he lifted himself to a standing position slowly and checked out the smaller clouds which would lead him to the other side.

They were dotted at random intervals, some close, others quite far and a few were moving either left or right, back or forth or up and down. Some looked solid while others looked faded. Charlie wanted to give up. He wasn't feeling well, knowing how high up he was. He closed his eyes and started to breathe slowly, relaxing each part of his body. He tried to meditate and forget where he was. He imagined being by a brook at home, using steppingstones to get to the other side. Visualising this helped him to be calm and he felt a warm happiness.

He opened his eyes and looked confidently at the prize ahead. He imagined the steppingstones on a stream to reach the embankment and claim the glass rod. He slowly stood up, arched his back, lifted his shoulders and looked at the nearest cloud, trying to imagine that the blue light below was water and the mountains going by below were part of the current. He stepped onto the first cloud and then brought his other leg across to stand on a smaller cloud. He was ready to step to the next, slightly faded one.

That was it. He made a start and had to continue. He didn't look back or down below the clouds. He stepped across to a slightly larger cloud but was horrified when his feet began to sink into it, as it started to fade. He began to feel hot. He moved quickly and took a chance, jumping on a cloud close by, just as the cloud he was on faded completely, exposing the depths below.

Charlie readjusted. His feet were stable where he was now standing but he started to feel woozy and his legs were like jelly. He couldn't sit as the cloud was too small. The next one was a short distance away but it was moving to the left and right. He decided to time his next jump to be slightly to the right and moving in that direction, in case he needed to step once or twice. At least it was in the direction of the clouds' movement. He made the jump and, almost immediately, leapt from it to another cloud that was close by.

He looked towards the rod which was getting nearer, but just not close enough. He then jumped across to a cloud which was rising and lowering, but he mistimed the jump and, as he leapt forwards, the edge of his foot caught the edge of the cloud as it was dropping. There was nothing for it but to leap quickly towards a small cloud which was slightly to the left. He missed it with his feet but, since he had flung himself forward enough, he was lying across it with his legs dangling from one side and his arms from the other. The cloud was so small that he was struggling to figure out a way to get up onto it.

He tried desperately not to look down as he felt faint when he saw the ground racing by, so far below. The next cloud was fading and the other reachable one was moving forwards and backwards. Due to his position, he decided that it might be the best one. He pulled his arms up and pushed his hands against the cloud to lift himself onto it. With his feet only just fitting on it, he was stuck in a frog-style position, facing the faded cloud. He had to go for it. He saw another cloud just ahead which seemed slightly larger and more solid. He did it. He leapfrogged to the faded cloud and then jumped immediately forwards to the more solid one.

To his dismay, he couldn't stay any longer as the cloud was starting to shrink. There were three more clouds ahead before he could reach the rod, but they were progressively further apart.

Charlie started his run-up on the remaining part of the cloud and leapt. He reached the next cloud and decided to keep going or he'd never make it. He leapt immediately to the next one and finally leapt to the last one. There was a long leap to reach the pillar with the floating rod. He didn't hesitate as he just wanted it over with. It felt like slow motion, but Charlie was a bit too confident and hadn't estimated the distance. His arms were outstretched, trying to reach for the rod, but he dropped and fell slightly short of it.

Reacting quickly, he managed to grab the base of the pillar and dangled there. The golden door and the clouds had vanished. There was only him dangling on the pillar in the air and holding on for dear life. He knew he couldn't get up the pillar. His fate was sealed.

At that moment, a thistledown floated by his head, and he remembered seeing one like it in the woods at the treehouse. It floated about, then headed away.

Charlie felt himself get weaker and tried desperately to hold on. Seeing the thistledown made him wonder if his magic might have returned now that the walls and clouds were gone. He closed his eyes, willing his strength to return, and attempted to meditate while still holding the pillar tightly. He felt the breeze that he desperately hoped for surrounding him. He wasn't sure about flying as he'd never tried it at that height. Instead of risking it, he took a gamble and released his grip on the base of the pillar. He began to fall but managed to whip his hands out towards the rod. It budged and was pulled from the top of the pillar.

The rod was in front of him, but he was falling quickly. With his heart pounding, he tried to maintain his concentration. He pulled back his hands with all his might and the rod flung itself towards him. He looked down and realised he was closer to the ground than he thought and was about to hit it. With the rod next to him, he released the energy to prevent a sonic wave. He desperately grabbed for it and prepared to meet his fate when his fingers, luckily, wrapped around it.

Everything slowed down and he went into a spin. The light became very bright as a mist accumulated around him, as though it was trying to hold him and cushion him from the impact. He heard banging in the distance and the sound of wood being split. He was afraid as he held the rod tightly. The intense splitting was nearby and, as the mist began to fade, he found that he was on his back. There was a loud crash as the garden gate was shattered to pieces.

Charlie suddenly realised that he was back in his garden, exactly where he had been before he left, although it felt like a few days had passed. He was disorientated and felt a bit wobbly. In front of him, amongst the wreckage, stood his headmaster with eyes as black as onyx stone.

Charlie spoke.

'Sir. Mr Grimauld, Sir?'

The headmaster stood with his eyes transfixed by Charlie before he spoke with that raspy voice.

'You have what I want. Get it now.'

'What do you mean?'

'Don't play the innocent with me.'

The headmaster twisted his hand and Charlie felt a tightness in his head, as he was lifted painfully to a standing position. The headmaster continued.

'The Book … now, or I'll sssqueeze your head until it popssss.'

Charlie felt like his head was in a vice, with a migraine starting. He tried to pull in his newfound power but it was hopeless. The tightening was too distracting.

He felt as though he was about to faint when a thistledown flew in front of him and randomly darted in front of his eyes. It seemed to emit a golden light, different to the one he saw in the cloud challenge. Then it shot towards the headmaster.

'What is this?' he bellowed, as he tried to swipe at it but it cleverly avoided his swaying hand. It was beginning to annoy Sinistre so he decided to destroy it. He clapped his hands trying to crush the seedling but it dropped downwards, narrowly avoiding him.

The distraction was long enough. Charlie closed his eyes and felt the breeze wind up his body with speed. He then looked at his headmaster, who was still being puppeteered by Sinistre. Standing poised, Charlie went into a spin and flung his hands towards him, who in turn swung his hands to crush Charlie's head. But it was too late as Mr Grimauld left the ground and began to spin.

The thistledown floated away and Charlie spun his finger faster, increasing the spin of the vortex. The headmaster was trapped in the centre, spinning violently. Charlie moved the vortex out through the smashed garden gate and into the back alley.

He walked around so that he had the full length of the alley in view and, with one last piece of magic, he pulled back his hands before pushing them forwards to send the headmaster spinning down the alley, at great speed. Once out of sight, Charlie opened his hands and clapped to disperse the vortex.

He had no idea how much time he bought himself, but he quickly unlocked the back door and ran up to his bedroom, where he packed his rucksack with the prophecy. He didn't have time to examine the parchments in the foil castle on top of his wardrobe, but he did notice that one of them seemed to have new markings. They went into the rucksack along with his newly-acquired glass rod.

Charlie checked his chest in the mirror and saw that the oval mark with the sky design was still there, except the edging had turned golden and the design was now a vibrant sky blue. It made everything feel so real.

He ran down to the front door and, as he was approaching it, his mum opened it.

'Mum …'

'Charlie? What have you done now? I know that look.'

'Mum, please can we just get into the car and drive? It's super urgent.'

'But, I've …'

'Mum, please!'

Jennifer realised the urgency in her son's voice and turned back to the car.

'Come on, and make sure to lock the door.'

His mum was already in the car when Charlie ran back into the house to lock the back door, and then the front door. He ran to the passenger side and jumped in. He could see that the headmaster was coming back into view, a reasonable distance away, down the road.

'MUM, GO NOW … QUICKLY!' Charlie screamed.

His mum quickly started the engine and sped off down the road. Charlie trembled as he looked back, but the headmaster was out of sight.

'Charlie, Love, what is it? What's the matter and where are we driving to?'

'Awww, Mum, just keep driving. I've got so much to tell you.'

'Charlie, are you in trouble?'

'Yes, I think you could say that.'

'With the police? Your school?'

'None of those. Now, please keep driving.'

'Right, well, I haven't eaten so I'll drive for about an hour and we'll stop for some food if you're hungry. Is that okay, Charlie? Maybe we can talk about this then?'

'Thanks, Mum. I love you.'

'I love you too, my beautiful son.'

With that, Jennifer gave him a reassuring smile and continued driving. Charlie was still trembling and it took at least thirty minutes into the journey before he managed to relax as there was no sign of the headmaster. He checked behind them constantly.

His mother instinctively carried on driving for an extra half-hour. Call it a mother's intuition that she knew to do this, as Charlie relaxed more the further she drove.

Eventually, they reached a Toby carvery restaurant at the side of the road.

'Are you okay here, Charlie?'

'Yes, thanks, Mum. That's perfect.'

They drove into a side street and parked behind the restaurant, amongst some large raised bushes. Charlie was relieved that they'd found a secluded spot to park. If the headmaster did come, he might not find them.

As they headed towards the restaurant, he was nervous, wondering how he was going to tell his mum and if he should show her the mark on his chest.

Inside, they were taken to their seats in a booth by the windows. It was as if his mother instinctively knew that's what he wanted. This was common practice, especially during the last few years. He would be one step ahead of her when she needed something, and it was the same the other way around. The booth was in a great spot, as they were hidden by other people in the restaurant but could see out of the windows if they needed to.

They sat down and menus were handed to them.

The waiter advised, 'Soup of the day is lentil. I'll pop back in a few minutes.'

This was it. Charlie had to come clean.

CHAPTER 13

THE SECRET GUARDIAN

Jennifer and Charlie remained quiet, looking at the menu. Charlie knew that it was important to tell his mother, but he was thinking about how to word it. He was concentrating so hard that they turned the waiter away twice.

They did manage to order their drinks and Charlie decided on one of his personal favourites, cloudy lemonade. With the drinks on the table, they eventually placed their order. Charlie carefully looked around before lowering his voice.

'Mum.'

'Yes, Cha?'

His mother held her hands out and gently rubbed the back of his with her thumbs. He felt reassured by this comfort.

'Mum, I'm not sure where to start but, honestly, if you don't want to believe what I'm about to say, I understand and won't hold it against you.'

His mother was intrigued and sat forwards to listen.

'Mum, the day I ran home from school, and we went back later. Well, I had been sent to the headmaster's office because my teacher assumed I was causing a fuss when I was being … bullied. He just didn't see it.'

'Charlie. Why didn't you tell me this before? You poor dear.'

Her eyes started to shine a little and she was itching to get up.

'No, Mum. I'm okay, honestly. You can stay there. But this is where it gets complicated.'

He recounted the events. From the day of bullying when the headmaster became possessed and the books attacked him, when he "borrowed" the book from Grimauld's desk not knowing why he was drawn to it, when he was warned of the deliveries; right up to his training and his reappearance in the garden when the headmaster had shattered the gate.

Charlie's mother didn't interrupt but listened intently to every word, occasionally raising her eyebrows and saying "aww" now and then. He stopped for a moment when they received their food. Charlie started with lentil soup, followed by the house-special burger and homemade triple-cooked chips. He also topped up his cloudy lemonade.

Jennifer urged Charlie to continue his story.

They finished their mains before Charlie ordered a sticky toffee pudding with ice cream, and his mother ordered the mixed fruit bowl. But, while they were waiting, Charlie was interrupted by something floating just behind his mum's head.

It was a thistledown, but it kept dashing towards the window. Charlie had forgotten to mention the seedling to his mum, and only then realised that he only saw one whenever the headmaster was about.

He looked towards the window. It was the headmaster, sniffing the air in search of something. It didn't take a genius to know what. Charlie signalled to his mum without a word; only a finger over his lips to ask her to remain silent. She looked across and, to her horror, she also saw the headmaster.

The thistledown then moved in another direction, beckoning Charlie to follow as it floated gently towards the ground, about knee height, and headed towards the toilets. Charlie indicated to his mum to follow and popped on his backpack, got on his knees and started crawling. Jennifer quickly grabbed her purse and left more than enough to pay for their meals, with a generous tip for the waiter before she followed Charlie. They got a few glances as they crawled along the carpet under the window. The headmaster looked through the window and scanned the people in the restaurant.

He missed them by a few seconds.

He did, however, notice that people were looking at something on the ground and decided to enter the restaurant, but not by the front door. He raised his hands and crumbled a part of the wall. People started to panic and scream, trying to reach the exit.

With the help of the commotion, Charlie and his mother managed to go through the door towards the toilets. They continued to follow the seedling, which led them to another corridor where they eventually reached a fire door. They left through the fire escape and the seedling disappeared back down the corridor they just traversed.

They reached the car and Charlie took a glance back at the restaurant. He saw a chair being launched into the air. Distracted by this, the headmaster was following each chair that was being raised.

Charlie realised at that moment, this thistledown had been looking after him and seemed to show up whenever he was in danger.

His mum quickly turned on the engine, leaving the car park, heading for the motorway to get away at the fastest speed possible.

She eventually spoke.

'Charlie, that's some story you told me in there.'

'It wasn't a story …'

'I haven't finished yet, Charlie. It was some story but, you know what …?'

'What?'

'I believe every word you said, and I think it's time we had a serious discussion. But not until we are safely away, okay?'

'Okay.'

Charlie felt butterflies.

They drove for some time, stopping only once for fuel. It was a few hours before they reached a motorway service station, where they drove in for a toilet stop and refreshment. Charlie made sure he took his bag in with him.

They popped into a coffee shop just at the entrance and ordered a frappé and blueberry muffin each. Again, they sat at a table where they could see out of the huge window, in case the headmaster appeared.

His mother asked him to show her the book that he'd taken from the headmaster. He obliged and, with a little shake, pulled it free from his bag. She was halfway through sipping her frappé and suddenly spluttered, and almost choked, when she caught sight of the cover. Some people stared at Charlie, but he reacted quickly and patted hard on his mum's back.

'Mum, are you okay?'

'Yeah, thanks, bless you. I'm okay now. I just drank my frappé the wrong way.'

She was transfixed by the cover design on the Book of Tallemseen, which was lying on the table. She looked up at Charlie and asked, 'Do you recognise that pattern, Charlie?'

'Well, I think so. It's what drew me to the book in the first place. I had to have it. Do you see what I mean then, Mum? Why are you asking?'

'It's the same tattoo that your father has on his chest. You probably don't remember as he always wore something over it.'

'What? Dad had a tattoo on his chest. I remember him despising tattoos and yet I think I remember something on his chest. It makes sense now what Jan meant by 'wearing it well like my fath—'

Charlie stopped speaking, realising that he'd just given away the part he wanted to leave out and hoped his mother wasn't paying attention. He tried to avoid the subject.

'Do you have any photos of Dad showing the tattoo, Mum?'

'You know what, Charlie. I think I do.'

She rummaged through her handbag, then checked the side pockets and pulled out some Polaroids. She looked through them one by one with a smile, yet a tear in her eyes. He held her arms to comfort her while she scanned through them.

It had been a few years since they last saw Roger Wafe. The photos were a reminder of the great times they shared and the loss they now felt. She pulled one out and laughed before passing it to Charlie.

'That's one of your dad there, Cha. We were on honeymoon in Greece and one of the rare times he wore trunks for swimming. It was hilarious, as it took him all holiday to summon up the courage to get into his trunks and have a swim. He could have controlled that ocean but was always afraid of it. So funny. But look on his chest.'

Charlie took the photo and there, emblazoned on his dad's chest, was the exact symbol that was on the front of the book of prophecy. The sky part of the symbol was exactly like the one on his chest.

He had a moment's flashback to the headmaster's office when he saw the book being closed and placed on the desk. He must have subconsciously recognised the image as that on his father's chest. The flashback was over. He realised why he had to have the book and was relieved that he wasn't going insane.

'Now, Cha. I'm just going to pop to the bathroom and then we best get going. Oh, and there's a fluffy thing on your arm. Take it outside, release it and make a wish.'

She left for the bathroom. Charlie looked at the thistledown sitting on his arm and wondered if he could communicate with it. He reached over and the seedling floated towards his finger. He jumped, not expecting the speed, then pulled the seedling towards his face and whispered.

'Are you okay?'

It bobbed up and down which reassured Charlie. He expected to see a seed in the centre of the fluff, but it was a tiny person. So tiny, it was hard to make out, but he could see two legs and arms on a body, and it was waving at him. He tried to discreetly wave back, then rubbed his brow to pretend that was what he was doing as he'd noticed a few prying eyes watching him.

He whispered, 'Thank you.'

He carefully placed his finger near his shoulder and it floated to settle on his jumper, just by his neck.

His mum returned, picked up the photos and popped them into her bag, while he put the book into his bag, ensuring they were ready to move on. They got into the car, then as his mum started the engine, she asked, 'So, Charlie. What was this Jan referring to when she mentioned you wear it well, like your father?'

Charlie felt embarrassed and slightly nervous. He'd told her almost everything but failed to let her know of the tattoo on his chest, which embossed itself in gold after the trial.

'Okay, Mum, before you drive off, I need to show you something but please promise me you won't get cross.'

The seedling moved from his shoulder and settled on the back seat as if it knew it was the right time to get out of the way.

'Okay, I promise Cha. What is it?'

Charlie pulled off his jumper and then lifted his T-shirt. 'This.'

There, in full light, was the tattoo design of the sky which was exactly like the design on the book and her husband. Her eyes widened and then she looked directly at Charlie with concern.

'Oh, Charlie. You're only a child. Why now?'

Charlie slid down his T-shirt and wasn't sure whether it was due to concern or if his mum was about to give him the third degree. He quickly explained that it simply appeared when he completed the teachings of the book, which then vanished, and that it only went gold on the edges when he got the glass rod. He pulled it from his bag to show her.

The seedling quickly flew to the rod and settled on it, trying to push down on it as a warning to keep it hidden. Charlie's mum noticed this and said, 'Charlie, put that away quickly.'

He was confused that she wasn't surprised that a seedling was there and that she understood what it was trying to communicate.

She started the engine and they sped off again, driving along the motorway at the highest speed allowed. Charlie expected the silent treatment, still wondering what his mum was thinking. He was surprised when she spoke.

'Charlie, there's something your dad and I never told you. Simply because we wanted to make sure you were old enough to understand, maybe at fifteen. But to be honest, it looks like things are happening already and you're barely twelve.'

She glanced at him, looking a little upset.

'You're just a boy, for goodness sake. I'll talk about it when we stop again, okay? There's something you have to know.'

He nodded and gave an 'okay' acknowledgement, even though he was more confused.

They drove a couple of miles further down the road where there was a sign for another service station ahead. The seedling started to move uneasily on the back seat before it floated towards the back of Charlie's hand, brushing against it to get his attention. The seedling balanced on his hand as he lifted it to his ear.

'What is it, little one?'

Charlie's mum looked curiously at him, then understood he was up to something and hadn't directed that question at her. This made him more curious about what his mum needed to talk to him about. He began to giggle as the seedling shuffled about in his ear. He closed his eyes to listen carefully, almost putting himself in the meditative state. He heard a whisper, and goosebumps started to form. He could make out the whispering above the humming of the car's noise.

'Charlie. Charlie, can you hear me?'

He laughed as the thistledown tickled his neck.

'Charlie. I'm Felina. I've been assigned to be your guardian until you're ready.'

He listened intently but couldn't hear anything. His mum was listening as she turned towards him with a frown, then continued concentrating on the road ahead.

The thistledown floated to the back seat and settled. Charlie started to feel on edge and the thistledown began to bob up and down, frantically trying to gain his attention. He looked back and saw a huge 4 x 4 in the distance. It was hurtling at great speed down the motorway and had already butted a couple of cars to the side.

'Mum, I don't want to panic you but please drive faster, and don't get off until we have a chain of roads that lead to several places.'

'Why Charlie? What is it?'

CHAPTER 14

CHARLIE'S ORIGIN

Jennifer didn't have to ask again, as she looked in her rear-view mirror. She could see the Land Rover in the distance and how it had blasted through a red Mini that just had no chance.

'Never mind, Charlie,' she acknowledged, as she put her foot on the accelerator, causing the car to quickly increase its speed.

Charlie felt the full force of the car's acceleration from the pressure on his back, against the seat. He checked the side mirror and could see that the dark green Land Rover wasn't far behind them and it was gaining. He glanced back and made out his headmaster, driving carelessly towards them.

'Mum, you have to go faster.'

'It won't go any faster, Charlie. But hold on.'

Traffic started to slow ahead, and Jennifer began to weave between the cars. The driver of the Land Rover didn't bother to dodge, he just ploughed straight through the cars like they were nothing. The cars went into a spin, and some catapulted and smashed against the side of the road, into the barriers.

Mr Grimauld had to be stopped. People were getting hurt, and Charlie didn't want his headmaster hurt either, fully aware that he was innocent and being puppeteered.

In the background, there were red and blue flashing lights as several police cars were in pursuit. Jennifer drove onto the hard shoulder as the traffic ahead was almost at a standstill. There was a blue sign ahead indicating they could leave the motorway, so it wasn't far. But the Land Rover was also on the hard shoulder and, no longer butting cars off the road, was gaining by the minute.

'Mum, there's not going to be enough time. I'm going to try something, but you've got to trust me.'

His mum nodded in agreement and concentrated on looking ahead.

'Okay, when we get to the turnoff, I want you to turn as though you are going that way, but then I want you to head at an angle to the side that leads you straight into the trees.'

'Charlie, the bushes and trees might soften our impact, but we could get seriously hurt and then he will collide straight into the back of us.'

'I know, Mum, but we must take that risk. If he goes on, others are going to suffer.'

'Charlie, I'm gonna trust you, okay? I just really hope you know what you're doing.'

The seedling started to bounce on the back seat. Charlie smiled and winked at it, as he looked back and saw that the Land Rover was almost upon them. So much so that it butted the back of their car, which wobbled violently from side to side. Charlie's mum kept great control.

Charlie closed his eyes, as they were on the approach to the turning.

'Mum, it's important that you let me know when you are making the turn, as I have my eyes closed.'

'Okay!'

Charlie's mum, now back in control, picked up speed. The Land Rover was momentarily slower, but soon started to catch up. Charlie felt the breeze entwine him, and his thoughts expanded as the breeze began to entwine the car. He was in a full meditative state, ready for the next step of his plan.

The turning came and his mum shouted "Now", just as they were driving directly towards the crash barrier at the side of the turning, with the Land Rover ready to give them another bump.

Jennifer screamed, held the steering wheel tightly and closed her eyes, bracing for impact. Charlie gave it everything it had as he pushed his hands downwards and, just as they were about to hit the barrier head-on, the car lifted and the tyres caught the tops of the bushes but continued to rise as they heard a loud bang.

The Land Rover had gone into the barrier at such a speed that it lifted and flipped several times through the bushes, coming to a halt as it was about to crash against the trees. The police caught up and blocked the road as people swarmed out of their cars toward the crash area.

Jennifer opened her eyes and quickly held the sides of the driver's seat to steady herself as she looked down through the window. They were above the trees and the roads looked like spaghetti.

They were flying!

They remained silent and the only sound was a gentle breeze as they continued to fly towards an empty car park, close to a lake and amongst trees, where they floated down slowly. As the tyres touched the ground, Charlie released his power a bit too soon, and the car dropped half a foot with a bump.

His mum left the car, her legs wobbling as she held the door to keep steady. The little thistledown was bouncing up and down on the back seat, and Charlie breathed a huge sigh and lay back in his seat.

There was no need for words. Jennifer controlled her breathing as best she could to stop herself from hyperventilating, as she looked at Charlie. He smiled and tried not to appear smug but he was slightly concerned about her.

After a few moments, he got out of the car and took her arm. He led her towards a wooden bench on the grass by the lake. He broke the silence.

'Mum, are you okay? Sorry, I had to do that, but it was the only way.'

Jennifer got her breath back, and replied, 'Charlie, that was incredible.'

She got up and wrapped her arms around him and continued, 'Oh, my son. You're growing up so fast. Please try and be careful when and how you use your gift. I know you had to use it then; I just hope no one clocked our number plate. But you need to keep this a secret.'

'I will, Mum. I promise. I had no choice.'

'I know, I know. You're just like your father, Cha.'

Charlie smiled, proud of that remark, but sad that his dad wasn't there to see what had happened.

'Charlie, I need to tell you something. We were going to wait until you were older, but after what I just saw you do, you need to know now.'

'Okay, Mum. I'm listening.'

The thistledown floated from the car, landing on Charlie's shoulder.

'Charlie, I didn't meet your father here.'

'What do you mean? England? Was it in Scotland then, or Wales even?'

'No, it wasn't anywhere here.'

'Okay, give me a clue. Which continent did you meet Dad in?'

'None of them, Charlie.'

Charlie was silent, confused by what she was trying to say.

'Charlie, I'll explain sometime how I met your father, but you need to know that he isn't a human being, as we know humans to be.'

Charlie was even more confused.

'What? Is he an alien?'

'No, no, Cha. Nothing like that. He is from here, but not just from here. He's an elemental master. He's from another realm and travels back and forth through a portal connecting Earth with his world.'

Charlie couldn't speak. He was at a loss for words but, after recent events, he wasn't as surprised as he could have been.

'We met after I stumbled through one of the two ways into his realm. Well, I was close enough that a creature pulled me in and caged me as a zoo animal in their world. It was your dad who found me locked up there and he rescued me, got me back to this world and destroyed the portal, so now only one remains.'

Charlie stared at his mum, not knowing what to say. He looked at the thistledown which was still sitting silently on his shoulder and then back to his mum.

'So, Charlie, I think you have gained his talent as you have the blood of an elemental master. They're very rare. They hold the power of the elements and rule the land. Your father chose someone to take his place on his throne and left his realm for me.'

'Wait … so Dad was royalty as well as an elemental master?'

'Yes, Charlie, he was. We were so happy together here and spent many wonderful years enjoying life. He sometimes took me through the remaining portal, where you came to be and that's where you were born. I'll never forget the shine in his eyes when you arrived and then we came back through the portal to here. They were incredible times. You and your father bonded quickly. We never returned to his realm after that.'

Tears formed in Charlie's eyes, as he was deep in thought about his father, rather than hearing about his origin. He couldn't believe that he had been created and born outside of Earth, in another realm.

'Mum, do you have any idea why or where Dad might have disappeared? Is he still alive?'

'I have a feeling, but I don't know where the entrance to his kingdom is anymore. About a month before he disappeared, he got a visit from a ghostly figure. I don't know what words were spoken, but he said that he needed to go back for a few days and that I was to stay and watch over you. And here we are, three years later.'

'So you knew where Dad was all along, and you didn't think to tell me about it.'

'Sorry, Charlie. I couldn't tell the police. Who would believe me? I couldn't risk anyone finding out that a portal … '

He interrupted.

'No, Mum. I'm your son. You should have trusted me and told me. I'd have understood. He's my dad and I had every right to know.'

He was angry. The thistledown decided to leave his shoulder and settle on his mum's arm, as she had become tearful and was attempting to reassure him.

'Charlie. Please listen. I'm so sorry.'

He walked away from her, towards the lake. He picked up a few stones and started to skim them across the surface of the water. A small hole, like a tiny drain, appeared in the water. He threw another stone at it and the hole began to grow.

'Charlie, please let me explain.'

'What's to explain? You knew that Dad had possibly gone back home a few years ago and never …'

He was cut short by the look of fear on his mum's face. He heard a sudden gush of water come out of the lake, behind him. A tentacle-like stretch of water rose from the hole, crashing down over him. He started to fight for his life, kicking his arms and legs frantically and trying to breathe, spinning erratically with water in every direction, as he was pulled down deeper.

He was normally a fantastic swimmer, but he was starting to weaken as he could no longer fight the water. One minute he was arguing on the bank of the lake and, the next, he was engulfed in water.

He thought he was swimming upwards but realised that he had lost all sense of direction. With his lungs filling with water, he began to panic. He was sinking and his swimming slowed, as everything became dark and cloudy. He desperately wanted to gasp for breath. He could just make out a huge dark image approaching him from the depths and thought he saw huge jaws, but he didn't have any strength and eventually succumbed to the waters, losing consciousness.

CHAPTER 15

THE LAKE

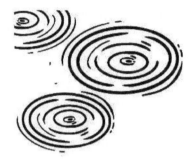

Charlie felt strange as he slowly regained consciousness. He dared not open his eyes after what he'd been through and felt as though he was floating, as his body gently rocked. He was breathing but felt restricted, as though a pillow was over his face allowing just enough pressure to breathe.

He heard a voice, although it was muffled and slightly distorted by bubbles.

'Hmmmm, you seem to be waking, Landwalker. Good. If you can hear me, keep your eyes closed for now or you may go into shock.'

Charlie had no intention of opening his eyes. He was already in shock from being taken by a wave and thought he was drowning. He was gently rocking and began to shake as he realised that he might have died and this was how the afterlife felt.

The voice came back a moment later.

'Now, lie still. What I'm about to do is not necessary but it'll subconsciously help you feel better about being here.'

Charlie was confused. Something was being applied around his nose and mouth and he scrunched his face as it felt uncomfortable.

'Yes,' the voice chuckled, 'I imagine you don't have a clue what's happening and wonder what's being applied to your face. I imagine it feels strange to you, but don't worry. All will be revealed, just one more thing to do'

He felt the strange sensation again, this time around his eyes.

'That's it. Ready. Open your eyes, but slowly, so that you can take in your surroundings.'

Whatever had been applied, Charlie was relieved that the muffled feeling around his nose, mouth and eyes was gone. He slowly opened one eye but quickly closed it tight again. He wasn't ready for that.

The voice came again.

'Ah, sorry, that's my fault. I hadn't told you that you are under water so it will feel strange when you open your eyes. I've applied a jellygil to them too.'

Charlie had no idea what a jellygil was but assumed they were covering his nose, eyes and mouth. He lifted his hand and gave a thumbs-up as he squinted to allow his surroundings to focus, and then he opened his eyes fully. It took him a moment to visualise everything and take in the realisation that he was under water.

He could make out something large, close to him, in the shadows of the cave, moving about slowly. It was hard to tell under water, but he thought that was where the voice came from, due to the direction of the bubbles.

'Hmmm, now then. That's something I'll need to teach you, as you obviously can't see very well, despite the jellygil coating your eyes. But don't worry, I'll explain how you will be able to see properly under water and great distances,' the voice chuckled.

The dark shape moved from the darkness of the cave into the light.

'There, that's better now, isn't it, Landwalker?'

Charlie was taken by surprise and swam back a little as there, by his side, was a huge talking walrus-type creature, with a long moustache dragging on the ocean floor from his whiskered nose. One of the large tusks, protruding from his mouth, was only half a tusk as the other half was broken off. Charlie remembered Tsangali and wondered if this was a common trait of the creatures of this world.

'Come on now, Landwalker. Have you not seen a walrum before?'

'Well, maybe something we call a walrus where I'm from, but never a walrum and certainly not one that talks.'

'Ahhhh, what a strange word to use, walrus,' he laughed. 'It sounds like a primitive version of me, I guess.'

The creature scratched his head with a fin which appeared to have fingers at the end of it. He certainly looked like a huge walrus, grey with a long moustache and a little tufted beard below his mouth.

'Oh my, how rude of me. My name is Aqualdium, and I'm one of the guardians of water. I'm assuming you have guessed that already' he said, with another laugh.

Charlie nodded and introduced himself.

'Hi, I'm Charlie, a human … well kind of. Actually, I'm not sure what I am at the moment.'

'Ah, there now, Landwalker Charlie. You'll discover who you are, I'm sure. Let's not worry.'

Aqualdium's smile was infectious and Charlie quickly felt at ease, smiling back. He began to look around seeing he was in a cave, obviously under water somewhere. It was lit up by, what seemed to be, an array of small light golden fish swimming in circles in the same area. They weren't in jars and seemed free, but they were more than content to swim together in the same circle, lighting up the cave with a beautiful bright glow. There were also shelves containing a collection of jars and gadgets.

Charlie was curious about where he was.

'So, Aqualdium. Where are we exactly, please?'

'Ah, great manners you have, Landwalker. I'm surprised you don't know. But then, you mentioned being human and I have never heard of a human until now. You are in the Kingdom of Watsurea and I am one of its guardians. Around you are elementals of the water.

'Watsurea? But how did I get here, to your home? Which I'm extremely grateful for, by the way.'

'Well, lucky for you, I found you drifting near my cave entrance. You were nearly dinner for an ecronum which was coming straight at you with its mouth wide open. It would have taken you if it wasn't for my heroics when I darted in and pushed you into my cave. I don't normally interfere with the natural order of things, but something called to me while I was out on a hunt. I wasn't sure what it was, but I had to trust it. So, I headed home as quickly as I could and, there you were, ready to be the main course.'

'Crikey, thanks so much, Aqualdium. I appreciate you saving my life.'

'Ah, think nothing of it, Charlie. You made me feel loads better, to be honest. But I must ask, how did you come to be here? You're nowhere near land and a land walker can rarely survive being under water. I only know of one and let's just hope we don't ever come across it, Charlie. Enough said.'

'I'm not sure, to be honest. One minute, I was arguing with Mum and, the next, I felt a heavy whack of water. Before I knew it, I was under water. I lost energy and felt sure I would drown, then I saw the jaws heading towards me and I woke up here.'

'Hmmm, there must be a reason you are here, Charlie.'

'Have you heard of a Tallemseen?'

'Yes. That's making a bit more sense, Charlie. Book of the prophecy. Tell me, can you see this?'

Aqualdium swam towards the rocky shelves, picked up a thin silver book and showed it to him.

'Well, I can see a book in your hand.'

'Yes, then, in that case, you must be the Chosen One.'

'Chosen?'

'You know the prophecy, as you have the book. Well, now it's time you learned about the power of water. I don't know what it will be, but your trial from this may not be easy.'

'Another trial? I guess that makes sense too.'

'You've been on one already?'

'Yes, the trial of air.'

'Wow, impressive, Charlie. I'm glad you made it here. So, the trial of water is your next quest then.'

Charlie looked at Aqualdium, deep in thought and attempted a smile. He thought back to when he was angry with his mum and left her on the bank of the lake. He wasn't sure if he would see her again, remembering how dangerous his last trial was. He wondered if she would be okay if, for whatever reason, he didn't make it. His thoughts were interrupted as a thick fin rested on his shoulder.

'Charlie, you look deep in thought. You were staring right at me yet didn't even see me moving towards you. I have great confidence in you, so please don't worry. You've already gained your first power in my kingdom.'

'How so?' Charlie asked, puzzled.

'Well, you can hear my voice and understand my words. Ask any of your land walker friends if they can hear these words and they will look at you and worry,' he laughed. 'You'll be able to hear the creatures of water now when you listen to them and you'll understand what those that can't talk need. You also gained another power as you sank because small gills have appeared behind those big circular things, sticking out on the side of your head.'

Charlie was confused and felt his ears. He could feel a few lines, like cuts, but they were moving, almost breathing, on the side of his head. It was a little unnerving.

Aqualdium swam towards some seaweed and slid his fin across it. Like a curtain, it pulled aside to reveal a mirror. Charlie swam over to it, feeling nauseous at the thought of the cuts behind his ears. He saw what looked like large gills and they were breathing as they opened and closed. He felt uncomfortable.

'So, you see, my friend. You can breathe under water. You don't need the jellygils around your nose and mouth. Your eyes don't need them either but it takes a while to adjust fully to see things. The one on your mouth is for your comfort as it's better than your mouth filling with water and you panicking.'

'Yes, true. Thanks, Aqualdium.'

'It's no bother. Now, let's learn some more. I'm not sure you know this, but elemental powers can be combined. We don't have to learn these now, due to the time we have, and you're already proficient with the ways of air magic. But just a quick example is that you can use the air vortex to create a whirlpool in water. It spins things and pulls them to the base of the spinning water. We have no idea of your trial, but it could happen at any moment, so we haven't any time to lose. I'm going to show you some things we can practise, Charlie, which are from the book there. You can learn them before you digest the rest of the book. It is very important.'

Charlie nodded in agreement. Aqualdium swam to the exit of the cavern and he followed. As he swam out, he was taken aback by the beauty he saw in the vast lake, surprised by the amount of sea life and the colour of the reeds, as well as the rusty old shop trolley and scooter with no wheels.

As a school of fish swam by, he could hear them talking amongst themselves. When they noticed him, they turned their tails, laughed and darted away.

'Now then my friend, the first thing you're going to learn is how to swim quickly, but don't get too excited or you may lose your way. Try it in short bursts only. Stop yourself by lifting your arms away from your body. I just wanted to make that point, Charlie, in case you shot away too fast while trying. Put your head down, use it to steer, slap your fins down to your side and bring your tail together so that it is straight.'

It took Charlie a moment to decipher but he soon realised that the fins were his arms and the tail were his legs and feet.

Aqualdium continued, 'I'll show you what I mean. It will shoot you forwards at great speed. The faster and harder you throw your fins by your side, the faster you will take off. Now let's aim for the large rock just over there, sticking up from the ground.'

He threw his fins to the side and, with his nose straight, darted forwards at speed. So fast in fact that, when Charlie blinked, he was already at the rock, waving his fin back at him. Charlie looked forwards and slapped his arms straight down to his side and straightened his legs. But instead of going straight, he went into an uncontrollable spin, almost hitting the cavern entrance if he hadn't pulled his arms quickly away from his body in time. He felt dizzy.

Aqualdium was already by his side.

'That was very close. I thought you were gonna cause yourself an injury. You did well but you had your head up straight. Remember, you will shoot in the direction the top of your head is facing if that makes sense. You need to put your head down and look forwards as best you can. I know it's restrictive, but you should be able to judge where you are by looking at the ground.'

Charlie regained his composure and smiled. He was ready this time. He looked towards the rock and noticed the rusty trolley between him and the rock. He knew that if he saw that, he would be going in the right direction. He put his head down, straightened his arms and legs, then catapulted forwards. In moments, he passed the trolley and noticed something shoot by him on his left. As he started to lift his arms, he collided with something which cushioned his impact.

He gained his composure and saw that Aqualdium had keeled over in front of the large rock and was holding his tummy. Charlie realised that he would have collided headfirst into the rock if it hadn't been for the walrum's quick action, using himself as a cushion.

'Oh dear, are you okay? I'm so sorry. Thanks for saving me.'

'Oooof, not a problem, Charlie. Just glad you're okay. You learn very fast indeed. Just remember that you need to weigh up the ground level quickly and be aware of distances to avoid collisions. I'm going to rest for a minute. Let's head back so you can read that book as you will need to learn all of it.'

With that, he swam back towards the cave. Charlie executed a missile zoom and stopped just before the entrance. Aqualdium smiled proudly at him as he entered the cave. Charlie followed and swam to a makeshift table, a rock that jutted out beside the shelves.

He opened the book that was laid on it and began to read. It didn't mention the trial like the previous book did but it taught some more useful water magic. How to produce water on dry land, how to raise and reduce water levels but bear in mind consequences elsewhere, since a balance in one place doesn't mean it is correct in another. On the water's surface, things may go catastrophically wrong if not done correctly.

He learned of the power to create tidal waves of different proportions and how this can also be applied under water to produce a kind of sonic water wave or barrier. He learned how to turn solid into liquid and back to solid. He practised freezing and boiling water, although he almost scalded himself before realising he'd best cool it down.

He learned about how water, the realm he was in, was created. He also learned about a great chaos that almost destroyed the realm of water but was subsided by an agreement made.

CHAPTER 16

IN TOO DEEP

There was so much to read, and a few hours had passed before he reached the end of the book. When he read the last page, about a spell which should only be used in time of need, the book pulled away from him and began to disintegrate in the water. It simply floated into a thousand tiny pieces which divided again, getting smaller and smaller, until the book was almost no more and shot towards Charlie. He felt a tingle in his chest and saw that his tattoo now showed the sea below the sky. The sea looked rough and full of large waves.

'Well, Charlie. It looks like you might not be such a land walker after all,' Aqualdium laughed.

Charlie was unable to laugh as he felt that uncomfortable feeling when something bad was close. Aqualdium's laughter was short-lived as an awful roar came from outside the mouth of the cave and a shadow darkened the hole.

The cave shook and, before he knew it, Charlie was pushed against the wall as a large rock fell from the cave roof. Aqualdium managed to move him in time, as the rock crashed and broke the table where he had just been sitting. Aqualdium put his fin to his mouth indicating to Charlie to remain quiet. The cave became very dark as the glowing fish distinguished their light; a defence mechanism to hide.

A dark creature rubbed against the entrance as it passed, collapsing rocks. Another roar sent shivers down Charlie's spine.

It was silent for several minutes. Neither of them moved, concentrating on listening for a sound. There was nothing.

Charlie whispered, 'I'm gonna take a look,' and was already at the cave exit before Aqualdrium could stop him.

'Be careful, Charlie. That didn't sound good.'

Charlie smiled and gave him a confident wink as he started to push himself through the hole. It was very quiet and there was no sign of life in the water as before. He pulled himself out of the hole and realised there was a dark shadow below him, which was quickly getting bigger. He didn't hesitate. He threw his hands to his side, straightened his head and legs and launched himself, as the nose of the creature dived and hit the ground where he had been a moment before.

Charlie gained his composure and turned towards the creature. He recognised the jaws; it was the ecronum. It opened its mouth, made another moaning roar and thrust itself towards him. He didn't hesitate as he quickly darted to the left and, although the ecronum turned, it wasn't fast enough. It shook its head in anger and quickly swam towards Charlie, opening its jaws, baring its teeth.

Again, he managed to avoid it. This time though, the ecronum struck its huge tail against the rock that he almost hit when training. The rock came hurtling toward him and he made a quick dash but, this time, he struck something firm which winded him. It was the ecronum. It had taken advantage of Charlie avoiding the rock and headed straight towards the place he would swim. However, it overswam so he hit it, but not enough to put him off-balance.

The ecronum took the opportunity to lash its fin at Charlie and it struck hard. He was hurtled towards the side of the lake, hitting it with some force as the mud became dislodged and fell, like a waterfall, towards him, pushing him down forcefully to the bed of the lake. He felt hopeless and could hardly move as his legs were already buried. He couldn't straighten his arms or legs as the mudslide continued to cover him up to his lower stomach.

He could see nothing through the falling mud. He was trying his best to free himself, but it was no use. He was stuck fast, and the mud was still falling. It was up to his chest when he noticed a dark shadow coming towards him. He thought it might be Aqualdium but, when he saw its teeth, he knew it was the ecronum. However, instead of attacking, it swam above Charlie and used its body to prevent the rest of the mud from burying him. It then began to wave its tail fin above him to dislodge the mud that was holding him fast and loosened it enough for him to free himself.

Charlie was confused and swam quickly over to some large rocks on the waterbed and hid behind them, peering across to check where the ecronum was. The water was very murky and he couldn't see. He waited until the mud started to settle before he saw that the creature was trapped in the mudslide. It lay still, almost disguised by the banks of the lake.

There could be no more danger.

Charlie swam back to the cave entrance to remove some boulders and rocks to help Aqualdium exit. But when a weak sobbing groan came from the ecronum, Charlie paused.

'Aqualdium, are you okay in there?'

'Yes, Charlie, I'm fine.'

'Can you hang in there a little longer? I need to do something.'

'Okay, Charlie. Be careful.'

He swam back to the ecronum and sensed that it was sad and in pain, by the sound it was making. He dared to swim towards the beast's jaws where he was upset to see a large swelling. He slowly touched the ecronum and gave it a gentle stroke, just above its jaws.

'There now. I'm a friend, okay? Thanks for helping me. I think I can see why you're in pain and I'm going to try and help you.'

In acknowledgement, the ecronum gave a reassuring calmer groan.

'I'm just going to get something, and I'll be right back.'

At the cave entrance, Charlie remembered that he could use the power of air with water and decided to try an experiment, unsure what the mix would do. He looked at the large boulders blocking the entrance, then closed his eyes for a moment before a pocket of air surrounded his body. He opened his eyes, pointed towards the boulders and pulled his arms back with full concentration. The largest boulder began to rock and shift a little. He pulled harder and it eventually came free. He turned slightly, then released the boulder in a safe place.

He turned and saw that Aqualdium was already out of his cave and pulling the smaller rocks from the entrance, clearing the way. Charlie swam over to him.

'Have you got any tongs?' he asked.

'I'm not sure what you mean, Charlie.'

'They help you pick things up safely that might be too hot to touch.'

By Aqualdium's blank expression, Charlie realised that he probably wouldn't need such a thing in water. He swam into the cave and searched everywhere but couldn't see anything that might be of use. He swam back to the entrance, where Aqualdium was floating and keeping an eye on the ecronum.

'Aqualdium, I'm going to do something which is possibly stupid. There is a long twisted coral-like splinter wedged deep in the ecronum's jaw which looks painful. I think that's what has been aggravating him. We won't know until I get it out.'

'What? Wait, Charlie. That's really understanding of you, but can you trust that thing, to help it? Are you sure about going into its mouth?'

'Yes, Aqualdium. I think it has a lot to do with its aggression. It saved me just now from being buried. That's got to count for something.'

'Then I'll go in and remove it, Charlie. You stay at a safe distance.'

'No, I need to do this. Your fins won't be able to wrap around it and remove it.'

'Can you not use your power to remove it, instead of going so close?'

Charlie thought for a moment and smiled.

'That's a great idea. Why didn't I think of that?'

They both swam to the ecronum, which was stuck fast in the mud and not able to move. Charlie closed his eyes and began to concentrate. There was nothing. He frowned deeply, trying his best to pull in the air but, again, nothing came.

Aqualdium started to make a noise rather like a walrus.

Charlie interpreted that as, 'What's wrong?' so he answered, 'I don't know. I'm going to try again from over there.'

Charlie swam away and started to concentrate again, but nothing was coming. It was as though his powers were gone. He started to realise that he wasn't breathing so well either. The jellygil around his mouth was expanding, thus reducing his breathing. He felt behind his ears and realised that he no longer had gills, so he was relying on the jellygil.

He knew he needed to act quickly as his breathing was becoming shallow. He began to use a meditation process that Jan taught him to keep calm and slow his breathing, thus prolonging his airtime so he could slow down possible suffocation.

He swam back to the jaws. This was it. There was nothing for it. He knew that his oxygen wasn't going to last much longer, and he wasn't prepared to let another suffer. He looked at Aqualdium and hugged him. He made a walrus-type noise, so it seemed that the loss of power also meant a loss of understanding creatures.

He swam into the jaws of the ecronum. He was aware that he was in danger on so many levels and needed to move quickly. He felt the raw inflamed area and the ecronum let out a huge roar which almost projected Charlie out of its mouth. He could see the hole where the coral was and lay against it, reaching in with his arm. As the beast's tongue tried to reach Charlie to push him away, he could tell that it was in pain.

He continued to feel about in the hole until he found something solid and twisted it. He gripped the coral as hard as he could and pulled. The beast's roar dislodged him and he was sent flying out of the jaw.

He swam back to the ecronum and spoke again reassuringly, 'Don't worry, we nearly have it. Let's give it one more try.'

Aqualdium made another walrus sound and pointed his fin to his mouth, which confirmed to Charlie that his theory was right. He wondered if he should swim upwards and reach the surface but he knew he wouldn't make it as his breathing was getting too shallow and he couldn't last much longer. He maintained his patience.

He looked at the jaw and knew that this would be his last attempt as the jellygil had hardly any air left and he was beginning to struggle.

He swam back into the gaping jaws and, without hesitation, plunged his hands into the hole and firmly gripped whatever it was. He pulled again but it would not budge and only hurt the ecronum more. He kept his grip and twisted. To his relief, it moved. He twisted it again and it started to loosen. The ecronum was still crying out but he embedded himself as an anchor on either side of its teeth, continually unscrewing the object.

His vision was starting to blur and he found it harder to breathe but, at last, he managed to dislodge the item and pull it from the hole. He escaped from the ecronum's jaws just as it closed its mouth. The object in Charlie's hand began to glow. He started to feel a bit better as he could breathe again. He even understood Aqualdium when he spoke.

'Charlie, are you okay? You did it.'

Charlie nodded with a smile. He turned towards the ecronum, brought in his power and raised his hands to dislodge the mud that was trapping the creature.

He knew from the glow on his chest that he had completed the trial of water.

The ecronum nodded toward him with gratitude as Charlie began to spin upwards uncontrollably, holding tightly to the coral rod. He closed his eyes, felt himself break through the surface of the lake, and landed heavily on the ground with a huge splash of water crashing down on him.

He was coughing and spluttering. He tried to catch his breath and heard a muffled voice which became clearer.

'Charlie, are you okay?'

His vision started to return and he saw his mum supporting him as he sat up on the muddy ground, still holding the twisted rod. He looked at her.

'I'm okay, Mum, sorry I yelled.'

He gave her the biggest hug.

'Charlie, that wave must have hit you harder than I thought. Are you sure you're okay?'

She placed her hands over his wet cheeks, studying his eyes for any sign of concussion.

'That was one freak wave. I wonder how that happened. Come to the car and get warm. Maybe pop your clothes on the back to dry and I'll turn on the heating. You're shivering.'

'Was I gone long?'

She gave him a strange look and felt the temperature of his forehead.

'Charlie, you were here all the time. You only got hit by a burst of water from the lake. Goodness knows what caused it.'

She helped him to the car. He undressed and lined his clothes along the back seat while she brought him a towel that she kept in the boot so he could get dry and wrap it around himself.

She looked at Charlie's chest and seemed a bit confused as she rubbed the markings. He looked down and saw that it had changed. Beautifully coloured water was now showing below the sky, with a golden border.

The twisted coral rod, which had been lying on the back seat, started to gravitate toward his bag as though a strong magnet was pulling it. He opened the zipper and it shot into the bag and wound itself around the glass rod, giving it a coral design.

As his mum turned on the car heater, all he could think about was his next trial. What would it be, and when?

CHAPTER 17

THE WARMING COALS

Charlie pulled the rod from his bag, examining it. He tried to untwist the coral, but it was stuck fast to the glass rod. He returned it securely to his bag, placing it in the footwell. His shivering subsided as raindrops started to form on the car window but he felt snug and safe in the warmth of the car. The little thistledown fairy was relaxed in the back seat as Charlie's mum started the car. She looked at Charlie and smiled.

'Are you okay now, Son?'

'Yeah, thanks, Mum. Sorry I had a go at you. It just came as a surprise, that's all.'

'It's okay, my love. You don't need to apologise. I'm only sorry I hadn't told you sooner.'

'So what does it mean? Am I not human? Where did Dad come from? Do you think he could be there now?'

'Charlie, it means that you are part human and part elemental, but I don't know the official name for that. Your dad is from the elemental realm, but I don't think he'd be silly enough to go back there. I'll tell you all about it sometime. It wasn't easy for us but we pulled through and I know that you will too.'

She smiled, trying to hide the pain she was feeling. She revved the engine a little and set off although Charlie didn't have any idea where they were going. He had to ask.

'Mum, where are we heading? We hadn't planned such a long drive, and I think we might be safe now. I hope Mr Grimauld is okay. I don't think it's his fault that he's always coming for us.'

'Yeah, that was quite an accident there but I'm sure he'll be okay as the police and ambulance were there straight away. I thought I'd give you a surprise and a couple of days' rest, as it's the weekend. I made a call from the café.'

'Oh! Where are we going?'

'Well, do you remember when you were younger, and we went through that long tunnel every year and you used to think we were going into a dinosaur world? Well, look ahead.'

Charlie looked as far as he could see ahead through the wipers, which were going back and forth. They were approaching the tunnel that took them from England into Wales. He was elated.

'Oh, wow. Haha, I remember now. Are we visiting Aunty Betty and Aunty Pamela in the valleys?'

Charlie's mum laughed at his excitement.

'If we get time. That's if they're in, of course. We're staying a couple of nights with your grandfather.'

Charlie loved Wales. He made friends so easily in the villages throughout the valleys. It was where his mum was born, in a little town called Bargoed. So, apart from being elemental, he was very proud to be part Welsh too.

It was great being in the tunnel. The sound was a little muffled and lights shone through tubes at the side, almost as though they were travelling through some sort of space station. The lighting made the walls very white. The exit was a tiny dot in the distance which grew bigger as they drove towards it. Charlie used to look through the forest trees when they came out, in search of a Tyrannosaurus rex or perhaps happen to spot a diplodocus munching the leaves. He almost swore he saw a diplodocus once until his friend, Kevin, who was spending time with them at that point, pointed out that dinosaurs no longer exist. It didn't put Charlie off imagining them though.

Charlie and his mum said out loud, 'Dinosaur Land' and laughed together. Even the little thistledown shook with laughter in the back seat.

They drove for another hour, passing lots of mountains and fields, often slowing to allow sheep to wander across the road. As they approached the valleys of Wales, the views were spectacular, overlooking the rivers and the tiny model-like houses below. Charlie's mum drove carefully as the roads were narrow, like one lane but meant for two-way traffic. At one point, the fencing at the side of the road was broken and Charlie could only assume that a car had lost control and plummeted over the edge.

They pulled up into a small street. The houses were very old and made of concrete with lots of tiny stones mixed in. The netting at the window in one house moved a little. That was where Grandad William Jenkins sat, with his elbows on the table and a rolled cigarette in his hand, watching the world go by. He was always people-watching.

'We're at Grandad's,' Charlie smiled.

The green-painted front door was already open and there was Grandad Jenkins, standing to attention, with a big grin on his toothless face; his dentures probably sitting somewhere in the house.

The rain had subsided when they got out of the car but the waft of lavender was strong from the front garden and butterflies and bees were loving life amongst the purple.

'Awww, Dad,' Charlie's mum called as she went up to her father and gave him the biggest hug.

'What're you doing ya then, Jen? You could've told me and I'd have made you both dinner, Love.'

'Awww, Da. I know you would, Lovely. It was a last-minute decision.'

'Well, your bedrooms are still made up from last time. You're always welcome, you know tha.'

Charlie got out of the car, carrying his backpack with the thistledown resting on the top, and grabbed his wet clothes.

'What are you doing, ma boy, wearing a towel in this weather? You'll catch your death of cold. Come in quickly, come and sit by the coal fire. Jen, why you let him travel like that for?'

'Hey, Pap. Great to see you.'

Charlie gave him a warm hug and entered the house, popping his backpack on the settee as he sat down cross-legged in front of the fire. He felt warm and, for the first time, so relaxed. He loved nothing more than the scent of a coal fire burning and, whenever he smelt it, he would always think of his grandad.

Grandad was very old-fashioned in his ways and still had one of those thin heavy irons that were heated over the coal fire to press his shirts, which were always pristine.

Charlie's mum popped back to the car to get some things from the boot, locked it and returned to the house.

'Shift to one side, Charlie. Let's pop this up for your mam.'

Charlie moved to the side as his grandad erected an old wooden clothes-horse which was folded in three with material keeping it together. He placed it like a triangle and Jennifer hung the damp clothes on it.

'They'll soon dry. Thanks, Dad.'

Charlie was always transfixed by the flames dancing around the coals. He would often run around the house to find any paper he could pop in it to watch the flames dance higher before they faded, leaving a red glow on the surface of the greying coals.

'Would you both like a warm cup of tea down you?'

They answered in unison, 'Oooh, yes please.'

Charlie picked up his rucksack and took it up to his bedroom. He already knew where it was as they had visited Grandad two weeks every year and had their own rooms, never used by anyone else and always kept for them. Rather than quilts on the bed, there were old thick sheets and blankets.

He sat on the bed, pulled the parchments from the pocket and noticed that there was writing on two of them. The watermarked one from the mini tsunami and the one from the tornado. The scorched one and the muddy one were still blank. He tried to match up the two with the designs on but it didn't make sense. There was possibly a map somewhere in there.

He took out the book and was about to start reading it when his grandfather called from downstairs. He carefully returned the book to the bag and indicated to the thistledown to watch over it. She acknowledged her agreement by bobbing up and down on the bag. He headed back downstairs, where his mum and grandad were sitting at the table by the window with tea and flat-looking scones, known as Welsh cakes, on a small plate next to the cups.

The tea was amazing although it had an unusual flavour. Charlie pulled a strange face when he tasted it.

'Tin milk,' said his mum, as though she knew exactly what he was thinking,

They had a bit of the usual catchup chat but missed out telling Grandad about the strange happenings.

Then his mum said, 'Well, Charlie. We'll be staying a couple of nights, so as soon as your clothes are dried, we can pop into the town and get some clothes and toiletries.'

She felt the clothing and they were almost dry. His grandad piped in, 'Charlie, shovel some more coal into the fire, will you? It'll soon dry those clothes.'

Charlie used the little spade and shovelled a good amount of coal from the bag in the corner. It was quite heavy. He carefully sprinkled the coal over the top as he had been shown previously. A couple of coals fell forwards, so he put on a thick heat-resistant glove to distribute them evenly. It wasn't long before they started to flame and he cuddled his knees, resting his head on them, fascinated by the flames.

'Come on, Dad. Let's start getting the dinner prepared. I'll come in and help you.'

They left for the kitchen while Charlie stared at the flickering flames in the coals and the red embers which flowed on the surface. The flames were dying down a bit, so he picked up the poker by the hearth and poked at them a little until the flames rose again.

He made himself comfortable but was distracted by one particular flame that didn't seem to burn from any coal or kindling. He stared at it curiously as it was sitting slightly above the rest and seemed to be slowly growing while the others settled.

His hypnotism was short-lived when he had the biggest fright and he jumped up, screaming. A face had appeared on the flame, with a mouth that was opened wide. It threw itself from the fire, engulfing Charlie who stumbled back.

The ground didn't feel carpeted anymore but was solid and cold like stone. He opened his eyes, realising he was no longer sitting in his grandfather's house. It was very dark with lots of flat stones dotted around, some with a red glow emitting heat and occasional flame bursts from the gaps in the stones.

There was a slight rumbling as the dust started to dance with the vibrations from what sounded like rolling thunder. A small, orange-furred creature, about the height of his knee, came into view, scurrying at speed. It looked like a rabbit but, instead of floppy ears, there were long trailing flames, as it dodged him at the last moment before carrying on.

There was a loud 'MOOOOooooove' but it was too late as something collided with Charlie while he was distracted by the rabbit creature. He lost his balance and fell to the ground, covering his ears, as the sound of metal on stone was deafening.

'WELL, DON'T JUST SIT THERE. HELP ME UP,' shouted something from the metal.

Charlie picked himself up and readjusted his towel, tightening it.

'Sorry, I didn't mean to get in your way. Are you okay?'

He walked over to the metal which seemed to be struggling and reached out his hand in an attempt to pull, whatever it was, up.

The armour managed, with Charlie's help, to stand and shake himself.

'Who are you to ruin my hunt?' enquired the armour, rudely.

'I'm Charlie and I just got here. Sorry about that, I didn't see you coming.'

'Well, surely you must have heard me?'

'I was distracted by that animal thing.'

'ANIMAL THING? You had no idea that was a flarune? Are you not from around here? How did you manage to touch my hand and not burn yourself?'

The metal armour had calmed down a little when it realised that it had stumbled across something unusual.

'I'm not from here, no. I have just got here, a few minutes ago.'

'But you're in the middle of a fire desert. You couldn't have just got here, even if you were the speediest jetboat rider. You're not even wearing armour, so you should have burned.'

'Honestly, I don't know and it's not hot enough here to burn. Where are we?'

'You don't even burn here? You're standing in the Realm of Inferblaze and you have no idea?'

'No. Honestly.'

The armour scratched its helmet.

'Hmmm, I'm Brune, the guardian of fire. I have a feeling about you. Come on, follow me.'

Charlie started to walk behind him, but Brune rose a little from the ground, with flames under his big boots, and was about to shoot forwards when he looked back and realised that Charlie was still standing. He landed back on the ground and looked Charlie up and down, as he stood with the towel around him.

'Where is your attire, anyway?'

'Well, ummm … it's drying by the fireplace.'

'Other than a fire palace, I've no idea what you're on about, young one.'

'No not palace, place.'

'Palace, place, whatever. Now, let's hush this and get back. Come along.'

Charlie approached cautiously as Brune held his arms out towards him, with metallic gauntlets, indicating him to come forwards. He then lifted and cradled Charlie as he again rose from the ground and started to speed forwards.

CHAPTER 18

PRACTICE MAKES PERFECT

They picked up the pace Charlie could hear the roaring of the flames under Brune's feet and the breeze created by their speed as they moved above the glowing embers which seemed to merge the ground into a dark red blanket.

Ahead, Charlie could see what looked like a flaming village with a huge bonfire in the centre, which was getting bigger. Firelights, like candle flames but the height of human beings, were darting around, eventually disappearing into the surrounding burning buildings.

They approached the Village of Fire. What Charlie originally thought was a bonfire turned out to be flaming towers. He was surprised as his towel was set alight by the heat. He was confused that he only felt warm when he should be burning. He threw away the blazing towel, covering his embarrassing parts with his hands, certain he heard Brune laugh. They were heading for the centre, between the burning towers, and the flaming gates began to open on their approach.

'Wow, this is incredible.'

Charlie couldn't help but be in awe of the burning splendour within the walls as they entered.

'This is Inferno Palace, Young One. You aren't from around here, are you?'

'Nope,' was all Charlie could say, spellbound by the intricate design within the walls as the gates closed behind them. The flames seemed tame within the glass. He saw many pillars and outhouses, with the palace ahead.

'Now, before I take you into the palace, we best get you something to wear.'

Charlie was placed on the ground where the cobbles were like glass with burning fires below them. Brune led Charlie to a small house on the left, calling to two small figures coming out of the flaming door.

'Make sure you're home before the light climbs, Bundle and Greta.'

'Will do,' they called back, as they left with small flames coming from their metallic armoured boots, heading toward the gates.

'They're my young firelets, Charlie.'

'Ohhhhh. Take after you then,' Charlie laughed.

'Only in some ways,' Brune laughed. 'They look more like their mother though.'

As he spoke, another flaming figure stood at the door, wearing a chainmail dress.

'Felura, this is Charlie. He's a very important guest.'

She disappeared back into the house without a word.

'Don't worry, Young One, she'll be okay. I think she's a little cross that I haven't returned with dinner.'

Charlie wasn't impressed. He hadn't realised until that moment that the flarunes were hunted as food.

'Can't you eat other things than those flarunes?'

'NO, WE CAN'T,' Felura shouted from the kitchen area as they entered. Brune kept quiet as he and Charlie looked at each other, knowing what each was thinking.

'Now, Young One. Let's get you something to wear.'

He went to the children's room, pulling one of Bundle's dark brown tunics from a flaming cupboard, which was fire-proof.

'There, Charlie. I think you'll feel better in this.'

Charlie put it on.

'Hmmm, yes, a little large as it's meant to reach your knees rather than almost touching the ground, but that's fine, Charlie.'

Brune took off his helmet and Charlie was surprised to see a pleasant old man with a beard, moustache and friendly face, although his skin was scarlet, his hair and beard were glowing orange.

Brune's attention was drawn to a shelf in the kids' room, where part of the wall had begun to glow brighter.

'Well, I think that confirms it, Charlie. You must be the child of the prophecy.'

'Why? Why does everyone think I'm the child of the prophecy? I don't get it.'

'I guess you wouldn't understand yet. You still have to find the others to make more sense of it,' Brune answered, while he moved a few books on the shelf, put his hand through the wall and pulled out a bright red book from behind.

'This is yours, I believe.'

'Thanks, Brune. I have been through two, so far.'

Brune looked impressed.

'Well done, Young One. Then you've only one to go after this one.'

He threw the book to Charlie.

'Are you hungry at all, or need something for your thirst?'

'I'm okay, thanks, Brune. I'd just had tea and Welsh cakes.'

Brune looked a little confused, but went to the kitchen. Charlie could hear a muffled row going on behind the closed door. He carefully touched a chair by the table to make sure he wouldn't burn in spite of the length of time being here, he's still weary. Then he sat down before opening the book.

It was filled with teachings about different styles of magic by fire. Charlie seemed to understand the lessons much faster this time, as he snapped his fingers in the air, causing a small flame appeared between them. He laid his hands out flat, as the flames grew to cover his palms. He read that he could hurl flames forward as a weapon or a warning to others. He kept his hands flat, merging the flames to form a huge floating ball of fire. He had to concentrate to keep it central. If the flame started drifting in one direction, he moved his hand in a circular motion to guide it carefully back to the centre.

He pulled his hands apart, the flaming ball growing bigger. He became stuck in that position, unable to turn the page for the next instruction. He couldn't use his air magic to blow the page as it also required his fingers and hands.

'Brune,' he called out.

The huge ball of flame between his hands was starting to look volatile. The shape distorted in several places, getting much larger and harder to control. Charlie began to perspire with fear.

'BRUNE!' he called again. The quarrel in the other room stopped, and Brune came through to Charlie.

'Charlie! What are you doing? Follow me carefully and don't trip, whatever you do.'

Charlie stood while managing to control the huge fireball floating between his hands. Slowly and gently, he started to walk cautiously towards Brune, not taking his eyes off the fireball. Charlie imagined that he had a cup of tea, filled to the brim, to carry upstairs to his parents' bedroom without spilling a drop.

As Charlie started to edge towards Brune, who was easy to spot beyond the fireball, a scream suddenly made him jump. The fireball started to shake violently with flames spurting out before pulling back in, as though it had its own gravity. Charlie stood still, holding his breath, as he tried to regain control. Felura held her mouth, realising her scream was a mistake.

Brune gave his wife a look, motioning towards her to stay calm and quiet. They let out a relieved sigh as Charlie regained control of the fireball, but he kept breathing carefully as he knew anything could still happen. Brune opened the front door, Charlie moved cautiously towards it. At last, after feeling his way over the step, he was outside.

'That's it, Charlie, you're almost there. When I say so, throw both hands up towards the sky and pull them apart a little but stay in that position. That fireball should fly upwards, okay?'

Charlie dared not speak as the fireball was still expanding, becoming harder to control. He nodded acknowledgement, moving further away from the building.

'Charlie, you are in a safe area now. Remember, when you are ready, throw that fireball upwards into the air and widen your arms to release it. Keep in that position though and don't move.'

Charlie gently chucked the large fireball upwards, fearing that it would escape. It slowly rose towards the sky.

'You should have thrown that a bit harder, Young One. It would then have been high enough to be safe.'

The fireball grew as it floated upwards. It was disconcerting to see it was growing faster than it was rising, causing it to slow even more.

'Charlie, why don't you pull your hands back, then push them forward as fast as you can? It may not work as it's purely a guess, but it should still be under your control.'

Charlie did as he was told. He pulled back fast then flung his hands forward. It was just the right time as the flames were becoming uncontrollable. It shot upwards at a faster pace.

'Good, but not fast enough. It's still too dangerous to explode it, Charlie. Try again.'

Charlie repeated the process. He could almost feel the weight of the fireball, shoving it upwards with a grunt, despite feeling a resistance. The fireball moved faster.

'Okay, now snap your fingers outwards, Charlie. Away from you, as if you have just found an efluge crawling up your body and you are throwing it away as far as you can.'

Charlie had no idea what an efluge was, but assumed it was some kind of creepy crawly, so he threw his hands forwards, opening and shaking them. At that moment, the fireball exploded with a brilliant white light as flames shot from all sides. There was the loudest of bangs as a shockwave threw everyone to the ground, even making the flames of the village flicker.

Charlie, Brune, and everyone else who was out at the time were thrown back onto their butts, their hands covering their ears. An even louder bang occurred, sending another shockwave which hit the village even harder, causing a couple of houses to be destroyed by the flames. The palace tower in the centre of the village lost the top of its ornate flaming roof. It was over. The fireball was gone, but the village was in turmoil.

Brune quickly pulled Charlie back into his house, shutting the door.

'Charlie, we need to leave now. Grab that book and get ready. I'll explain the magic of the jet feet as we go. You can help me capture a flarune too, so my wife can make us supper.'

So, that was what they had been arguing about, Charlie assumed.

There was a loud knock at the front door. Charlie grabbed the book before Brune grabbed his arm and took him up the flaming stairs to the bedroom at the back. Brune opened the huge window, cradling Charlie in his arms before he crouched down.

'Charlie, we need to crouch and concentrate all your energy towards your feet. Believe that you can leap and fly.'

Brune leapt, his feet propelling a jet flame, ejecting them out the window. Before they knew it, they were flying through the main city gates. Charlie glanced back and saw several people, huddled in groups at the front of Brune's house.

'Brune, why are they all there? Was it because of me? Why didn't we just fly over the walls instead of through the gate?'

'Charlie, don't worry about them. The wall has a force field above it so that nothing can fly in and potentially destroy us.'

Charlie grabbed Brune tightly, trying to avoid looking down. He remained quiet and wondered where they were heading. Eventually, they began to lower to the ground, but could see Greta, Brune's daughter, flying towards them alone.

Charlie noticed the look of concern in Brune's glowing eyes.

'Greta, where's your brother? He's meant to be with you at all times.'

'Father, please come quickly. He fell into the Beluvian Pit. He's stuck fast and can't move.'

'What were you doing at the Beluvian Pit? I have always forbidden you from going near it. Get yourself home now, Greta. I'll talk to you later.'

She was about to continue but her father shook his head in disgust. Seeing the look on her father's face, she knew she better head straight back.

'Charlie, this might be dangerous. I don't want to put you in any danger. Will you wait here? We will continue this once I've got my son. If you see a flarune, then please capture it. You will enjoy it. Read the book, it'll teach you things you can use.'

Charlie nodded in agreement, understanding the urgency in his voice. Brune ruffled his hair before he crouched, ready to jet off, leaving Charlie alone.

He took out his scarlet book to continue reading it. He learned a lot about harnessing fire magic, different hand and body gestures, creating fire bolts from the sky, and performing a gesture while imagining he had a spear or bow and arrow, which then appeared in flames. Again, he learnt the same casting spell he read in the other books, a spell which should only be performed in an emergency of the utmost danger. No explanation was given about what it did though.

On the last page, he reached the instructions regarding the jet stream, which he was excited to learn about. After several attempts, he managed to position his feet correctly, jetting around a large boulder several times until he was confident with the speed and height, being careful not to go too high. When he landed and approached the book, it began to disappear. Just before it went, it shot towards his chest and the black outline of a flame appearing in the tattoo between the sea and sky.

He thought about Brune having gone to the Beluvian Pit to rescue his son. If only there was something he could do. He began to get bored as he sleepily surveyed his surroundings. He was ready to drift off to sleep when he caught sight of a light, hopping around in the distance. He stayed still as it bounced closer.

CHAPTER 19

DANGER AT THE BELUVIAN PIT

Brune arrived at the Beluvian Pit and called to his son, 'Bundle, are you okay down there? Stay perfectly still.'

There was a moment of silence before he heard rubble crumbling.

'D-Dad, help me.'

'I'm coming, Son. Stay as still as you can now, don't make a sound. I'll work out how to get to you.'

There was a rumble from below. Brune knew that time was not on his side and he needed to act quickly. Just as the fire guardians hunted flarunes, the hunters of fire guardians resided in the Beluvian Pit. Known as trollflames, they were already on the move underground, getting ready for the next hunt.

***

Meanwhile, Charlie was surrounded by the bouncing flarunes. They were hopping about innocently, having fun while he remained quietly behind the stone. He was meant to capture one but did not want to.

He took some biscuits from the tunic pocket that Brune's son must have left there and crumbled them in his hand. He held it out from behind the rock, slowly and gently, then slid out into the open so they could see he was unarmed.

The flarunes stopped hopping, staring up at him, with their flaming noses up in the air, sniffing. Eventually, the largest one held up his paw and the others remained still as he slowly hopped towards Charlie, sniffing cautiously. He hopped about, getting slowly closer, sniffing all the time.

Charlie whispered, 'Hello, I'm Charlie. Don't worry, I won't hurt you, I promise.'

The flarune stopped and its flaming ears seemed to straighten upwards, as though listening carefully. Then it responded.

'You speak our tongue, Charlie. That's unheard of. No creature here understands it and yet you can speak it. If you can understand me, don't say anymore. Just close your hand and wave it up and down.'

Charlie obeyed, closing the hand holding the crumbs, waving it up and down. The other flarunes began to hop around excitedly as if this was a miracle. He could hear a lot of conversations at once. The large flarune put his paw up again.

'Silence, family. Stay where you are. I wish to speak with this creature alone. Stay on guard, quietly.'

They hopped into position, surrounding the rock, as the large one approached Charlie cautiously. He jumped up and settled on Charlie's knee, where he crossed his legs to get comfortable.

'I'm Rayfire, father of my family here, and one of the last remaining flarune families.'

'The last?'

'Yes, Charlie. We've been hunted for centuries by the fire guardians and our numbers have greatly diminished. We've suffered terrible losses but we can't reason with them because they don't understand us. We mean them no harm.'

'I'm sorry to hear that, Rayfire. Thanks for letting me know. How come you're telling me this?'

'Because a prophecy told of another creature, similar to the last, that will be able to speak our tongue.'

'Similar to the last?'

'Yes, another. There was one before you who looked like your kind. It was very unfortunate what happened to it.'

'What? What do you mean? What was his name? What happened? Did he look like me?'

The conversation was short as the ears of all the flarunes lifted in unison.

'We have to leave now, Charlie. The trollflames are on the move.'

'Trollflames?'

'Yes, they hunt everything. They don't care. If it moves, they'll eat it. They'll even eat the fire guardians.'

'Where are they on the move to?'

'They reside in the Beluvian Pit. It was your kind that created a hole that opened in the ground, filling it with these creatures we'd never seen before.'

'Oh no!'

'What is it, Charlie?'

'Brune is at the pit as his son fell in and he's gone to rescue him.'

'Charlie, there's nothing you can do about that now. You should get into that fire fortress.'

'We can't leave them.'

'We can't save them either, Charlie.'

'But how fast are these trolls?'

'They are clumsy and slow, but still dangerous.'

'Rayfire, we need to help him rescue his son. Maybe this is your calling?'

'How so, Charlie?' as Rayfire's interest was piqued.

'You said that hole was opened by my kind. If it can be opened, there has to be a way to close it and, if you help Brune, surely he would see you differently?'

Rayfire seemed unsure, but Charlie's words held merit.

Charlie continued, 'And I have no idea where that pit is, so I need your help to get there.'

'Okay, Charlie. We'll help you get there and nothing more as I can't lose any more of my family. We will leave you when the pit is in sight.'

'Agreed, Rayfire. Thank you.'

Charlie opened his hand when Rayfire tapped it. He took the crumbs and hopped back to the others, giving them each a piece, explaining that he would lead Charlie to the Beluvian Pit. He told them to head back home. There was a dispute amongst the group, and they all decided to go with Charlie, just in case Rayfire got into danger. He eventually agreed but they had to move quickly.

He called out, 'Charlie, are you ready? Try to keep up. We should hurry if we want to rescue Brune's son.'

Charlie nodded prepared his jet feet, as the flarunes packed together and began to hop away. He followed, a little wobbly at first, but his speed picked up. He dodged several boulders through the glowing embers of the dark rocky desert. He almost lost his balance at one point, but managed to remain on course. After several minutes, the air was illuminated by a huge firelight flare which shot skywards.

They could see the glowing red pit ahead, but there was no sign of Brune.

'He must be down there already,' cried Charlie, as Rayfire looked down and nodded in acknowledgement from the edge of the deep sinkhole. Although the creatures of that realm were impervious to the heat, Charlie felt that it was significantly warmer there. He wondered if that explained the dry, stone landscape.

The flarunes gathered to peer over the edge. Suddenly, Charlie's jet feet turned off and he fell, rolling several times. He stood up, his body and pride a little bruised, but wiped himself down before heading towards the edge beside the flarunes.

Charlie crawled closer on his hands and knees. The depth of the pit became apparent as he suddenly felt nauseous but tried to hide it as he cautiously peered over. He could see two figures at the base of the pit, with one slightly covered by a huge boulder.

'Are you okay, Charlie?'

'I think that's Brune down there and the other one must be his son.'

'Okay, everyone, we are gonna stay and help, Charlie. Let's head down cautiously. This pit will be dangerous and the trollflames are already on their way. Charlie, you should stay up here and keep safe.'

'It's okay, I'll be careful. All my life I've played it safe and stayed back, I'm not going to do that anymore. I'm coming with you.'

'Okay, but please be cautious as the trollflames may have prepared traps.'

Charlie nodded as the flarunes began to make their way over the edge, carefully hopping onto jutting rocks along the side. He closed his eyes and tried to summon the breeze so that he could float down, but it was no good. His powers were no longer working, which was why the jets suddenly stopped as he approached the pit.

He became nervous about the height. It was made worse knowing he could not use his magic. The flarunes made it look easy. Charlie concentrated on each step. He tried forgetting about the depth, imagining that every footstep he took was on the ground. He found his first foothold, gaining confidence with each step, knowing that he was getting closer.

The flarunes were close to the bottom of the pit, but held back to wait for Charlie's instructions. None of them dared to be the first to approach the fire guardians because Flarunes were hunted by them. They looked up to check on Charlie. He wasn't too far. Pieces of rubble were vibrating on the ground and they could hear Brune groaning, trying to push his son away.

Rayfire hopped back up the side of the pit towards Charlie, who was holding the edge of a stone tightly, having made the mistake of looking down. He froze and was frightened. His legs felt like jelly which made him grip tighter. It wasn't too far down but it was far enough.

Rayfire called to his family, 'We haven't got much time. Gather around below Charlie and brace yourselves to catch him.'

He spoke gently to Charlie, 'Listen to me, you've got this. Let go and fall backwards. My family is waiting to catch you.'

Charlie closed his eyes tightly.

'Charlie, the trollflames are gaining on us. They're close and we have to get this done. If you don't fall now, we have to leave.'

Charlie opened his eyes a little. He had a flashback to the wrestling class remembering how it helped him gain strength against his bullies. Falling was one of the biggest steps in wrestling, particularly falling with style. He was brought out of his thoughts when Rayfire shouted his name.

'Okay, I'll do....'

He didn't finish what he was saying as Rayfire hopped onto his hands and he was falling backwards. He landed softly, as he found himself on a soft and fluffy pile of flarunes. They were all okay and he thanked them. Rayfire joined them and pointed his paw towards Brune.

Charlie ran over to Brune, who was clearly in pain as a boulder had trapped his arm.

'Charlie, why are you here? Please take my son to safety and leave me here. I can hear the rumbling in the ground and you're all in danger.'

'No, Brune. My friends are here and want to help you.'

The flarunes bounced together into view as Brune's face showed surprise. Charlie looked up, something piquing his attention. It sparkled on the side of the pit. It was long, with a white flame.

'I can see part of the wand I need.'

'Charlie, we don't have time. If we don't move this boulder now, Brune will be in serious trouble,' cried Rayfire.

Charlie had started to head towards the wall so he could climb up to retrieve the fire rod.

'CHARLIE,' shouted Rayfire again.

Charlie stared at the piece of the wand. He knew how important it was, and without it, everything else was useless. It didn't take him long to choose. He sighed and shook his head as he ran back to the others.

'Right, everyone. On the count of three, let's push as hard as we can. Come on, Bundle, you can help too. We're gonna get your dad out safely.'

Bundle and the flarunes gathered around one side of the boulder.

'Rayfire, you grab Brune's arm and be ready to drag him out when we get this up high enough.'

Rayfire obeyed and went to Brune's loose arm. Brune was initially apprehensive and waved his arm at the flarune to usher him away. He eventually relaxed and allowed Rayfire to hold it.

'Okay, everyone. On three.'

CHAPTER 20

THE RESCUE

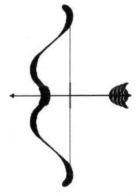

The flarunes looked confused when Charlie called, 'On three.'

He realised then that not all of his words were understood in that realm. So he clapped his hands three times and pushed at the rock, indicating what he meant. They seemed to acknowledge his meaning and braced themselves.

He then clapped once, twice and, on the third clap, they all used their strength against the boulder, which budged slightly. It was so heavy they couldn't hold it very long, so they dropped it and heard a painful groan.

Charlie did not dare to look, but then the groan turned to laughter and the flarunes were helping Brune onto his feet.

'My my, the little ones helped me. I never thought I'd see the day,' said Brune, rubbing his arm which had been trapped under the boulder. 'Thank you, flarunes, and to you, Charlie.'

'You're welcome,' Charlie smiled with a blush.

Brune looked around and spotted Bundle hiding behind a rock, a little further back.

'Bundle, come now, my son. Don't worry. You're not in trouble. Just remember to listen to me next time, okay?'

He appeared from behind the rock and the flarunes hopped wildly, trying to push towards Bundle and Brune, with high-pitched squeaks saying, 'Get out quickly, they're almost here.'

Charlie clearly understood what they were saying. He looked at Brune and Bundle and repeated what they had said.

'Can you understand them, Young One? Come on, Bundle, let's go.'

The flarunes began to hop towards the rock outcroppings on the side of the pit, while Charlie looked towards the fire rod he had seen earlier, wondering how he could get it.

'Charlie!' Rayfire cried out, just in time, as a flaming arrow whistled by his ear and hit the wall behind him.

Some of the flarunes leapt from the rocks onto the trollflames' heads to cover their eyes. They were clumsy creatures to start, and the panicking and bumping into each other caused them to fall over. The distraction was enough to help Charlie get to the side and start the climb, ignoring the fire rod he so desperately needed.

The flarunes saw Charlie was well on his way and they began to leap back to the side. One of them was grabbed, being thrown hard against the rock jutting from the wall. As it went limp, the trollflame laughed in triumph and proceeded to bite it, swallowing half before throwing the other half into its fiery mouth.

Charlie saw what happened but there was no time to grieve. His height phobia disappeared as despair took over at the death of the flarune who helped him escape. Teary eyes blurred his vision when he tried to locate the next ledge. Burning arrows flew up towards them as they climbed the Beluvian Pit walls. An arrow was heading towards another flarune, but Bundle shielded it so the arrow bounced off his armour.

They were getting closer to the top. There was a cry from below as the rest of the trollflames emerged from the cave and a deep gurgling voice called out, 'FOLLOW THEM. LET NONE ESCAPE OR WE WILL DINE ON YOUR CORPSES.'

The creature dribbled goo from his flaming mouth as he called out these orders. He wiped it on his dirty ragged tunic, staring with hunger at the escaping creatures above. The archers hung their bows over their shoulders and began the climb.

A couple of the flarunes were already at the top, looking over to help others. Brune was next over, but the trollflames were gaining on those flarunes still climbing.

Rayfire called to Charlie, 'Keep going. I'll try my best to keep these things away. When you get to the top, make sure you leave as fast as you can. Don't worry about me. It's important that you are safe and will hopefully bring peace to my family.'

'No, Rayfire, you can't do this. You've lost one already, I'm not …'

'Charlie, we need you to get out and save us all. If it costs my life, I'm fine with that as long as you're all safe up there. Now hurry. Go.'

Rayfire managed to hop away in time to avoid his paw being grabbed by a filthy claw slammed against the edge he was standing on. He landed on the trollflame's head and pawed at his eyes. The creature screamed in agony and lost footing while trying to protect himself. He plummeted into a few other trollflames that were climbing behind him, so they all lost hold and fell back down into the pit. Rayfire had hopped off and grabbed a ledge just in time to avoid the fall.

Charlie looked upwards and continued to climb. The height didn't seem to bother him anymore with so much going on. It looked as though the others managed to get out, leaving just Charlie and Rayfire left. Charlie turned to see Rayfire drop another trollflame into the pit.

'Rayfire, we're safe. You can come out now,' he called. But the timing was not good as he felt a tight grip around his ankle which was cutting into his leg. It was a thorn noose bind, one of the traps set by the trollflames.

Rayfire noticed Charlie's plight and hopped up as fast as he could. Hundreds of trollflames were gaining speed. A gang was fast approaching Charlie. Rayfire used this to his advantage and skilfully bounced across the row of their heads, managing to throw several of them off-balance. He got to Charlie's foot and began to gnaw on the vine that entwined itself tightly around his ankle, already drawing blood. It was tough work, but he managed to get through the shoot, allowing Charlie to continue his climb.

'Charlie, do it for our kingdom. Close this pit,' the flarune cried out, as Charlie was being helped up over the edge by the others. He turned and saw Rayfire hopping on the heads of the trolls that were near the edge, toppling them back into the pit. His last hop wasn't so lucky as one grabbed his paw and managed to pull him into his fall.

'Noooooooooo,' Charlie screamed.

He hobbled quickly away from the pit until he felt his power return. It felt like the wall of heat which hits you when exiting a plane after landing in a hot country.

He stood tall and shouted to the others to get back. Despite the throbbing pain in his ankle, he closed his eyes, lifting the surrounding boulders and rocks into the air. He summoned a vortex spell and they spun in the shape of a funnel. The last of the surviving flarunes was out of the pit but there was no sign of Rayfire. Trollflames were starting to appear at the edge of the pit. One looked over and caught sight of the vortex of rocks which was heading straight for them.

'GET DOWN,' the trollflame roared to the others as Charlie launched a hail of boulders and rocks towards the pit, knocking the trolls into it. Some limped to the cavern as the rocks began to fill the pit, smashing against, causing a landslide of other rocks, crushing trollflames in the path of the avalanche.

Despite feeling exhausted, Charlie continued to pull large rocks and boulders into vortexes, determined to fill the pit. Disgusted by what he witnessed, he continued as if possessed by a burning need for revenge.

Brune walked up behind him, resting a hand gently on his shoulder before saying calmly, 'Come on now Young One. You've done it. There's no need for more.'

Charlie broke from his trance of anger, relaxed his power, the spinning rocks dropping heavily from the air. He collapsed to the ground, sobbing. Brune placed his hand on his shoulder as reassurance.

'You let it out, Charlie. Don't worry. I'm the only one aware of this. You're allowed to grieve. You did well. Take a look.'

Charlie, still sniffing, looked towards where the Beluvian Pit had been. A new mountain of rocks stood in its place.

'I did that?' he snuffled.

'Yes, Charlie, you did. You're a true hero.'

'It wasn't just me, Brune. It was all of you and our fallen ones below.'

'Aye, Charlie. It was.'

They sat for a moment in silence looking towards the mountain. Bundle came to join them and the flarunes silently hopped over, huddling around Charlie as the glowing red veins of the black mountain stood tall. They silently mourned together.

'I now name this Beluvian Mountain. A memorial for our lost friends.' Charlie then paused, before saying, 'I'm sorry, flarunes.'

The flarunes fluffed up to give Charlie comfort and one reassured him by saying, 'Charlie, it wasn't your fault. You have saved us from any future attacks from the pit. You've closed it and that's what our fallen ones and leader would have wanted. They didn't fall in vain and, because of you, we all get to live.'

'Thanks,' was all Charlie could say, as he was still trying to contain his sorrow for Rayfire and the others.

'So, Charlie, I think we need to get you back to ours, clean you up and then find your home,' said Brune, the clang of metal indicating he was getting up onto his feet.

He then turned to the flarunes and said, 'I'm not sure you guys understand me, but I want to thank you all. From this day forth, I'll make it known that you are no longer to be hunted but welcomed in our homes, although give me about a week to decree this law so everyone is aware.'

The flarunes quivered and stared at Brune, blankly and cautiously, with their fiery ears in the air. Charlie smiled and translated what Brune said. They exploded with excitement and were hopping everywhere in celebration, bouncing around Brune to show their gratitude.

Charlie left the scene, walking towards the base of the mountain, where he knelt, touching the rocks.

He whispered, 'I'm sorry, Rayfire. I wish I could have saved you and not the other way around. It was my fault, as a moment of greed caused this. It was never meant to be this way. Thanks to you and the bravery of your flarunes and the fire guardians, they are now at peace with one another.'

His tears sizzled against the base of the mountain.

'Maybe I should call it Rayfire Mountain after you, my friend,' he said, as he looked up towards the flaming stars and comets in the sky, imagining them to be the spirit of his friend.

Charlie was disturbed by rubble falling from the mountain close by, as a flame came through a small hole. He stood back, preparing himself as more rubble started to come loose. A small orange furry head popped out from the hole.

'Thanks for that touching speech, my amazing friend. It was great to hear and all that, but you didn't leave much wriggle room for me to get out, did you?'

'Rayfire! But how?'

Charlie pulled him from the hole and hugged him.

Rayfire laughed and said, 'Come on now, Charlie. Let's not get emotional, my warrior. I was just lucky enough to know how to dodge and shelter.'

From a short distance away, everyone realised what was going on and ran with excitement to greet Rayfire. There were lots of hugs and exchanges of conversation as Charlie interpreted it all for the fire guardians and the flarunes.

'We must lay a memorial here and never forget the sacrifice and bravery of our fallen friends', suggested Charlie.

'We'll be sure to do that, Young One,' answered Brune.

'Thanks again, Charlie,' Rayfire said proudly. 'You were very brave, and we are all eternally grateful. You've closed the pit, made a mountain and averted the danger. Oh, and before I forget, I believe I have something that belongs to you.'

Everyone stopped and looked towards him, even Brune and Bundle, although they hadn't understood what he said. Rayfire reached into his slightly dishevelled fur and pulled out a glowing white flame rod from a hidden pouch.

'This, I believe, is yours, Charlie. I forgot to mention that I came back up via the rod as I knew what it meant to you and what you sacrificed.'

He raised his paw towards Charlie, holding the fire wand. Charlie was struck by emotions but he didn't take it immediately.

'Thank you, Rayfire. You should have left that. Your life's more important.'

'Okay, I'll just pop it back then,' Rayfire answered, jokingly.

'Haha, no, it's okay. But please hold it for a minute as, when I touch it, it will take me home. I just want to thank everyone first.'

'Ah, in that case, you're not having it then,' Rayfire laughed and Charlie laughed with him.

Charlie got up, hugged each flarune and shook their paws, thanking them for their bravery. He then hugged Bundle who gripped him tightly until Brune tapped him on the shoulder, to get him to let go. Finally, Charlie jumped up on Brune and held him tightly around his neck.

'Ooooh, now, Young One, you've almost as tight a grip as my son,' he laughed.

'Thanks, Brune, I have learnt from the best. Please look after these flarunes, as saving you was all down to them.'

'You have my word, Charlie. I never thought we would bond with the flarunes and I know that's down to you.

You're a greater warrior than you think. I have a feeling we'll see you again.'

'I hope so, Brune.'

Charlie smiled as he released his grip as Brune placed him gently on the ground. He then approached Rayfire.

'Yes, Charlie, I heard everything you said to Brune. No idea what he said, though,' and they both laughed.

'Look after them, Rayfire. They may need you again someday. Thanks again for agreeing to do this. I could never have done it without you.'

'Thanks to you, Charlie, our kind is at peace with the fire guardians now. I would never have imagined that in my lifetime. Anyway, we've kept you long enough now, Kiddo. You best get going.'

Charlie stood up and waved to everyone. He held his hand out for the fire wand and Rayfire passed it over. His chest shone through his robe, which, the meaning of, he now understood. Then a red glow surrounded him as he flew through the air and, with a bump, rolled along the ground away from the coal fire, knocking over the clothes horse.

'Are you okay in there, Charlie?' his mother called from the kitchen.

He was back at his grandfather's home.

'Yes, Mum. Sorry. I was just taking my clothes from the horse as they're dry now and I'm heading up to have a shower.'

'Okay, dinner won't be long.'

'Okay, thanks.'

Charlie took the fire wand and clean clothes before he made his way upstairs. He threw the rod towards his bag and almost hit the thistledown, as he forgot she was there. She just managed to dodge it. He smiled and asked her to carry on guarding the bag. She bobbed up and down in agreement as he gave her a proud beam, thanked her, and then went to have a much-needed shower. He checked his chest in the mirror and, sure enough, the flame design was a beautiful array of red, white and orange.

The fire wand on the bed started to vibrate before shooting into his backpack, where it infused itself with the glass rod with the coral design.

The wand was almost complete.

CHAPTER 21

HOME SWEET HOME

Charlie returned from the shower, dried himself and got dressed before he realised that the fire wand was no longer on his bed, where he left it. He reached for his bag and, as he expected, there it was; entwined into the wand, adding a new vibrant scarlet flame to the design.

He pulled out the book of prophecy and read the pages which had now turned from a jumble of words to legible sentences. He read through the trials of air, water and fire and felt a little uncomfortable as they seemed to be written as a log of his journey. Since he just completed his recent adventure by fire, the next page was unreadable.

'Charlie!' called a voice from downstairs.

'Coming,' he called out in response.

He returned the book to the bag with the wand.

'Thanks, Thistledown, for looking after these. I'll be back up shortly.'

The thistledown bobbed up and down again in acknowledgement. He headed downstairs breathing in the beautiful aroma of a roast dinner. He was not keen on vegetables but, with his grandfather's amazing homemade gravy, everything tasted wonderful. His plate was empty in no time.

'Thanks, Grandad. That was amazing, as always. How do you do that gravy?'

'Haha, glad you enjoyed it. I'll show you sometime. Have you any room for homemade rice pudding?'

'Mmmmm, yes, please. I'd love some,' Charlie smiled.

His mum nodded in agreement when her dad looked at her, raising his eyebrows for a response. He toddled off into the kitchen and Charlie decided to ask his mum a question he never thought he would ask.

'Mum, when we get home, can we look at some skydiving charity events? I'd like to give it a go, please.'

Jennifer looked at Charlie, surprised.

'Charlie, are you sure? You're petrified of heights. Remember when we had to call the fire brigade because you'd managed to get up a tree and couldn't get back down? You clung on to that branch for dear life.'

'Yeah, I remember. No need to rub it in,' Charlie blushed, and laughed.

'Why would you want to do this, Charlie? I don't mind if you really want to, but I'm intrigued.'

'Well, I guess for two reasons. The main one is that it's great to give to charity as it makes you feel better for helping others.'

'Okay, and the other?'

'Well, I seem to be doing so many things lately that need me to be good with heights. I've got a little better but this will help me even more, I suppose.'

'Okay, Charlie. Very brave of you. We can certainly have a look when we get home. We'll be heading back tomorrow if that's okay. We hadn't prepared for a visit and you're back to school on Monday too.'

'Oh, yeah. I forgot about that. Thanks for reminding me.'

'Hopefully, with the police capturing your headmaster, it'll be safer too.'

'Yeah!'

At that moment, Charlie's grandfather re-entered the dining room. He was holding a huge old-looking bowl, obviously still hot as he was wearing oven mittens, and placed it on a heat-resistant mat in the centre of the table. The scent of the golden-brown pudding, made with nutmeg, smelt amazing. He returned with dishes for them all and a giant spoon.

Noticing Charlie give the spoon a bit of a look, his grandfather explained, 'I got this from my Navy days as a chef, Charlie. One of the few things they let me keep, well kind of,' and they laughed.

As his grandfather broke the surface, mixing the skin into the rice pudding, it took Charlie back to a time with his mum and dad. How they had laughed and told jokes together. It brought a tear to his eye and made him more determined to find out what had happened and if his dad was still alive.

'Charlie, are you okay?' his mum asked, bursting the imagined family-past bubble.

'Yeah, I'm okay, thanks. Just thinking about Dad.'

His mum gave him a reassuring smile.

'I'm sure he's okay, wherever he is. Hopefully, he'll find his way home. Never give up on that, my dear,' she said, as she rubbed his back and he nodded with a smile, before finishing his rice pudding.

'Oh wow, Grandad, that was the best rice pudding I've ever had. Thank you.'

He hugged his grandfather, took the dishes into the kitchen and began to wash them, which he found to be therapeutic. His grandfather soon joined him with a tea towel, ready to dry, and his mum put the dishes away.

Afterwards, they sat together by the coal fire and his grandfather told Charlie old war stories of his adventures as a chef at sea. It was getting quite late, so Grandad made a Horlicks for each of them, a warming malted milk drink sweetened with honey. It was great for relaxing them and helping them sleep, ready for the journey home the next day. That night everyone had the best sleep in a long time, a much-needed rest.

The next morning, refreshed and alert, Charlie and Jennifer headed downstairs to the aroma of smoky bacon and eggs as Grandad was already in the kitchen, cooking breakfast. It was wonderful and they were both well-fuelled for the journey. Grandad passed Charlie two small bags, each with leek and onion crisps and a small bottle of Dandelion & Burdock, he'd also wrapped egg and mayo sandwiches in cling film.

'Just for the journey home, mind,' advised his grandfather, with a wink.

'Awww, Dad, you really shouldn't have, you've done so much for us already,' said Charlie's mum, as she gave him a peck on the cheek and a big hug. Charlie followed suit.

'You've both got everything now, haven't you? Make sure you have a safe journey.'

Charlie patted his backpack carefully so as not to disturb the thistledown who was resting in the bag's lining. He nodded that he'd got everything, gave his grandfather another hug, and his mum looked quite tearful as she ushered Charlie out. Goodbyes were always emotional.

They made their way to the car, Grandad having already closed the front door was a sign that he was also tearful, but didn't like to show it. They saw the netting twitch at the window, by the chair he always sat in to watch the world go by, with his elbows on the table and tobacco rolled. He didn't smoke while they were there but from the red glowing ember behind the netting, it was obvious he just lit a cigarette.

As they drove off, Jennifer beeped the horn twice and Charlie turned to wave. He could see a waving arm appear from under the netting until they turned the corner out of sight. Charlie seat-belted and made himself comfortable.

The journey was fairly quiet, as usual. Whenever they left Grandad's home, they always felt sad, which made them quiet. They'd play the odd game of "I Spy", to see who could spot such and such first, and then Charlie would fall asleep for the rest of the journey.

They pulled up outside their home at last. Charlie was the first up to the door while his mum was getting some bits from the boot. He unlocked the door and a lovely aroma of flowers came out from the house. The air fresheners had kicked in. He went back to the car and carefully got his bag from the back seat.

His mum sniffed the air, and said, 'Ahhh, great to be back, isn't it, Charlie?'

Charlie nodded with a smile. He felt more relaxed than he'd been in a long time. He took his bag up to his bedroom and pulled out the parchments from the side zip pocket. The thistledown popped onto his shoulder and they both puzzled over them. Three of the parchments now displayed a print of some kind on both sides, only one still blank: the muddy one. He puzzled over the three of them as he turned them individually to make them fit, but no matter what he tried, he could still make no sense of them.

'Hmmm, still don't get it yet. One more to go.'

The thistledown bobbed up and down, signalling she was listening. He returned them to their hiding place in the tin foil fortress at the top of the wardrobe. He then pulled out the book of prophecy, the Tallemseen, and checked its pages. Those he had already read were still legible but the last quarter of the book remained a jumble. He popped it back into the base of the wardrobe under the loose wood.

He pulled out the wand. It was the first time he had managed to have a good look at it since the adventure at his grandfather's. It was an intricately beautiful wand made of glass with a scarlet flame entwined around its full length and infused with a coral design. He placed it next to the book, covered them with an old dark sheet and hid them under the floor of the wardrobe.

He discarded the bag back in the wardrobe after he pulled out his notebook and pen. He placed these in his bedside drawer and lay back for a moment, deep in thought about the ordeal he'd faced.

His mother called up to him, 'I've just phoned Grandad to let him know we're home, he said you'd left a robe or something.'

'Oh, okay. Thanks, Mum. He can keep it there for when we head back.'

'Okay, but I don't remember you having a robe before.'

With that, she'd gone back into the lounge. Charlie looked at the thistledown, who was resting on his tummy.

'Well, there's one trial left and it doesn't take a genius to know that it's earth-related. I wonder if we will understand each other when that's done. Shame it wasn't first,' he laughed.

He got up and pulled out his tablet to search for parachute jumps, and found a tandem dive which piqued his interest. He was feeling better about heights, determined to conquer his fear. He looked at the thistledown who was jiggling about. As though he knew what she was saying, he answered.

'I know, I know. I don't want to use magic for skydiving. I've got to do it myself, humanly, if that makes sense.'

The thistledown acknowledged his answer and settled. He found out that if he could raise enough charity sponsors, his jump would be free. He decided to do that so there would be no expenses for his mum. He completed the online form.

'Right, I best go down and keep mum company and let her know what I'm planning. Would you please look after the book again?'

The thistledown jiggled in agreement and went to the top of the wardrobe, settling on a piece of tin foil in the throne room that Charlie had created. He gave a little laugh and headed downstairs.

His mum was staring at the computer screen silently.

'Mum?'

She jumped and dropped the glass of juice she was holding.

'Charlie, you really shouldn't do that. You need to let me know you're there. You frightened the life out of me.'

'Sorry, Mum.'

She went to the kitchen with the now-empty glass that luckily didn't break as it had a soft landing on the thick carpet. Charlie looked at her screen and saw that she was reading an article about Mr Grimmauld. The headmaster survived the collision and been arrested for several offences which included arson, speeding on a motorway with reckless driving, escaping from police custody, and assaulting several members of the public including emergency service members.

'Wow, that's awful,' Charlie said aloud and was deep in thought for a moment. As his mum returned with a cloth, he asked her, 'Do you think he meant this? Like, do you think it was him?'

His mum looked confused. Charlie tried to explain what he meant as he knew his headmaster was acting out of character.

'Mum, can we see him?'

'Who?'

'My headmaster. Please?'

'Oh, that's who you were talking about. Why would you want to see him? He almost tried running you through, Charlie. He's dangerous.'

'But I genuinely don't believe it's him. I think somehow, something's controlling him. He just wouldn't do this. Pleeeease.'

After everything that had happened, she understood what Charlie meant and she smiled.

'I'll see what I can do for you, Charlie, No promises though.'

'Aww. Thanks, Mum.'

Charlie went over and hugged her, wetting his sock in the process as he forgot about the spillage. They looked at each other and laughed.

It wasn't long before there was a knock on the front door. It was his Aunty Kathleen with his little cousin, Louise.

'Hi, Charlie,' she said. 'Go on in then, Louise, and play with your cousin, Charlie.'

They both entered and hugged Charlie. His mum came to see who it was.

'Aww, Kath. What are you doing here?'

'Well, I was just passing the area, to be honest, and we never did get to visit that day we planned after that commotion you had, bless you. Just thought, as it's still early afternoon, why not come give a quick visit?'

'Aww, you're always welcome. You know that. You're lucky to have caught us to be honest. We've just got back from visiting Dad in the Valleys.'

'That's lovely. How was he? I'm gonna have to take our Louise up there soon, to see him.'

They continued their conversation as Charlie took Louise into the living room. He reached for a board game, but thought of a better idea.

'Hey, Louise. Do you wanna come over to the Pastures with me? Have a look around the woods to see what we can find.'

'Really? That'd be amazing. Remember when we found that white snake thing?'

Charlie laughed and said, 'Yes, I remember, haha. That was a slow worm but it did look like a baby snake, I suppose.'

Charlie checked with his mum and aunt before they got ready and left for the Pastures. They went across the fields, where they spotted a couple of butterflies, an Admiral and a Cabbage White, unusually flying together. They then headed towards the wooded area, not noticing two figures watching them, at a distance, with great interest.

CHAPTER 22

FOLLOWED

The short-cut grass began to give way to long grass and mud tracks towards the trees. Charlie discovered an unusual caterpillar gnawing on a leaf. He went to take a closer look, when a boot appeared from nowhere, crashing down on the leaf. It was shuffled left and right to make sure that the caterpillar was crushed into the ground.

'Well, look what we have here. An idiot and his girlfriend, frolicking in the woods, aye Dennis?'

'Yeah, Griff. Do you think they need to see more of nature?'

Dennis laughed and grabbed Charlie tightly around the back of his neck. Louise was taken by surprise and began to run but Griff grabbed her arm.

'No, you don't, little girl. You're gonna witness what we put your idiot of a friend through.'

Dennis and Griff led them further into the woods. Griff's grip on Louise's arm only tightened as she struggled, while Dennis gripped the back of Charlie's neck tighter too, but Charlie was worried about his cousin.

'What do you both want? We've done nothing to you.'

'Fun, you idiot. What else would we want?' Dennis asked as they led them towards the brook.

Their feet sank deeper into the mud as they continued. Dennis struggled as his weight was making it harder for him to walk, so Charlie took an opportunity to wiggle from his grip and push him backwards. Dennis did not expect that as he fell into the mud. Charlie ran behind Griff and threw his arm around his neck into a sleeper hold position he learnt in wrestling class. Griff loosened his grip on Louise, where he left a red mark on her arm. She began to tear up.

'Run home, Louise, quickly. I'll hold these guys off. Don't worry, I'll be okay.'

Louise, being light, managed to run through the mud easily without sinking. She checked on Charlie again before she ran from the woods.

Dennis was up, grabbing at Charlie which only made him tighten his grip on Griff.

'Try that again, Dennis, and I'll put your mate here to sleep.'

Dennis was taken aback by Charlie's confidence, but then he began to laugh.

'What? Why's that funny?' asked Charlie.

'You, Charlie. Full of bravado and strength,' Dennis laughed. 'But not for much longer. Let him sleep, I don't need him anyway. I want that book you have, Charlieeee.'

The pretence dropped. Dennis's eyes turned black. His voice became raspy and deep, not like his usual. Charlie released his hold on Griff, who fell to the ground, holding his neck and trying to catch his breath. He turned to Dennis.

'Den, what's wrong with you?'

Charlie answered, 'Sorry Griff, I don't think that's Dennis anymore.'

'Oh, Charlie, ever the assstute one. Thought you could defeat me in a mere car collisssion. Can't say much for your headmassster,' as he laughed again, menacingly.

Charlie's assumption was right. He froze for a moment realising the danger.

Griff picked himself up and went to punch Dennis, who just raised his hand and grabbed Griff's fist with ease, laughing. He started to slowly twist it and Griff cried out in pain. Dennis's nose almost touched Griff's and he said, 'Try that again, puny mortal, and you'll die along with him,' as he looked towards Charlie.

The ground began to rumble like an earth tremor and it was getting stronger as Dennis released his grip on Griff. The force knocked the three of them off-balance when, suddenly, a hole appeared in the ground between them and started to grow.

'That'sss impossible. That can't be happening here,' said Dennis, looking very confused. His body started to contort in pain as the hole grew larger. None of them could escape as they were stuck in the mud.

'Dennis, or whatever you are, what's happening?'

Griff looked at Charlie, confused and very frightened. The hole at their feet was still growing. It was black inside but they could see a shimmering liquid.

Dennis screamed in agony as the invading entity left through his lips. It struggled to escape as it was being drawn unwillingly towards the hole which was almost at the boys' feet. It was trapped, with its form being distorted until it touched the blackness, where it took on the shape of a lizard-like creature.

At that point, Charlie heard his mum and Aunty Kathleen calling out, but it was too late. The hole opened and pulled Charlie, Griff, Dennis and the lizard inside. They screamed as they plummeted, feeling for something to get a hold of, but there was nothing.

It was so dark, they could see nothing; not even their hands in front of their faces. Their screams lessened as they slowed a little and the blackness around started to lighten to deep grey. Charlie could see Griff and Dennis, although Dennis looked unconscious. Griff was still waving his arms, as though he was screaming, but muted. He then tried to swing his arms as though he was attempting to swim towards Charlie. Charlie relaxed a little until he caught a glimpse of a monstrous lizard-like creature.

The grey started to turn a shade of yellow and the four of them were slowly disappearing into it. Charlie looked around for the lizard but could no longer see it. Nor could he see Griff or Dennis. Griff's hand reached through the yellow and grabbed Charlie towards him. Charlie gave him a reassuring hug as they landed on a circle of brown grass. The surrounding yellow squeezed them together for a moment, then seemed to open up, releasing its hold as it began to spread. Charlie and Griff released the hug and found themselves standing in the middle of a large blooming yellow flower. They stepped off onto the grass.

Griff was frightened and asked, 'Where are we? What happened?'

Charlie crouched down to check on Dennis who appeared by another flower, still unconscious, but he was breathing.

'Come and help, Griff. Let's get Dennis over to the shade of that tree.'

'Fat chance after what he tried to do to me.'

'That wasn't him, Griff. Something was controlling him.'

'You going all exorcist on me, Charlie? That stuff's just made up for the horror, you know that?'

'Look, he needs our help, so let's put him over there and then we can figure out what to do.'

'Why are you so calm? Why should I do this for you? Have you managed to drug us somehow?'

Charlie was struggling, trying to drag Dennis on his own. Griff tutted but did help and they lifted him over to the shade of the tree, as it was quite hot. When they put him down, Charlie laid him in the recovery position by placing him on his side, with his leg lifted slightly to anchor him, and his arm outstretched. Charlie had already checked that his airway was clear by looking in his mouth. He looked up at Griff who had gone very quiet. He was standing there, just staring silently up at the sky.

Charlie walked over to him and looked up. Three suns were shining brightly but they each had a different colour. One was a slight shade of yellow, the other was a slight shade of blue and the third had a tint of red.

They stood in awe at the sight. Charlie turned to check on Dennis, but only saw the tree and the flattened grass where they'd placed him. There was no sign of him. Charlie tapped Griff on the shoulder, who was still mesmerised by the sky.

'What is it now, Charlie?' he asked, in his usual bitter voice.

He looked across and could see that Dennis was missing.

'Where'd he go?'

'I dunno. He was there a minute ago. No idea where he's gone.'

They both called out for Dennis but there was no sound. They searched the long grass but there was no sign. They even walked around the tree and Charlie climbed it to survey the land. There was nothing, apart from a few grassy hills, lots of coloured flowers in bloom and trees dotted about.

Charlie wondered about flying but thought better of it, as he didn't want Griff and Dennis to know that he could conjure magic.

'Where are we?' inquired Griff. 'How the heck did we even get here?'

'I'm not sure.'

They both had filthy trainers, caked in mud, and the bottoms of their joggers were just the same, but there was no mud here and the trees were a lot sparser. There were quite a few giant flowers of various colours, in full bloom with open petals.

Charlie could hear voices, very faint, but they were there. He kept a straight face so as not to alert Griff. He had an idea.

'I'm feeling a bit tired,' he said, and with that, he lay on the grass and put his head to one side, with his ear to the ground. He could hear voices underground and then noticed some small sticks moving about the field at ground level.

Griff grabbed Charlie around the neck of his T-shirt and pulled him up.

'What do you think you're doing, Wafe? Trying to sleep, while my pal is missing, is a no-no. We find him now,' and he shoved Charlie back against the tree.

'Okay, you're right, Griff. I dunno how to say this, but we need to work together.'

Griff folded his arms, sneering at the suggestion, and turned away.

'Look, I don't like it any more than you do, but it's the only way we're gonna do this.'

Griff looked down and eventually, with a little reluctance, he agreed. He pointed towards a few small mounds close by, in the grass.

'They weren't there before.'

Charlie noticed the short stubby sticks on top of each mound, and tiny indentations.

'I wonder what they are.'

Griff didn't hesitate and pulled at one of the sticks. Charlie heard a cry from below, 'No, he's got me here. He's yanking at my shell.'

'Griff. Leave them alone,' Charlie called.

Griff turned to Charlie, surprised at the tone of his voice. He then began to stomp on the mound and Charlie could hear, 'Owwwh' with every stomp. Griff then ran towards Charlie, tripped him up and raised his foot above his head, stopping just within an inch of his nose.

'Just remember this, Wafe. I'm in charge. Don't you ever tell me what to do, okay?'

Charlie didn't answer, so Griff pushed his trainer down onto his nose. He pushed it a little more, just enough to hurt.

'Okay, Wafe?'

'Yes, okay.'

Griff held his hand out to Charlie, who grabbed it, pulling himself up.

'Griff, did you hear anything when you grabbed those sticks? Please don't grab them again. They might be toxic or something. I've never seen them before and I'm just thinking of you.'

'Hmmm, hadn't thought of that,' Griff said as he wiped his hands on Charlie's top. 'There was a squelchy sound, I guess.'

Charlie walked over to the mounds.

'What're you doing, Wafe? You just told me not to go near them, so what're you doing?'

Charlie held his hand up to silence him and crouched by the mound and spoke quietly, 'Hello, I'm Charlie. I'm not going to hurt you, but please try not to move too much. If you understand me, shake that thing on the top of your hill.'

'Charlie, why are you trying to imitate that stupid squelching sound? You buffoon.'

Charlie smiled when the stick shook slightly.

'I just wanted to imitate them, Griff. You find that if you can imitate sound …'

'Am I that interested? Let's just go look for Den. He's probably woken up and gone for a wander.'

Charlie whispered to the ground, 'I won't hurt you, I promise, but please stay hidden for now because this guy can be trouble.'

The ground trembled around him as four mounds lifted, revealing large round creatures. They were as high as his stomach, with arms and legs, and they each held a spear. Their faces and body looked like one huge acorn. They looked as though they were wearing woolly hats with stalks coming from the top.

Griff screamed and fell backwards as they headed towards him, pointing their spears.

'We no like twubble,' one of the acorns said angrily to Griff, as he lay helpless on the ground.

Then they all chanted, 'We no like twubble.' Getting dangerously close to Griff and poking him with their spearheads, they all chanted, 'We no like twubble.'

'It was him,' Griff pointed accusingly at Charlie.

A larger mound started to lift and an acorn creature appeared wearing a golden crown. Standing next to Charlie, he folded his arms and looked towards Griff.

'Rid the trouble,' one of the acorns cried, and they all raised their spears above their heads, ready to thrust them into Griff.

Griff held his arms over his head and screamed out, 'Help, Charlie. Please.'

CHAPTER 23

BULLY ME THIS, BULLY ME THAT

Charlie raised his hands, and called, 'Wait.'

The acorn creatures paused for a moment, looking at their acorn leader who was standing next to Charlie. The leader lifted his hand, gesturing for them to wait, as he led Charlie to a tree, out of earshot, and spoke in a kindly voice.

'So, Charlie, I have noticed the foul way your friend treats you and is quick to blame you. Is he a friend?'

'To be honest, he picks on me at school, but I don't want any harm to come to him. I think there's a chance he might change. He deserves that chance, I guess.'

'You are a wise one indeed, and I will tell you what intrigues me.'

'What?'

'You're able to understand us and speak our language. Only a Chosen One can do that. By the way, how rude of me, my name is Otu, leader of the dillichups. We live in the land of Terriana and I am a guardian of the earth.'

'I'm pleased to meet you, Otu. I'm Charlie, Charlie Wafe. I believe I'm the Chosen One you mentioned because I've been to three realms now and this is my fourth.'

'I'm impressed indeed, Charlie. May I?'

He proceeded to place his hand on the neck of Charlie's T-shirt. Charlie nodded and allowed Otu to look at the tattoo of the three realms.

Griff called over, 'Am I okay to go now, please?'

Otu turned to the others and nodded for them to lower their spears. Griff ran to Charlie who introduced him to Otu and then proceeded to talk with him.

'Otu, we're looking for a friend of ours.'

Griff sniggered at Charlie, not knowing what language he was speaking. Charlie ignored him and continued, 'His name's Dennis. He was lying unconscious by that tree. We turned our backs for just a moment and when we looked back, he'd gone. Not a trace of him.'

'We've not come across him, Charlie. But we'll certainly help you find him.'

'One more thing. Unfortunately, something came in with us. In my world, it looked like a dark shadow, a mist, which had control of Dennis, but it tried to get away when we were sinking here, it got caught in the ground too. It turned into a huge lizard and half of its skin was peeling.'

Otu did not like the news.

'It sounds like Sinistre, Charlie. If he's after you then he must know you are part of the prophecy. He either wants to get the book or destroy you or, even worse, both.'

'Why though?'

Otu looked around and advised him not to carry on the conversation in the open. He put one arm around Charlie and the other around Griff, but Griff was having none of it.

'Griff, if you don't let them do what they're trying to do, you'll be in danger. They're helping us,' explained Charlie.

'When did you start talking like that though? And why should I trust you?'

'You don't have to, but I'm not the one who keeps picking on you, am I?'

Griff was quiet and let the dillichup grab him. Within moments, they were being dragged down through the mud into a network of underground tunnels with various carvings on the walls. Otu instructed the others to take Griff to a guest room. He then turned to hug Charlie again and they sank into a deeper tunnel system which was even more elaborate than the previous one. Considering it was underground, it was very vibrant and colourful.

They entered a large room which looked like a study, with lots of books on one wall and a huge wooden desk in the centre. Otu led Charlie to the desk and offered him a drink, but he refused. He then left the room and eventually returned with a small brown book, which looked very old.

'This, Charlie is the book of the Earth's elemental magic. You'd be wise to learn all of it and add the final part to your chest. But before you do this, I need to tell you about Sinistre. He was one of the earthly creatures known as the Lezarios. They still reside here, but in smaller numbers now, across the river in a dank swampy area. He was an elemental but became hungry for more than just the element he was created for. Another dark, evil beast, which already has the power of the four elements and much more, promised Sinistre any element he chose if he would serve him and do his bidding.'

Otu paused for a moment as he could see Charlie was astounded by what he was being told. He asked if he would like a drink now and Charlie nodded. He returned with a hot yellow milk-like drink which had a lovely flavour of lemon mixed with passionfruit. Charlie prompted Otu to continue.

'Sinistre was told to claim the head of a royal from the element he wanted. He chose the fire realm of Inferblaze, not too far from here. He killed Prince Kye and took his head to the beast. The beast granted Sinistre his wish, the power of fire which, combined with his power of earth, made him unstoppable. He created a war between us in Terriana and the inhabitants of Inferblaze, and we were enemies for a long time.'

Charlie was horrified.

'That isn't the worst of it, Charlie. Sinistre destroyed many lives for this beast and wiped out several elemental families. Some are now extinct. Together they were unstoppable and managed to merge bodies and reanimate them. As far as we know, the only creatures they created that exist today are the trollflames and the demonuettes. Trollflames live in a magic pit in the fire realm of Inferblaze, called the Belluvian Pit. The demonuettes live here in the dark lands on the top of Lezaragons Mount.'

'I know the trollflames, Otu. I fought them and they won't threaten anyone again as I closed the pit on them. It's Beluvian Mountain now.'

'That's perfect, Charlie. Seems that you truly are the Chosen One, which is why Sinistre thinks you need to be destroyed, or the book. The more you learn from the book, the more it puts Sinistre and this beast in danger and weakens their ultimate plan.'

'What plan?'

'Charlie, we're easy pickings for them, they're after a much bigger prize. A world that we can't cross into, yet.'

'Yet?'

'You have witnessed it, Charlie. Sinistre has been crossing the threshold to your world to destroy the book or you, or even both. Here, he's a species of Lezaragon; a cross-species of fire and earth, in his lizard state with continually peeling skin due to the cross changes. But he can only cross into your world as energy, and can only become physical by taking a host, one of your kind, while he is there. However, he must return to our realm after a certain period as his energy depletes there. If he were to remain in your world, eventually he would disintegrate and only exist in the shadows.'

'So, he is vulnerable then, but how can we prevent him from getting back?'

'In your world, Charlie, there's only one way here and one way there. You have discovered four openings for your elemental challenges. It's the only time they open in other areas and well, this is your last.'

'But where can I find the portal when I'm in my world?'

'I don't know much about your world yet to understand but, as long as you hold that book, I think you have the key, which is why they want it so badly.'

'And what about the beast?'

'Nobody knows, Charlie. We wonder if Sinistre has gone rogue and the beast no longer exists. We already know that he is mustering forces here to cross into your world and take hosts, creating a new world of evil and darkness. They think the book holds a key to sustaining themselves without returning here to recharge.'

'How come you know so much?'

'From the only creatures that can exist in both your world and ours. I think they call it a thistledown in your world. Have you ever seen one?'

'Yes, I have. It's in my room now, guarding my book.'

'You impress me, Charlie. I feel that you have become attached to it even though you've not yet completed the Earth's elemental challenge.'

'I don't have to. It's kinda just there, right when I need it. It has saved my mum and me a couple of times now.'

'It's a guardian, your personal guardian. Each elemental has its own variety of creatures. You happen to have one of the best, which is actually called a pixiedown. I believe that, in your world, you have a thistle flower which spreads a seed with a kind of fluff around it called a thistledown funny enough. Our sprite could only venture around your world disguised and the thistledown is a close resemblance. Here, they are also called Earthen Fairy Sprites, Pixiedown for short. You'll see them flying around the meadow with a glow to them of various colours depending on their rank. You can easily see them here as they are much larger inside this sphere, compared to your world. But if you look closely inside yours, you'll see the same little creature.

'Wow, yes, I did notice it a long time ago.'

'Anyway, Charlie, I best let you get on and read that book. I feel time's almost upon us.'

'What about Dennis? We have to find him and be sure he's safe.'

'We will, Charlie. But you must learn everything in that book because I think, with that knowledge, it'll help you find your friend.'

'Well, it's not like he's my friend, but he is human after all.'

Otu smiled with admiration as he exited the chamber, leaving Charlie with the book.

Charlie found it difficult to concentrate, worrying about Dennis, but he began to read. Since he was able to understand the earth creatures, he wondered if he could communicate with the pixiedown. It was something to try if he managed to get back home.

He read how to make the ground soft and solid, how to create and enlarge a crack in the ground, how to make it shake, and then make it calm. He practised what he could on a small scale and managed to keep good control, based on his experience of the previous three books, especially the fireball scenario. It wasn't without a few mishaps, as books fell from the shelves and something dropped in the background, shattering on the floor.

Charlie managed to get two-thirds of the way through the book before he began to yawn and his concentration dwindled. His eyes closed longer between blinks than they should and he was fighting to keep them open. He stifled a large yawn, made himself as comfortable as he could and fell asleep. It didn't feel long before Charlie woke with a jump as Otu placed a hand on his shoulder.

'Come on, Charlie, I'll take you to your room. Bring the book with you. The day has made you very tired. We'll set off early to find this Dennis of yours. I've already sent out a few patrols to search for him overnight.'

A very sleepy Charlie followed Otu along the corridors until he came to his room. The door closed behind him, and Charlie was surprised by the beauty of the room but found it hard to take it all in as the large bed in front of him looked so inviting. He managed to undress before he flopped onto the bed and, within seconds, he was fast asleep.

***

Earlier, when they arrived in Terriana, Sinistre was using his remaining energy to claw his way out of the flower's petal that had him in its grasp. He eventually managed to tear himself out of it, snarling at the bulging yellow flowers around him, knowing that Charlie must be in one of them. But he was too weak to gamble or waste his precious energy trying to figure out which one.

He was frustrated that he was so close to stopping Charlie's progress but he'd failed again. He scuttled away over a few hills, but stayed close enough to spy and try to gain an advantage over them. It couldn't be that hard, as they were now in his domain.

He could see the flowers had opened, but one of the figures was collapsed on the ground and lay motionless. He spied another figure prodding at it but it did not move. They were too far away for him to see who they were. Sinistre licked his lips with his unusually long tongue and his mouth watered, showing his jagged teeth. The black slits in his eyes widened and narrowed, trying to get focus, and he hoped that the one on the ground was Charlie.

He was interrupted by sounds below him. He placed his ear to the ground and sniffed the air while listening. He knew something was coming and he had to act quickly. He looked towards Charlie and the others, deciding to risk getting behind the tree to check who was lying there. They were concentrating on the one on the ground, so he used this distraction to slither closer to the tree, taking one mound at a time. He was close enough to hear muffled voices. He managed to get behind the tree, out of sight as he disguised himself by fading his colour to match the brown bark.

His face turned quickly towards a mound that had started to appear discreetly through the ground. He could hear Charlie's voice heading away from him and had to act immediately. He peered around to see Charlie talking to someone, while looking at the sky. This was his chance. He had no idea what he was going to do but instinctively snapped into action.

He placed his claws underneath the body which was still alive as he felt its warmth against his cold arms. He lifted it and ran away as fast as he could, over the hill, before Charlie noticed the body wasn't there. Sinistre crouched as low as he could when he noticed Charlie climbing the tree. The bundle in his arms started to move a little and groan.

'No, you don't,' Sinistre hissed and gave the boy's head a thud with his tongue, which seemed to have a heavy ball at the end, and made him unconscious again.

Sinistre patiently waited another minute before checking again. Some dillichups had appeared and Charlie was watching them as they gathered around the other boy. Sinistre took the opportunity to scurry away, carrying his captive. He glanced back and could only see fields and hills, as he continued towards a darker area of the land with caves, where he knew the dillichups would never venture.

He took the boy to a cave where there was a broken wooden chair and a table on which were bones, a few bits of rope and wax candles that had almost melted away. One of the candles was still lit and flickered precariously, ready to go out at any moment. Sinistre dropped the boy against a piece of rock that was sticking up from the ground. He grabbed a rope from the table and tied him to the rock so that, if he woke, he couldn't escape. Sinstre sat on the broken chair, looking at the dancing candle flame, as his grin showed his grotesque teeth in the candlelight and he said to himself, 'I've got you now, Charlie.'

He laughed hissingly to himself. It was obvious he now had a plan. He grabbed a quill with his claw and started to scribble on parchment.

***

Back in Charlie's guest bedroom, some time had passed before he woke up. He suddenly realised he wasn't at home, so he quickly got up, knocking the book to the floor. He had no idea what time it was or how long he'd been asleep, but he began to panic and wonder if Dennis was okay, or not.

CHAPTER 24

THE CELEBRATION OF THE BOOK STUDY

Charlie grabbed the book and went out into the hall. He knew he was in a network of underground tunnels and assumed Griff must still be in one of the chambers above his floor. Charlie scanned the book to see if there was any kind of magic he could use to find him but couldn't see anything.

He spotted a hole in the ceiling and closed his eyes. He opened his arms slightly and raised them slowly, so that his body rose up through the hole to the next floor. Four dilluchups approached him in a relaxed manner, holding their spears vertically. One beckoned Charlie to follow and he obeyed, so as not to rock the harmony.

Surrounding him, it felt like they were guarding him rather than forcing him along. He entered a large room at the side, where Otu was sitting at a table with Griff. They were enjoying some kind of cereal in bowls which resembled upturned acorn crowns.

'Come and sit, Charlie. Help yourself. There are all kinds of food choices for the morning snack,' Otu invited. 'This Gritt seems very hungry.'

Charlie chuckled and didn't want to correct Otu about Griff's name, as it might have been his accent, but it gave Charlie a certain one-upmanship that he had been called Gritt.

'Thanks,' he replied.

He sat at the table, pouring some red and green ball-type cereal into his bowl. He reached for the jug which contained what looked like orange milk.

'Any news on Dennis yet?' he asked, while he reluctantly poured the orange milk onto his cereal, with his nose turned up a little as he was unsure of how it would taste.

Otu indicated towards Griff that he needed privacy to talk to Charlie. It wasn't long before Griff was full and the dilluchups escorted him back to his room. The moment they left, Otu turned to Charlie.

'Charlie, my apologies. He was up much earlier, and we explained to him as best we could, with hand gestures and this letter, that Dennis is okay at the moment, but you need to know that Sinistre wants you to go alone to the Lezaragons Mount.'

'He wouldn't have understood a word you said. You could have just said it in front of him.'

'You can't be too careful. But Sinistre requests you, Charlie, and nobody else. He said that he will give you a choice in which there is a chance to have Dennis returned.'

'But is he okay?'

'We have to trust this message. It was left on the ground by the tree you were both nearby. It also explains that, as long as you go alone, Dennis will remain alive.'

'So why am I still here? I should've left already.'

'No, Charlie. Don't be too hasty. He's given us the time and place to meet. It's at Lezaragons Mount when the light starts to fade, a day from now. I suggest that, while you have the time, you digest that book and your food, as you will need all your strength.'

Charlie licked the food. It seemed to have a pleasant fruity flavour but he could not identify it. He ate it all and felt much better for it. The guards returned to escort him, with his book, to the end of a corridor where they stood on a grassy circle which then raised them to the surface. Otu followed, not too far behind.

'Okay, Charlie, it's time you learnt the rest of that book,' Otu encouraged.

Charlie carried on from where he'd left off and the powers were on a much grander scale. He looked at a variety of creatures around him and spied some birds on the tree branches. He concentrated hard on one of them and his mind was transferred to that bird. He could see through the bird's eyes as it flew over to his body. Otu looked in disbelief as the bird perched on Charlie's shoulder.

'Is that you, Charlie?' he asked, and the bird chirped, giving an acknowledging nod. It suddenly flew off, disorientated and Charlie gave a sudden jerk as his mind returned to his body.

'Charlie, I'm impressed how you took control of a creature so quickly. You only jerked because your mind switched too quickly. As gently as you take the creature, it should be the same when you return to your own body. Keep practising that one and you'll be amazing.'

During the morning and afternoon, under the light of the three suns, Charlie continued to learn about the spells of Terriana. There were just a few more to look at when he came across the spell he'd seen in the other books.

'Otu, I have seen this spell in the other three books but I can't practise it because it's only to be used in my darkest hour. It mentions that even then I may not be at a level to do it. What is it?' he asked as he showed Otu the spell.

'I know of this. I'd let it go, Charlie, as it's an ancient summoning spell and, in all the realms here, no elemental has ever been able to pull it off, not even the strongest elemental guardians. So, I'd just skip over that for now.'

'I know it off by heart now anyway, so I guess I'll just move on.'

He turned the page and learnt the last couple of spells. He realised he could create mountains, hills, dips and valleys. Luckily, he was practising out in the wilderness of Terriana, as when he tried to create a hill it became a mountain and, when he tried again, he created a split across the ground which opened and became a valley.

Unfortunately, when he tried to close the valley, he meant to create a hill but couldn't control it so it shot up like a mountain. He got upset and felt he couldn't do it, throwing the book away. Otu gripped his wrists and beckoned him to sit down for a moment with him.

'Charlie, you have this. You just need to relax. You are getting stressed so you're not able to hear the support which the land and trees are giving you.'

'What do you mean?'

Otu was still gently holding Charlie's hands.

'Close your eyes, Charlie, and listen.'

He closed his eyes but couldn't hear anything. He began to feel even more frustrated. Otu could feel this as Charlie's hands were getting much warmer.

'Charlie, breathe in for three, hold your breath for three, then exhale for three. Keep your eyes closed, relax and listen carefully for any sounds. A breeze in the distance, the creaking of old wood, or the sound of a flowing river. Listen.'

Charlie kept his eyes closed and used the breathing technique to relax. Otu could feel his pulse slowing.

Charlie could hear a gentle breeze and pictured the details in its path. He felt the terrain around him and could see it in his mind. When the breeze circled a tree, he saw it in his dreamlike state. When it hit a rock and became distorted, he could see the rock. A visual map of the layout of the land, including the creatures and even himself and Otu, began to appear in his mind.

'That's it, Charlie. I believe you can see it now, can't you? Push your power to the map that's forming in your mind. You can only change your surroundings though, no further. Do you see the valley you just created? Try to make it …'

Otu didn't need to finish the sentence as, with a smile, Charlie had freed one of his hands and waved it in a gentle rhythm across the valley. The land gently pulled up into level ground again.

He then released his other hand and waved it slowly towards the tip of the mountain he had created. As he slowly pulled his hand downwards, the mountain became a hill. He then distinctly heard the breeze whisper to him, 'Thaaank youuu, Charrrrlieeee.'

He opened his eyes. He realised he just learned three powerful and useful spells all at once, which seemed to flow together. He felt relaxed and peaceful as the Earth spell book began to rise and shake in the air, suddenly starting to spin and fade, before shooting towards his chest, forcing him back onto the soft grass.

He composed himself and shook his head as some of the dried grass was in his hair. He looked down his top and saw a black outline of an island with a tree, where the flame was part of a campfire on a hill, with the sea below and the sky above. There was no colour to the land and Charlie knew that his final trial was imminent.

The riddle which the headmaster had recited in his office, with Sinistre in control of him, started to make sense. But Charlie wondered why Sinistre, gave away four deliveries and trials if he wanted to be rid of Charlie? Why did he not take the book of prophecy then? Had he not recognised it? Charlie was confused by these questions but didn't allow them to cloud his mind.

He knew he had to get Dennis back and it probably wasn't going to be easy.

'How do you feel, Charlie?'

Charlie felt butterflies in his tummy as he replied, 'That was unbelievable. Wow, I'm blown away.'

He tried to stand but his legs were like jelly. To hear the land speak through the breeze was the most surprising of all of the spells.

'The land thanked me for levelling it out, Otu. That's absurd.'

'No, Charlie. That's earthen magic for you. You're naturally powerful, but be very careful how you use that power. It can consume you. You need to judge if the advice given to you is sound or of evil intent. Remember that not all the land in this realm is good.'

Charlie understood and nodded his head.

'Come on now, Charlie. It's getting late and the light's starting to fade. You've been out here for most of the day.'

They returned underground and went through one of the side doors in the top-level corridor, where there was a long table which seemed to be the length of a football pitch. The dillichups, who were seated there, all fell silent before they stood to raise their goblets, cheering out to Charlie, and a feast was laid on the table in celebration. Griff, who had just joined them, was confused. Otu smiled at Charlie and led him as well as Griff to their seats.

'You've earned it, Charlie. You've learned the magic and history from all four of the elemental books and you have a huge task ahead tomorrow, trying to rescue your friend, Denise.'

Charlie laughed as he imagined what Dennis would think if he knew he was known as Denise in this world. Denise and Gritt. Charlie sat beside Griff and, for the first time, they seemed to get on as friends, as they celebrated with the dillichups into the evening. Griff even started to learn the language and felt quite pleased with himself.

Eventually, everyone retired to bed. Charlie had a lot going through his mind as he lay staring at the ceiling. He still didn't fully understand the rhyme that he'd heard in the headmaster's office. He wondered if Dennis was okay and then began to wonder what the next trial would be.

Eventually, he managed to fall asleep.

CHAPTER 25

KIDNAP

When Charlie woke up, the dome lanterns in his room were still off which disorientated him regarding the time. He sat up to stretch and wakened one of the whispoths in its intricate globe. It was enough to get its wings beating fast enough to emit a warm electrical glow that lit the room a little.

Charlie stifled a yawn and stretched, before approaching the wash basin at one side of the room. He practised some water-enchanting in the bowl before splashing his face, then sat back on the bed. All he could think about was whether Dennis was okay and what Sinistre had planned.

He was hypnotised by the whispoth as its flittering wings within the globe when its little wings began to slow down, dimming the light. He closed his eyes and listened. He heard feet clattering along the ground some distance away, but then the sound of something else, which was out of place, scuttling along on all fours. He heard silent raspy breathing and was disturbed by the same shiver he got before something dangerous happened. He suddenly shot to his feet and called out, 'Sinistre.'

Suddenly, all the lights came alive and his door was flung open by Otu. Charlie explained. 'Sinistre's here somewhere, Otu. He's above us but I'm not sure exactly where.'

'Wait here Charlie. We'll go and check. Are you sure it was him?'

'Yes, I would know that breathing anywhere.'

Otu ran into the corridor, taking a number of the guards with him. Charlie suddenly had a terrifying epiphany and quickly got ready before running into the corridor.

'Take me to Griff's room,' he commanded the guards.

They surrounded Charlie and ran at speed towards Griff's room. They rose a level to the next tunnel system and turned into a dark corridor. Charlie knew something wasn't right as the whispoths hadn't activated the light.

'Guards, stand to the side,' Charlie commanded, as his pulse started to race.

He clicked his fingers and two flames appeared. He threw them together between his hands and, concentrating, he slowly pulled them apart so that a ball of flame grew. He looked ahead and shoved his hands forward into the pitch-black corridor. The flame lit the sides as it travelled along.

Charlie and the guards backed away as the flame lit up a huge dark lizard on the ceiling, holding a limp Griff who was dangling by his arms. Just as startled, it hissed in anger at them with jaws dripping and its huge fangs showed in the light of the flame.

The guards composed themselves and readied their spears to launch.

'No,' Charlie cried and stood in the way of the spears. 'He has Griff, you might hit him instead.'

The guards looked at each other in agreement. Charlie turned and started to run towards where Sinistre had just been. He created another flame and sent it to light the corridors ahead. He continued to create and thrust the flames in intermittent projections as he raced forwards. He then worked his jet boot magic and sped down the corridors. Eventually, with the help of a fireball light, he caught a glimpse of Sinistre's tail as it disappeared around the corner at the end of one of the tunnels.

Charlie maintained control and managed to turn the corner, but his speed made him reckless as a tongue suddenly shot from the wall to his side. Somehow, he had not spotted the dark shadow against the wall which was hiding Griff from view. The lethal tongue whipped out and landed squarely on the side of Charlie's head with a painful crack. He lost control, flying straight at the wall ahead, slamming against it at quite a speed. He collapsed to the ground and some soil piled on top of him. Sinistre leapt next to him and bared his teeth, right above Charlie's face, with goo falling onto his forehead. He could hardly move as he felt a throbbing pain in his head and a warm liquid running down his face.

Sinistre laughed in his face and rasped, 'Thisssss isss gonna be eassssy, Charlie the Chosssssen One.'

Then, as fast as he came, he leapt away just as the guards caught up. Charlie collapsed back onto the rubble and the blurred figures of the guards moved closer. Then it went dark as he lost consciousness.

***

Charlie regained consciousness and could make out strange murmurs around him, but he couldn't open his eyes. It seemed as though he was listening from underwater and didn't understand the words, but then the voices started to become clearer. He opened his eyes slightly and the light hurt them at first, but he managed to keep opening them wider. He was lying in a bed and felt a tight grip around his head, which was throbbing with pain. He gently lifted his hand to find out what was squeezing it and felt the material.

Charlie called, 'Hey' and the murmurings around him stopped.

He was relieved when he saw Otu appear next to him and a few of the others.

'Did you find him? Did you help Griff?'

'Sadly, Charlie, we couldn't help him. By the time the guards got to you, Sinistre and Gritt had already gone. I'm so sorry. I have no idea how he did it without alerting someone. This is my fault.'

Charlie raised his hand to the rough crown top of Otu's head and stroked it reassuringly.

'Don't feel bad. Nobody is at fault for what happened. He's unpredictable and we can learn from it. Anyway, what's the time?'

'Our suns are at their highest point, Charlie. You were out of it all night and the early part of today. You must rest as you had quite a bang to your head.'

'I can't rest, Otu. He has Dennis and Griff now. I just hope they're okay. I must meet him at the Lezaragons Mount, as planned.'

'Well then, just rest a little longer, Charlie. You need it. We will lead you to the base of the mount and we'll let you climb. I'll follow and will remain out of sight.'

'No, Otu. I don't want to put you in danger. The base of the mount is fine. He wants me alone so I don't want Dennis to suffer because I made the wrong choice and allowed you to come.'

'I understand, Charlie.'

A dillichup approached, wearing spectacles that somehow balanced on his face despite having no nose, or none that you could see. His crown was tinted blue and he brought a cup of green liquid over to Charlie, as Otu stepped to one side to allow him through.

'Hello Charlie, I'm Professor Nate. How are you feeling? You had quite a bump, you know.'

'I'm okay, thanks. Just a little bit of a headache, to be honest.'

'You're very lucky that's all you have.'

Nate sat next to Charlie, dripping the drink gently onto Charlie's lips. He coughed a little and turned his nose up.

'Urgh, what is that? It's disgusting.'

'It's good for you, Charlie. It'll help the bone in your head heal quicker and stronger.'

'The bone?'

'Charlie, if you'd hurt your head any more than you did, I don't think you'd be here now. You have a major cut to your head and the bone at the top was slightly cracked. We got you here in time to start the healing process. The crack closed quickly and fused much faster than we thought possible. It's still soft but this drink will help solidify it.'

Charlie had no idea how close he'd come to death in that tunnel. If it had happened in his world, he would have been in a critical condition. They had nothing there to soften bones which would push together like putty and solidify them. If he had survived, he would have had to live with a cracked skull. He took the cup in his hand and drank the rest, trying not to breathe through his nose as it had the stench of a putrid swamp.

The professor continued, 'That's better, Charlie. Well done.'

He removed part of the bandage from Charlie's head and smiled with relief before removing the rest of it.

'You heal very well, Charlie. However, you must rest a little longer. Your head should feel much better after a couple of hours.'

Charlie lay back and Otu stood and clapped his hands twice. The whispoths in the globes slowed their wings and the room dimmed. Charlie drifted back to sleep.

***

It only felt like a moment later when Charlie was shaken gently by Otu.

'Charlie, it's time to go shortly. We've made some food for the journey to help you stay strong.'

Charlie blinked a few times to wake up and immediately felt that his head was much better.

Otu continued, 'Charlie, you must try not to worry too much although it's understandable, given the situation. We'll be with you every step of the way to the base of the mount. If you need us, or something goes wrong, just let off a fireball as you did in the hallway and we'll see it.'

Charlie smiled gratefully and hugged him. Otu was quite stiff in his stance as he was not used to hugs. Dillichups were so curved that, even if they tried, they could hardly reach around each other.

'Thanks, Otu. I'm just gonna have a quick wash.'

Otu went with the guards and stood outside in the corridor. Charlie got up and jumped into the showering area that contained a barrel with holes in it. When he pulled the cord, it sprinkled him with a shower of warm water. He had a fright when he saw how red the water was when he washed his hair and realised that it was his blood. His head felt fine though and, after the shower, he checked it in the mirror and it seemed to have no sign of damage or scarring. It wasn't long before he was dried and dressed. With a big sigh, he looked back at his room, taking everything in, before he opened the door and went into the corridor to signify his readiness.

Otu gave him a reassuring nod and smile. Charlie followed him and some guards along the corridor. They rose to the next floor and continued along. He didn't recognise the tunnel they were going through but knew it must have been where the accident occurred. He felt uncomfortable as they passed the area which now included a barrier of bamboo sticks to prevent others from going through. There were a few dillichups with yellow crowns who were presumably the maintenance crew. Earlier, Charlie worked out that the crown colour signified their occupation or role.

He saw more bamboo in the roof further along and Otu explained, 'That's where he dug out and escaped, just as we arrived, Charlie.'

At last, they reached the end of the long corridor where they rose again and the ground seemed to move to the side as they surfaced. Charlie was blinded by the brightness, as his eyes adjusted after being so long underground. He smiled, closed his eyes, breathed a deep intake of fresh air and held it for a moment before releasing it slowly. He opened his eyes as Otu led him to a small table set up with food.

'We thought it would be a good time to have food out in the open, before we set off, Charlie.'

Charlie smiled and they sat down to eat. The chatter was amicable and the whole setup helped him stay positive and focused. The food was delicious and much-needed. The only gross thing was the drink that Professor Nate brought over to him, which was a medicine to help his wound heal, even though it looked and felt much better. Charlie swilled his mouth afterwards with refreshing water with a hint of lemon. He was slightly nervous, as it reminded him of the Last Supper he'd read in Sunday school once.

'This is it, Charlie. Are you ready to go now?'

He looked at Otu and said, 'Yes, as ready as I'll ever be, thanks. Let's do this.'

They began to walk along the meadows with the guards surrounding him. Charlie took in the beauty of the areas they travelled through, often looking up at the sky.

'Is that Ryskia up there, Otu?'

'It probably would be, Charlie, as you would be out in the open and get noticed from afar if you flew up there.'

Charlie laughed.

'No, Otu. Not risky. I meant is that the realm of Ryskia up there?'

Otu laughed as he realised his misunderstanding.

'Oh, Charlie. Sorry. Yes, it's a part of Ryskia. Many of them reside on the clouds up there; an entire civilisation living above us. I'd forgotten that you've been there.'

'Yes, it was only for a short while, but it was truly amazing.'

As they carried on, a thought came to Charlie and he asked that they stop for a moment. He went towards a tree, and as Otu was about to follow, he raised his hand signalling him to stay where he was as he needed a moment of privacy. Otu obliged and stood his ground, advising the guards to do the same.

CHAPTER 26

THE CALL FOR REINFORCEMENTS

Charlie walked around the tree and sat down, with the dillichups out of view on the other side. He closed his eyes and went into a deep meditation as he whispered words into the breeze of Terriana, repeating them several times. He opened his eyes, looked up and smiled hopefully.

Charlie returned to the group before they continue travelling until Lezaragons Mount came into view. Shrouded in dark clouds, the peak was completely hidden except when silhouetted by flashes of lightning. As the group moved closer to their destination, Out wrapped an arm around Charlie, whose face was tight with fear or concern – or both.

'This is it, Charlie. We can go no further with you.'

Charlie looked up at the mount, wondering about his two bullying friends.

Otu continued, 'Charlie, they'll be fine. If anyone can save them, you can. I'm confident of that.'

Secretly, Otu was petrified and wondered if Charlie was ready. But it was too late as they were there, and Charlie had to go on by himself. Charlie, however, turned to hug Otu again before shaking hands with each of the guards.

'Thanks, everyone. Please don't worry. I'll see you soon,' he said, as he smiled and waved.

They all raised their hands and gave a cheer as he started off. He used the jet boots' spell and began to glide up the side of the mountain, towards the dark sky. He remained close to the mount so that, if the jets failed him, he would only have a short fall to the ground. Heights didn't bother him much anymore. He'd had so many close calls that, by surviving each time, he was reassured that there was nothing to fear as long as he was careful. His current fear was concentrated on the unknown within the dark cloud, which was getting closer.

When he was near enough to the top, he lowered himself to the side of the mountain, getting a safe foothold. The climb took longer than expected as he slowly approached the peak. He looked up at the dark cloud he was approaching, where he saw a few flashes and heard a roll of thunder. The first few noisy blasts made him jump, but he was getting used to it.

He suddenly shuddered with cold. It meant that Sinistre was on his way. He tried to light a flame in his hand to keep himself warm, and to help with visibility, but it didn't appear. Charlie, now within the cloud, saw glowing eyes, deep and red. He began to walk cautiously toward them.

'Charlieeeeee, Charlieeeeee. I knew you'd come,' the raspy voice called out from ahead and gave a nasty chuckle.

He heard some muffled noises, and as he got closer, the dark cloudy mist rose skyward, he could see Sinistre holding a wriggling bundle in one arm. Another bundle, not so wriggly, was dangled in sheeting over the edge of a sheer drop, only being held up by a small protruding piece of rock.

Sinistre leaned his head to one side, admiring Charlie's fearless demeanour, but was determined to change that. He waved his free hand, wafting away the remains of the dark mist, allowing Charlie to see everything much more clearly.

'Charlieeee,' Sinistre hissed, showing his sharp but broken, filthy teeth as drool spilt from the side of his mouth. 'It's good to see that you survived. I want you to witness this moment. The moment you fail in your quest.' Sinistre laughed.

'I'll not lose to you,' said Charlie, loudly and confidently. 'Now I'm here, you stick to your end of the bargain and let them go. You can have me instead.'

'Oh, Charlie, I intend to.'

He laughed menacingly again.

'You see, we have a situation here, and you have a few choices. A game if you will. Firstly, I will look to drop both your friends at the same time, which of them would you try saving if any?'

'Is there another choice, Sinistre?'

'You agree with me, here and now, a time and place to bring me the book.'

'And if I refuse?'

'Then you've sssealed your fate and that of your friendsss, as well as another important thing,' Sinistre answered, angrily.

'Do tell, Sinistre,' Charlie said, as he smiled confidently, knowing it would annoy the lizard who was standing menacingly in front of him.

Sinistre held out his free claw, displaying a wooden stick.

'I will dessssstroy the thing that you need, Charlieeee.'

Charlie noticed that he hissed more as his anger increased but, there was no denying, he needed the wand. He attempted to ignite a flame in his palm, but nothing came and he realised that this was part of the fourth trial. He knew he couldn't touch the stick yet as it would leave Griff and Dennis in danger. He had to think quickly.

'What the heck would I want a stupid stick for?' he said, playing dumb.

Sinistre's eyes opened wider with surprised curiosity and said, 'Then, I guess you won't be needing it, Charlie.'

He dropped the bundle from his shoulder, snapped the stick in two and dropped the pieces over the cliff edge. Charlie's heart dropped but knew he had to hide his hopelessness, as it could be made worse.

'Maybe I overessssssstimated you, Charlie,' said Sinistre, as he gritted his teeth tightly in anger. 'Now here'ssss a dilemma for you, but do you even want to sssssssave them?'

'What do you mean?'

'You had my word. You showed up and I will releasssssse them, now that you have sssssssurrendered yoursssssself to me. Get rid of the wretched creatures for what they put you through in sssschool. Yesssssss, I ssssssssaw it when he was my hosssssst. It was most pleasurable to watch the fear in your eyesssssss,' he said as he looked in Dennis's direction.

Charlie was not unnerved by Sinistre's attempt to belittle him. He was more relaxed, realising the plan earlier was coming to fruition. He spied something approaching in the distance but he proceeded to gaze into Sinistre's eyes.

'Enjoyed it, did you? You like that sort of thing, aye?' Charlie laughed. 'Shame you can't have me, innit?'

He stepped closer. Sinistre stepped back and almost teetered over the edge as he almost lost balance when he hit some rocks with his heels.

'ENOUGH!' he bellowed, picking up Griff and unhooking Dennis from the protruding rock so they both dangled over the drop below.

'Will it be Griff, or will it be Dennissssss? It is time for you to decide, one or the other.'

Sinistre laughed just as lightning struck and thunder rolled. He released the grip on Griff and Dennis. Both dropped, plummeting to their doom.

Sinistre's arrogance betrayed him as a large blue streak came from above and Charlie ran forwards, leaping over the edge of Lezaragons Mount. He dived and picked up momentum, speeding towards Griff. He attempted to use his jet power but nothing happened. He concentrated on Griff, reaching out to him. He almost missed, but managed another grab, pulling him into his arms.

He mouthed to Griff to stay calm as the force of gravity was strong against them. Charlie looked across and saw a giant furry creature capture Dennis in mid-fall, catching him in soft fur. Dennis, panicking, turned towards a hut in the centre of the creatures back that had just caught him. The dragon turned his attention towards Charlie, who still had a tight hold of Griff. By then, the ground was getting much closer than Charlie would have liked, even though he'd managed to slow down by showing Griff how to open his arms and legs and keep them flat resembling paragliding.

Sinistre stood on the mountain, looking down at them, absolutely livid as there was nothing he could do. He could not fly and knew he'd be doomed if he leapt. The lightning sizzled around him as he raked the ground with his claws, enraged.

Charlie tried reassuring Griff, visibly afraid of the approaching large sabre-tooth fang, visible from the mouth of a giant tiger's face heading straight for them. Griff couldn't scream, the gag was too tight around his mouth. Griff fainted in terror from the approaching monster. But it was no monster; it was Charlie's faithful friend, Tsangali, the blue dragon from Ryskia, the realm of air.

Tsangali roared with laughter as he headed quickly towards Charlie and Griff. He dipped his head and dived below them at the same speed as their fall. He slowed a little to allow Charlie to touchdown with Griff in his arms, then slowed gently. They were almost at the base of the mount when they slowed down enough to be safe, narrowly avoiding the jagged edges of the rocks below.

Tsangali began to fly up, away from Lezaragons Mount, as the dilluchups cheered from below. The thunder at the mountaintop was fierce. Charlie dragged Griff across the fur towards the hut where Jan was waiting to greet them. She'd already managed to drag Dennis onto some blankets in her hut. Charlie checked his magic and raised his hands as the air lifted Griff. His power had returned and he gave a satisfied grin to Jan who looked at him proudly. He carefully floated Griff onto the bed next to Dennis and released him. They both lay there, peaceful and safe. Jan and Charlie untied them and removed their gags. They spooned some healing warm milk from a large vessel, slipping it gently through Griff and Dennis's lips. They drank it all before Charlie and Jan went outside and let them rest.

'Charlie, you've grown so much inside and in power too, I see. Congratulations on making it here. It's lovely to see you again, my wee boy. I never doubted you for one moment. That was some power you gained to be able to whisper to Tsangali from such a distance. I'm proud of you and of what you've become.'

'Thanks, Jan. Means allot. Otu was on a one track path to the mount, that I was worried he wouldn't allow me to stop at the tree on route and use my message whispering magic. So grateful it worked and the message found you.'

She hugged Charlie and smiled broadly. Charlie welcomed the hug as it reminded him of his mum and the comfort of home.

***

Back at the top of Lezaragons Mount, standing on the edge of a peaked plateau, Sinistre was angry and screamed, 'Noooooo!' He scratched the surface, making deep claw marks in the rock. He started to claw at his face, which bled as he pulled loose skin away. Anything within reach, he tore to shreds as his anger exploded beyond his control.

Sinistre went to the edge and leapt downward, using the crevasses and jagged rocks to assist until he eventually landed on the ground. He heard the dillichups celebrate in the distance and scowled. He bounded on all fours along the rocks and grass towards the guards. They scattered fast as he clawed one down to the ground and proceeded to rip him apart.

Otu threw a spear in his direction but Sinistre raised his head at the last moment, caught it in his crooked teeth, biting down on it so that it splintered into bits. The others gathered into a large group, raising their spears. Sinistre hissed at them, they stepped back cautiously. He then turned and left them to lift their fallen comrade.

He ran across the fields and fire lands to one of the two locations where the four elemental realms meet in this world. Called the Cave of the Dark, it tunnelled at least a thousand human miles away, to a place called the Palace of the Light.

Sinistre stood at the entrance of the cave and fearfully gazed at it for a moment. He had no plans to enter the cave at any time so diverted around to the side and removed shrubbery from the ground where a circular puddle was hidden. It glowed with swirling colours.

Sinistre slowly placed his claw into the pool and writhed in pain as his body began to disintegrate as he sank into it.

From a lonely tree on a remote island in the centre of a lake, a dark smoky entity entered the human world and took flight. It was a very angry Sinistre, knowing exactly who his next host would be.

***

Charlie sat on the small stool outside the hut on Tsangali's back, staring at the royal blue fur and the way it waved gently in the breeze of flight. Jan sat on another stool next to him.

'What's on your mind, Charlie?'

'Well, the prophecy book Tallemseen hasn't revealed too much yet. Do you know anything of the tale of this prophecy?'

'I do, Charlie, but only a little. Apart from you, no one knows the actual words on the pages of the book. What I do know is that it speaks of a Chosen One who will have the power to stop the darkness and close the portal so evil creatures of our world can't spread out across your world and make it their home, using humans as their hosts. The only way to prevent the portal from being closed is to destroy the book before the Chosen One learns its secrets or destroy the Chosen One himself.'

Charlie was about to continue but was distracted. They could hear mumblings of Griff and Dennis, a sign they'd woken. He turned to Jan and asked, 'How do we get home?'

'There are two ways, Charlie. You need to find a wand to take you back or go through a portal that is in the dark lands, but we don't know exactly where it is located.'

'I have three wands infused into one, Water, Air and Fire. Sinistre split the last one into two pieces and chucked it down the mountainside.'

'Then go find the two pieces, Charlie. That wand still survives because you can use the magic of the earth. Hold them together and the wand will mend itself.'

'That's great. So, we just need to land and search for them.'

'I best head back in, now we can can hear the boys are stirring. Good luck, Charlie. I'm sure I will see you again soon!'

Jan waved her hands in the air toward the hut. Charlie looked puzzled. 'Just enchanting the home, bracing for a bumpy landing, Charlie.'

'Ah, I guess that makes sense.'

She hugged Charlie again and went back to the hut.

Charlie went to ask Tsangali to land at the Lezaragons Mount in Terriana. He grinned, nodding his acknowledgement before turning around, heading back to the mountain.

By then, Griff and Dennis were on their feet and came out of the hut. As Charlie neared them, Dennis rushed at him ready to land a punch but Griff ran between them and pushed Dennis back so that he fell to the ground.

'Leave Charlie alone, Den. He saved our backsides from hitting the rocks and being mashed by that creature.'

Dennis got up and went nose-to-nose with Griff, saying, 'And you think we'd be here if it weren't for him?'

'Yes, Den, we would be. We were the ones that went after him, remember?'

Dennis was quiet for a moment and then looked at Charlie.

'What's happening, Charlie? What is this place? What's going on? How can you understand these monsters?'

They heard a friendly booming voice cry out, 'Ready to land.'

All Griff and Dennis heard were growls and roars. They were afraid as they looked at each other blankly.

Charlie advised them, 'Griff and Dennis, lie down and brace yourselves for the landing. We'll have time for questions later.'

They obeyed and they all lay on the dragons back, gripping the fur tightly in each hand.

CHAPTER 27

THE PERILOUS JOURNEY

While the boys gripped the dragon's fur, there were a few strange bumps as Tsangali flew upwards, almost vertically, towards the dark clouds before levelling off. The darkness became thicker around. Lightning bolts flashed in the clouds as they glided just below them. The rolling thunder were extremely loud, making Dennis and Griff jump. Eventually, the dragon landed on the top of Lezaragons Mount and Charlie stood up. Dennis and Griff remained where they were, trembling and gripping the fur tightly.

'Come on guys, we don't have much time. Knowing Sinistre, he's that giant lizard-thing by the way, he's not going to be here. He will have gone back to our earth by now. He's erratic and, luckily, acts before he thinks.'

'Luckily?' asked Griff, as he stood up cautiously.

'Yep. He will be going for the book, which is why we have to hurry.'

'Okay, where do we start?' asked Dennis, who was now standing with them.

Charlie waved to Jan who was looking at him with admiration. She smiled and waved back, holding a chequered rag in her hand and dabbing her eyes with it as she turned back to the hut, looking sorrowful. Charlie felt touched and sad as he walked to the edge of the paw. He slid down the shiny marble-like claws which were a mixture of sky blue and royal blue. Griff and Dennis were reluctant at first but eventually followed. They dismounted and joined Charlie on the mount as he turned toward the bright golden eyes of Tsangali.

'Thank you, my friend. I'll see you again, someday,' he said as he smiled and stroked the top of the dragons claw.

'Mmmm, you know how to calm a dragon, don't you?' Tsangali laughed. 'I'll always be here for you, Chosen One.'

Having shielded themselves behind Charlie, Dennis and Griff had no idea a conversation was taking place. The dragon raised his head, winked at Charlie and then walked to the edge of Lezaragons Mount before taking flight. The wind caused by the dragon's wing flaps messed up the boys' hair but they managed to stand their ground though. Hiding a tear from the others, Charlie thumbed the wayward tear. In that moment Tsangali was already a speck on the horizon.

He was ready.

'Right, you two, come on. We need to find two sticks. It was just one but Sinistre snapped it, trying to destroy it. They are crucial to getting us home. Each end is broken but they should piece together.'

'Sticks? How the heck are we meant to find two pieces of stick on this great mountain if they're so small?' Dennis quizzed.

'Sticks on this mountain are non-existent. Most are made of charcoal or dead shrubbery, as nothing survives here. These two are alive and will look out of place.'

Griff asked, 'Charlie, what if Sinistre gets hold of the book you mentioned? What's so special about it?'

'That's why we need to hurry, Griff. If Sinistre gets a hold of that book, it could destroy our chance of getting home and saving our earth. The moment I put the two sticks together we should, in theory, reappear at the exact time and place we left our world. So as long as he hasn't reached the book and we keep together, it'll be fine. We'll work it out.'

'And if he gets the book before we get out?'

'It doesn't bear thinking about. It could mean the end of the two worlds, as we know them.'

Griff paused for a minute, then asked, 'So if we successfully put the two sticks together, would that mean that my pal here is going to have that thing inside him again?'

Charlie didn't want to answer but felt he had to be honest.

'Yes, it does, Griff, but we would be prepared, as we have the advantage of hindsight.'

Griff and Dennis didn't look confident, especially when they saw what was next to Charlie's feet. Their eyes widened as they saw the deep claw scratches in the rock surface with bits of skin and blood around them.

'He's pissed, Charlie,' said Dennis, still staring at the marks.

'Come on guys, we can't dawdle. Let's start looking.'

Charlie walked to the right and said, 'He dropped one of the sticks over here.'

He then walked along the edge, slightly to the left, pointed downwards and said, 'And the other here.'

Dennis and Griff composed themselves and scooched carefully, as close to the edge as they dared, and looked down whilst holding on to each other. It wasn't vertical but it was the most dangerous drop they'd ever seen and they wondered if they would survive a fall if it came to it. Dennis spoke first.

'Charlie, if you think we are going down there with you, then you've got the wrong guys.'

'Dennis, we have to go down together. The moment we find those sticks and bind them together, you both need to hold my arm because as soon as they touch, boom, we'll be back home.'

'We know you're gay, Charlie, but we don't have to join in your gay ways and hold arms,' Dennis mocked.

He was stopped short as Griff thumped him in the stomach.

'Leave Charlie alone. Did you not hear what he said about the book? While you're name-calling, that thing is in our world going for the book and if he gets it before we get those sticks, well … Charlie?'

'Thanks, Griff. Basically, to remind you. If Sinistre retrieves the book and destroys it, there will be no stopping the evil creatures of this world from taking ours. They will eventually make it their home and possess all the bodies of the human race. There's absolutely nothing we can do about it if he wins this. Our world will be in utter chaos and they'll go from strength to strength. They will take down the good creatures of this world too.'

He lowered his voice as he thought about the end of this sentence, without saying it aloud, '... and I'll probably never find out if my father is alive or not.'

Griff seemed to catch Charlie's emotion as he patted his back and whispered, 'I'm sorry, Charlie, for the way we were with you.'

Charlie nodded and smiled. Griff turned, speaking to Dennis.

'Charlie's alright, you know. He saved us, man, and it's time that we show him what we're made of and help him. So, come on, Den, this is the least we can do. We got this.'

Dennis sulked a little but quietly came around to the idea. He cautiously peered over the edge at the steep drop below.

'Okay then, Charlie. What's the plan? How're we gonna do this?'

Charlie discreetly clicked his fingers to see if he could ignite a spark but, as he feared, he had no powers to help them and realised that it must be a part of the challenge set for him.

'What're you doing?' asked Dennis.

'Nothing. Right guys, thanks so much for being here. I must warn you both, this mission is going to be dangerous. We're going to have to ascend this Mount. I can't deny, it'll waste valuable time that we don't have. So we'll need to work as fast as we can together okay.'

'You're sounding all grown-up, Charlie. We'll be calling you Sir next,' Dennis replied.

Griff gave Dennis a warning stare.

Charlie's eyes were diverted towards a cloud behind them, where something caught his attention. A hundred small glowing red eyes were staring at them from within the cloud.

'Um, guys. I think we need to get over the edge as soon as we can, out of view. Just don't look behind you, okay? Try not to make any sudden moves. Just move slowly, let's go.'

Asking someone to not look behind is one of the worst mistakes you can do, as Dennis and Griff, discreetly at first, looked behind them and immediately noticed the eyes. Suddenly, there was an ear-piercingly loud evil squawk that caused the three boys to block their ears and freeze.

Hundreds of crow-like creatures with bright red glowing eyes were heading straight for them, in a dive formation. The boys leapt off the edge of the mount and grabbed the rocks which prevented their fall, as streams of the creatures sped over them, barely missing them but too fast to redirect.

The crows began to turn in perfect unity which could have been described as beautifully graceful if they weren't so terrifying. Their evil shrills cut the air as they flew directly at the boys, who turned their faces to the cliff and closed their eyes, waiting for the inevitable.

Nothing happened.

Charlie turned and saw that the birds had become erratic and were dispersing, as a volley of spears hurtled towards them from the clifftop. When he saw who was standing on the edge, he felt more confident.

'Otu!' he called.

'Good to see you, Charlie. Shame it's not under better circumstances. We saw your big blue friend coming back to the top of the mountain and knew you had to be here. We decided not to sit around and let that creature get away with what he's done so I gathered up some troops to come and see if you might need help and it seems as though you do. Now, get going, Charlie, and do what needs to be done and we'll try and hold these demonuettes off as best we can.'

'Thanks, Otu. You're amazing.'

Otu smiled and waved Charlie on as the demonuettes were gathering again to face him and his army. Charlie, Dennis and Griff had to hold their ears as the birds squawked loudly again before dive-bombing over the clifftop above them.

'Come on, Den and Griff, let's go find those sticks. If you spread out your hand, they are the length from your wrist to the tip of your middle finger.'

They nodded in acknowledgement and started to descend cautiously, checking each crevasse and hole carefully. Charlie lost a foothold as the side of the cliff crumbled. He held tightly to the jagged rock edge as his feet dangled in the space until eventually he calmed down and found a good edge where his feet could rest as he looked for another foothold.

'Damn, that was close,' he said to himself.

Dennis called out, 'Charlie, I think I've found one.'

He pulled the wooden half-stick out and proudly waved it about precariously.

'Great, Den, that's it. Now, put it in your pocket safely and we'll look for the next piece. It's going to be further this way, towards me, so let's continue and move to our right as we descend.'

Dennis seemed to listen, for a change, which was probably because of the new-found authority in Charlie's voice. He put the half-stick into the pocket of his joggers and zipped it securely, then followed Charlie.

The battle cries from the dillichup army above became louder and the squawks of the demonuettes were still ear-piercing, as they lured the army closer to the edge. Charlie was worried about the dillichups but he knew how important it was to retrieve the wand. Otu wouldn't be happy if he abandoned the search, knowing what was at stake. He paused for a moment to make sure he was safe, then attempted his magic again by clicking his fingers, but there was nothing, not even a spark.

A couple of stray demonuettes flew from the battle above, towards Charlie. They tried to distract him and make him lose his balance by flapping at his face. He gripped hard and tried to shove them away with his free arm, but they just glided around him with ease and continued flapping against his face. He began to feel the sting of the attack. One of them was about to sink its sharp blood-red jagged beak into his eye but a large hand grabbed it around the neck and proceeded to bang its head hard against the rock until there was a snap and it went limp. The other crows flew back to the battle above.

Dennis released the dead bird which dropped to the land below and a few other demonuettes, that had been flapping around Griff's face, were disturbed by this and dispersed. Charlie smiled at Dennis.

'Griff and I hunt a lot of birds back home,' he grinned.

'Thanks, Den. Let's carry on before they come back.'

'Charlie!' Griff called from a distance to the right of them. 'I think I see it, but I don't think you're gonna like it.'

Dennis and Charlie began to edge along, eventually reaching the wide ledge where Griff was standing. He had his back to the cliff and was pointing at a large thin rock in front of them which was like a tall stalagmite. Lodged at the top of it, they could see the other half of the stick.

Charlie suddenly realised that a flock of demonuettes were starting to surge to their left.

'Guys, turn around and brace yourselves, they're back. Make sure you keep your faces to the cliff,' he warned.

All three managed to turn and find a secure handhold in the rocks as the demonuettes screeched and squawked their battle cry and began to dive at them, pelting their full weight against them. Their beaks were so sharp that they tore the boys' clothes and cut at their skin. Suddenly, Griff cried out in agony as one managed to pierce deep into his thigh.

Charlie recognised a voice, calling from above, 'Watch out, Charlie.'

He turned to Griff and Dennis, warning them, 'Hold on and pull in as tight as you can.'

They did so as a volley of spears pelted downwards. Some caught their prize as a large number of demonuettes were pierced and gave out their last squawks. Those that managed to escape dispersed to regroup.

CHAPTER 28

WHERE'S MUM?

Charlie took a moment to realise he'd spotted something sitting on Griff's hand, the one holding him up safely against the cliff face.

'Griff, are you okay?' he asked, trying to keep Griff's attention away from it.

He was surprised that Griff couldn't feel it and assumed the pain of his wound outweighed the tingle on his hand, where an efluge perched. A spider-like creature with eight legs permanently ablaze which has the nastiest bite. It was currently looking very relaxed.

Griff had his other hand pressed against the wound on his thigh but he could see that Charlie was distracted.

'Yeah, I'm just a little cut, that's all. Nothing too bad, it'll heal. Just had a big green beast chew my head off too, that kind of thing,' he tested but didn't get a reaction. 'Charlie, you're not listening to me. What is it?'

'Griff, listen to me now and just stay calm, okay?'

'Why do I hate it when someone says anything like that?'

'Well, it's just that you have a spider sitting on your hand. Don't look at it and stay calm.'

'Great!' Griff responded, but he stood perfectly still and calmly kept facing Charlie until Dennis looked across at Griff to see what they were talking about.

'What the fuck is that thing?' Dennis shouted.

Charlie turned to Dennis and said angrily, 'Den, shut your mouth. If your friend moves suddenly, he'll fall because the bite of that thing is very dangerous and extremely painful.'

Dennis went quiet but Griff was starting to shiver. The two front flaming legs of the efluge rose slightly and it stood tall.

Griff checked out the drop to judge if he could jump but it was too high. He spotted something glinting below that seemed to be coming closer. Charlie remembered that he had been told that efluges generally travel in groups.

'Guys, stay perfectly still and try to relax. I should warn you that I don't think that's the only spider. We might feel them on us soon.'

Charlie began to perspire as he looked up towards the dark cloud, still flashing above, and could hear the battle still going on. To relax he lowered his breathing, as he had learned. He spotted several holes appearing in the rock face around them.

'Close your eyes and hold fast,' he instructed the others.

Den didn't speak but Griff whispered, 'Charlie, I've been trying to tell you something. I don't think those spiders are the only creatures to worry about. Nor those birds up there. Just look down if you get a chance.'

Charlie slowly turned to look down but caught sight of Dennis's arm. Several efluges were sitting there and had their front two legs upwards. He could see their mandrills protruding covered with a flaming liquid. Charlie decided to remain quiet and perfectly still as he closed his eyes, just as he saw an efluge crawling onto his hand.

Dennis gave a bloodcurdling yell as fangs suddenly penetrated his finger and he let go of the rock. Trying to remain as still as possible, Charlie and Griff looked on in terror as Dennis's arms started to flail in the air and he fell backwards. There was nothing they could do. Charlie froze in fear, waiting for a thud as he heard Dennis screaming, but it suddenly went quiet.

Charlie felt a strange sensation bounce along his arm and he saw the efluge run towards a hole in the cliff. Little orange paws grabbed at it and he heard a crunch. It was a flarune, eating its prey. Then a familiar voice came from behind him.

'Well now you're awake, Charlie, I think you might have dropped this.'

The voice was deep, calm and friendly. Charlie instantly recognised Brune and some flarunes riding along on his large shoulders. They leapt towards the cliff wall and the efluges ran back into their holes. Brune was referring to Dennis and Charlie was relieved to see that he was carrying him.

'Brune, it's great to see you and the flarunes. Perfect timing, my big friend.'

Brune gave a deep laugh.

'Well, this one here is one of yours, I guess, and he looks a little worse for wear, I must say. He's fainted so he has, Charlie.'

Brune looked toward Griff and said, 'Ooooh, I think I best help your friend over there too. Guards, take him up top.'

Two others in metallic armour flew to Griff. They grabbed him and safely took him to the top of the mountain.

'But what made you come, Brune?'

'When you called for Tsangali's help earlier, Charlie, I realised that you have not mastered the whispering method yet because we heard your call, although at the time we didn't understand it. We decided to check in on you and, well, here we are. Let's get you both up there, Charlie, and I'll tell you about it.'

'Brune, just to let you know, the dilluchups up there may be having trouble with demonuettes.'

'Don't you worry, Charlie. You don't have to tell us twice. Come on, we're on it.'

Brune moved closer to the cliff so that Charlie could wrap his arms around him before he powered his jet boots and carried Charlie and Dennis to the top of the mountain. They soon reached it and found Griff, sitting there, looking rather shaken. The scene was a carnage of dillichups and many more demonuettes. Otu was battling three demonuettes who were pecking at him. His guards were aiming spears at them, keeping them at bay, but they looked exhausted.

Brune placed Dennis carefully on the rock surface and Charlie jumped down from his back.

'Look after these two, Charlie, we're gonna help the dillichups and finish this for you, okay? We'll talk after.'

He patted Charlie on the shoulder, turned and ran toward the battle followed by the other fire guardians and flarunes. Griff was petrified and sat on a rock next to Charlie. He held out his hand to hold Charlie's. Charlie held it tightly, smiled reassuringly and knelt next to him.

'Don't worry, Griff. We've got this, okay? They are our friends and they are here to help us.'

'But, Charlie, how did this happen? Are we dreaming? I'm honestly sorry about what we put you through.'

'Awww, don't mention it, Griff. It's okay, honestly. I'll tell you about this place someday but now's not the time. But just know that we're safe now.'

'But what about the book though?'

'I feel that it's safe at the moment, Griff. We'll know when Sinistre has it, but I fear he's getting closer all the time, for sure.'

'But it would be okay if he did have it though, wouldn't it? Like you said, as soon as we manage to get back, everything will be as it was at the point we left.'

'Yes, but there may be a bit of a problem with that. Although we, who have crossed worlds, go back to exactly as we were, anything that happened in our real world while we were here will remain.'

'So, just to understand this; if Sinistre destroys the book before we get back …'

They spoke the last part of the sentence in unison, '… the book will be destroyed.'

It looked as though the demonuettes were at last being defeated. A few of them gathered in a small cluster and retreated into the dark clouds. There was a roar and everyone gave a valiant cheer before tending to the dying and wounded.

Otu and Brune came to Charlie's side.

'Brune and Otu, I can't express our gratitude. Honestly, thank you.'

Brune answered, 'It's never a bother, but why are you still here in our world? What're you up to Charlie, to risk yourselves like this?'

Otu then added, 'Yes Charlie, he's right. And what happened to Sinistre? We felt the backhand of his anger, that's for sure.'

Charlie briefly explained everything that happened.

'Charlie,' Otu replied, 'click your fingers now.'

'Why?' Charlie queried, not sure what Otu thought would happen.

Then Brune responded, 'Just try it, my boy. Click your fingers. Have confidence.'

Charlie looked at his hand, clicked his fingers and a flame appeared floating above his hand. His face glowed and then he threw it towards the cloud. Griff was impressed by the magic trick.

'But how?'

'It's because you brought us all together, Charlie,' replied Otu.

'Well yeah, but are we not forgetting Watsuria though? I haven't involved them.'

Brune interrupted.

'Actually, it was your friend from Watsuria, Aqualdium I believe, who heard your signal for help. He surfaced to our land from the sea and explained your message to us. As I mentioned earlier, I'd heard something, but the truth was that I hadn't a clue what the message said at the time and dismissed it as we were all busy rebuilding the damaged roof of the palace. There was a lot of noise.'

'You are all amazing. Thanks so much. I should now be able to do this.'

He released Griff's hand and stood at the edge of Lezaragons Mount. He pointed his hand towards the stick that was sitting on top of the stalagmite below. He closed his eyes for a moment to concentrate, feeling the air around him, and the stick began to float upwards to his hand. He grabbed it with a satisfied smile.

Dennis was starting to wake. Griff was watching the whole thing with his mouth wide open in disbelief.

'Thanks again to all of you. I guess it's time we must head back now. I really hope to see you again. Do you need anything before we go?'

'Just to know that you stay safe, Charlie. You did well,' Otu replied.

Brune answered, 'Exactly what he says.'

They all laughed.

Charlie looked at Dennis and Griff asking, 'Are you both okay now and ready to go?'

'Yeah, deffo.'

Dennis pulled the other half of the stick from his joggers and passed it over to Charlie, who placed the cracked ends together.

'Right, you two, hold onto my arms. We're off.'

Griff and Dennis held an arm each. Just as Charlie was about to tap the sticks, he felt a sudden shiver, the warning he got when there was danger. He saw a vision of his wardrobe and the pixiedown flying erratically around as claws tried to capture her. Then the wardrobe shattered in bits and he could see the edge of the book of prophecy.

Charlie quickly regained his thoughts and brought the stick together. A spark flew from the crack between the sticks, binding them together and then, with a sudden blinding light, the three of them fell back towards the ground.

They were lying in the woods with their backs in the mud and Charlie could hear his aunt calling his name. He quickly popped the wand into his pocket. She called out again and he realised something was missing. They were back in the moment they had left but his mum's voice was missing.

'Charlie, what is it?' asked Griff, seeing the look on his face.

'My mum was calling before we left but I can't hear her now.'

A snigger broke the air and Dennis laughed an evil laugh, as Griff and Charlie realised what was happening. Dennis's eyes were as black as onyx, confirming that Sinistre was back where he started, before the mud engulfed them.

CHAPTER 29

FELINE CAPERS

Dennis stopped laughing and began to look in pain as he shook vigorously and dark smoke with glowing red eyes seeped from his mouth as he collapsed unconscious on the ground. The dark mist was a bit greyer than Charlie recalled. It hovered and circled Griff and Charlie's heads, scanning them before it shot away.

At first, they were frozen, then Charlie went over to Dennis, to check his pulse and administer first aid, just as his aunt came into view from amongst the trees, with Louise who had led her there.

Kathleen grabbed Griff's shoulder and started to shake him, shouting, 'What did you do?'

Griff remained silent and his eyes watered a little. Charlie quickly got up and pulled his aunt from Griff.

'It wasn't his fault, Aunty. Dennis collapsed and Griff was about to call the ambulance.'

Griff understood the instructions and continued with, 'And I was about to let Charlie know my mobile had died.'

Kathleen contacted the ambulance as Louise ran up to Charlie, hugging him.

'Awww, Louise. I'm okay. The boys were playing but they were a bit rougher than they should have been. We're all okay now. I had to get you home because I didn't want you to get hurt.'

That was it. Another semi-truth from Charlie just to keep the peace and avoid further questions or having to explain the unexplainable.

'Where's Mum, Louise?' Charlie asked.

Louise became tearful. Kathleen finished her call to the ambulance service and turned to Griff.

'You keep an eye on Dennis as the ambulance is on its way.'

Griff nodded and went over to sit with Dennis. Kathleen went over to her daughter and hugged her. She explained to Charlie what had occurred.

'Charlie, your mother's hurt. An intruder got into the house and barricaded Louise and me in the kitchen. We heard things being broken and your mum screaming but, by the time I managed to get the door open, the intruder had left although I didn't hear him or her leave. Charlie - wait!'

That was enough for Charlie. He started to run home before Kathleen finished. Seeing the blue and white tape around his home, where the front door was smashed to bits, was enough to give the clue that it wasn't good. He went straight for the tape to get through but a police officer stopped him.

'You're not allowed in here, Son. It's a crime scene and nothing's to be disturbed while Forensics are collecting evidence.'

'It's my home and Mum's in there, let me through.'

Charlie started kicking up a little and the officer had to hold him.

'Now, now. She's not here. Stop struggling, you won't find her in there.'

The officer was struggling to hold Charlie when his aunt appeared, calling him from the roadside, which helped calm him a little.

'Where is she then?' Charlie asked as he relaxed.

His aunt nodded to the police officer and put her arms around Charlie, leading him away from his home.

'Charlie, your mum was unconscious but breathing when we found her on the ground outside your bedroom. It looked as though she'd cut her hands and there was a lot of bruising, perhaps caused by the struggle, but she is okay as far as we know and was taken to the hospital. It all happened when your cousin, Louise, came running to me in the kitchen saying that some kids had got you. We were just about to leave and that's when the kitchen door slammed shut and was barricaded.'

Charlie remained silent and stared at the damage.

'Would you like me to run you to the hospital, Charlie? We'll go and see her.'

He nodded silently but, as his aunt went to guide him to her car, he said, 'Wait. There's something I need to do first, if that's okay, please?'

Kathleen was confused but she nodded and opened the back door for Louise to jump in. She got into the car and started the radio as they waited for him to get back.

Charlie sprinted to the alley and ran up to his back gate. He could hear the police radios on the other side and knew it was useless to try going in. Then he spotted the neighbour's ginger cat sitting on top of their garden shed that was raised above the fence.

He stared at the cat in deep meditation and began to mimic it, licking his paws, and then glancing suspiciously at Charlie. He realised that he had to keep his composure as he was now inside the cat's mind. Through its eyes he looked at himself, standing at the back gate.

'This is weird,' he thought. 'I must sort my hair out soon. It's looking a bit dishevelled.'

Charlie, now inside the cat's mind, stood on all fours and surveyed his garden from the shed roof. There were a couple of officials carrying clear plastic bags out, containing pieces from the house. He went to walk but tripped slightly. It felt strange to have four feet, especially short stumpy ones. How the heck can a cat balance and be so majestic with these clumsy feet, paws or whatever? He gazed up towards his bedroom and then checked the back door, which was propped open with the kitchen bin.

He had to be careful as he'd only practised this once back in Terriana. He hadn't thought about how a cat's legs might move and it was hard to concentrate. He took another look at himself, staring with empty eyes in his direction, and thought, 'It seems safe enough to stay where I am in that alley.'

He started to place one paw in front of the other, with the back ones at the same time, circling the shed roof until he had the balance and movement right. When he was satisfied, he walked towards his garden and leapt onto a branch. His back two legs missed as he grabbed it with his front two paws; his claws sank into the wood so he didn't fall. He then managed to twist his back two legs up and gained composure on the branch. It was so difficult as in Charlie's mind he had two legs and had timed the leap to the tree perfectly, but he hadn't factored in the weight and length of his body and the two legs at the other end.

He stealthily moved along the branch and leapt, landing smoothly on the grass just at his back door. No one noticed as he quietly slipped in and passed through the kitchen door to the hall. That was when he saw the destruction.

It was as though the house had been the scene of a raging stampede. A man wearing plastic waved at him and growled, 'Grrrrrrrr'. Charlie laughed as he realised how stupid it looked from a cat's perspective, and he ran upstairs to his room. It was like a bomb had hit it, but it seemed that the officers hadn't entered it yet as items were barricading the door, although it was easy for a cat to get through and that's what he did.

He crawled through the space in the doorway with ease to look around. The tin foil fortress he'd built on top of the wardrobe was flattened in the corner but the four pieces of parchment were still there. He saw that they all now showed a design. He tried to lift them to read but realised that paws are not great at picking up sheets of paper. His bag was open on the broken bed and he eventually managed to place the parchment pieces inside using his mouth and paws. He could see the corner of the Tallamseen Book of Prophecy at the base of the wardrobe. Luckily, it was still there. He went to pounce towards it but something was tugging at his whiskers.

He shook his head and rolled onto his back, flailing his paws, as he tried to see what was pulling his whiskers. It didn't work so he headed towards a broken mirror by the bedroom door. As he peered into it, he leapt back with a meow and knocked a pile of rubble to the floor. His reflection had frightened him as he momentarily forgot that he was in the mind of a cat.

Footsteps were thudding up the stairs and seemed so loud in the ears of a cat. Charlie ran quickly through a hole below the bed as the officers arrived at the door and shone their torches.

'Don't move anything yet, we've not tested this rubble,' one of them said.

The other voice replied, 'Okay. Let's get the team up here next and retrieve evidence of what happened.'

They headed back down and Charlie manoeuvred himself from under the bed and sped towards the wardrobe. He could now see what was pulling his whiskers as it stood in front of him, trying to prevent him from going near the wardrobe. It was the pixiedown and Charlie saw the little fairy pixie clearly inside the fluffy shell. He tried to speak but all that came out was a plethora of meows. He was getting frustrated, so he headed back to the mirror, tapping on it for the pixiedown to watch. She understood and floated cautiously towards it.

The cat breathed onto the glass and then, using its paw, started to write the letters C H A R but soon reached the side of the mirror as paws are bigger and clumsier than fingers. Suddenly a pleasant lady's voice said, 'Oh my, Charlie, is that you?'

Charlie sprang back as he was taken by surprise that the pixiedown could talk. Regaining his composure, he nodded, and she started jumping in the air for joy, before heading towards the book.

He tried to bite into the edge of the book so that he could tug it, but it didn't budge. The pixiedown floated nearby, pointed a small stick at the book and surrounded it with sparkles. She beckoned Charlie to move back, then proceeded to raise the book onto the bed, and into the open bag. in a mini tornado of dust.

Luckily, the three parts of the wand were still in the school bag so there was nothing further they needed. They stopped and heard people coming upstairs, chatting. Charlie looked at the window and the pixiedown performed magic to create another mini tornado to open the latch. The cat leapt and used his paw to prise the window open.

Policemen were still in the garden, so they were careful not to attract their attention. Charlie could see that he was still in the alley, in a trance. He leapt back to the bed and tapped on the bag before leaping back to the window. The footsteps were getting close to the bedroom doorway and they were grateful that the bed and wardrobe prevented the police from having a clear view of the room. They had to act quickly.

The pixiedown used her magic to raise the bag towards the open window. The cat leapt to the neighbour's fence to let her know where the bag had to land, then he jumped off the fence into the neighbour's garden. The pixiedown managed to float the bag out through the window and it was almost at the fence when the bed moved and the officers came into view. One thought he saw something drop as the pixiedown released her magic in fright and floated out of the window unseen. He went to the window and looked out. There was only a cat in the neighbour's garden and police in the garden below. Luckily, he didn't spot the bag that was dangling on the neighbour's drainpipe near the window.

The pixiedown rested next to the cat, clearly exhausted. Once the officer had moved from the window, the cat leapt back onto the fence and, with the other officers busy in the garden compiling bags of evidence, he began to shimmy up the drainpipe. He paused and slid a little as his claws couldn't get hold of the plastic. Regardless, he continued up and managed to free the strap that was caught on a screw at one of the pipe joints.

The bag dropped with a thud on the fence and, as the cat diverted the officers' attention, the pixiedown used a little magic to push it so that it fell into the neighbour's garden. Meanwhile, the cat leapt down into the alleyway, walked up to Charlie and gazed into his eyes. As Charlie's mind drifted back into his body, the cat sauntered away, as if nothing had happened.

'I never want to be a cat,' he muttered, as he unlatched the neighbour's gate and retrieved his bag. Luckily, the neighbours kept their curtains closed when they watched TV in the living room.

CHAPTER 30

THE TALISMAN OF ENHANCEMENT

As Charlie closed the gate, the pixiedown settled on his shoulder.

'Charlie, it's great to see you again. I was so worried.'

'Wow, I can hear you now! That's awesome! I'm sorry I couldn't hear anything before. Come on though, we need to get back to my aunty's car because Mum is in the hospital and she's taking us to see her.'

'Charlie. It was your mum who caused all this.'

Charlie stopped rushing down the alley.

'What?'

'It was your mum. Well, not your mum exactly, as Sinistre used her as a host and I didn't realise until it was too late. All I could do was fly around her head until she swatted at me and destroyed the wardrobe. She saw the book and was about to pick it up but then she collapsed on the ground, as though Sinistre simply disappeared.'

'Oh, my! That must have been when we returned so he was forced back into Dennis.'

'Dennis?'

'Long story. Hopefully, Mum is okay. Let's go see her.'

'Sorry I let you down, Charlie. I was shocked. She took me by surprise.'

'No. Please don't feel bad about it. I think your distraction stalled her in the nick of time, to be honest. And it wasn't Mum, remember? There's something I need to add to the bag.'

Charlie pulled the wooden wand from his pocket and, as he unzipped the bag, it started to emit a brilliant white laser beam. The other three, already entwined, floated out of the bag and the wooden wand floated next to them. They melded together into a magnificently decorated wand of the elements of fire, earth, air and water. It moved into the bag and the design on the front cover of the prophecy book began to glow, brightly golden. Charlie had to cover his eyes and the pixiedown hid behind him.

He could hear his neighbours coming out of their houses. The gates in the alley were opening just as the light subsided and the books front design separated from the book, falling into the bag with a black leather-lace string attached. Charlie quickly zipped up the bag and left the alley.

'Come on, pixiedown, we can look at this later. I think we have brought too much attention to ourselves.'

They went from the alley where everyone was gathering, confused by the light that had appeared. When they couldn't see anything, they returned to their daily lives.

Charlie got into his aunt's car and the pixiedown settled on his shoulder.

'By the way, Charlie, my name's Felina,' she whispered in his ear.

Charlie smiled in acknowledgement and Aunty Kathleen started her engine to head to the hospital. Felina sat on Charlie's shoulder, on the opposite side to his cousin, so that she remained hidden, but was close enough to his ear to keep in contact.

Charlie fumbled about in his bag to find the design that had fallen from the book. He managed to grip it and pull it out. It had become an talisman with the same incredible design as that on his chest. There was a crest of the sky, the ocean below, the island and tree in the middle and a burning flame at the centre. The flame had turned into an elaborate crystal firestone which glistened orange in the sunlight.

'Ooooh, that's pretty. Where'd you get it from?' asked Louise.

Kathleen managed to glance in her rear-view mirror and saw the orange glow of the crystal as it lit up the back of the car.

'Wow, Charlie. What is that? Is it your mum's?'

'Not sure, it was just in my bag. I must have got it on one of my school trips and forgot about it,' he replied.

Felina whispered in his ear, 'Charlie, I suggest that you read the book as soon as you can. That talisman looks like it is full of magic to me and I think it may show you more, now you've completed your four trials. Maybe those parchments have answers too.'

Charlie accidentally said, out loud, 'Good idea!'

'What is, Charlie?' asked his cousin.

'In a minute, when I've finished looking at this, I've got a little puzzle we can play.'

'Oh, wow!'

He looked closely at the talisman which was the same design tattooed on both his chest and his father's. As he placed it around his neck, it dropped level with his tattoo and was exactly the same size.

The central stone glowed as a gentle breeze wafted against Charlie. He closed his eyes, breathed in and held it in meditation. A warm strength covered his body and he felt safe for the first time in a while. He smiled.

'That looks pretty, Charlie, and it glows,' Louise said, with a glow in her eyes too.

Charlie straightened his top over the talisman, to hide it. They were almost at the hospital when he pulled out the four parchments, each now with a design on them. He budged up and placed them on the seat between him and his cousin.

'C'mon then, Lou. You've always been great at puzzles. Let's try and make something with these pieces.'

Louise clapped with excitement and started to twist the pieces; even turning them over to try and make them fit. Sometimes they fit two together, other times three, but the final piece just didn't fit, no matter which way around they did it. They tried several times before they pulled up at the hospital. Even Felina was baffled.

When Aunty Kathleen was parked, she turned and stared at the pages.

'Hmmm, wait a minute.'

She stretched out and turned a parchment a few times, turned another one over and then folded it so that it was diagonally across the top of the other three and covered a third of the design of each piece.

It worked.

As she finished the fold, the paper sealed itself into an odd-shaped single parchment with an island she seemed to recognise. With a satisfied slap on it with her finger, she confirmed, 'That's it. But I'm impressed by how much puzzles have changed these days. How have those pieces become one picture with no sign of any breaks in it? It baffles me.'

She laughed and asked, 'How are you gonna use that puzzle again, now that it's fixed itself?'

'Wait, Aunty Kath. Does it mean something to you?'

'It looks identical to a place in Scotland where your mum, dad and I used to go when we were younger. It's at the northern end of Loch Lomond but there was an area we stopped at much further up the road, on the way to the Falls of Falloch, I think it's called. There was an island in the mist and it looked stunning. Quite scary, in some ways, yet beautiful at the same time. Well, it looks exactly like that island, and there was even a huge tree in the middle of it, even though the island was small. I thought I recognised it as I put the puzzle together.'

'Wow, thanks, Aunty.'

Charlie rolled the parchment carefully and popped it back into his bag as they exited the car. He looked at Felina and quietly said, 'We need to get there somehow, Felina.'

She agreed.

He slung his bag over his shoulder as they entered the hospital. He waited with Louise while his aunt went to reception to get directions.

'Right, come on then, you two.'

They followed her as she led the way along corridors and up some lifts. In one of the corridors, Charlie spotted Griff.

'Griff, how is Dennis?'

'Awww, Charlie, he's okay, I think. We've just been moved up here after waiting ages in Outpatients. His parents are in there at the moment, so I popped out to give them some space. He's unconscious but stable. How come you're here?'

'My mum. We had an intruder and she was attacked. She is in recovery here.'

'Oh no, sorry, Charlie. I really hope she's okay.'

There was a pause and Griff continued, 'Thanks, Charlie, for getting us through that place and helping us escape. I'm sorry for what we did to you at schools.'

'Honestly, as I said, don't worry. It's totally cool. Glad we can be friends now and put that stuff behind us.'

'Yeah, of course. Thanks mate,' Griff said, hugging Charlie. 'You best go see your mum. They're waiting for you,' he said, nodding towards Charlie's aunt and cousin.

'Okay. See ya later, Griff, and wish Dennis well from me.'

'Will do, catch ya laters, Mate.'

Charlie caught up with his aunt and cousin. After a few more corners, they arrived at his mum's ward. They entered and could see how fragile she looked, lying in the bed. She was battered and bruised, with her arms and legs bandaged.

Charlie ran to her.

'MUM, aww, Mum,' he said as tears started to form.

Jennifer tried to lift her bandaged arm to comfort him but it was painful, so she rested it and spoke.

'Charlie, it's okay. This isn't your fault. Yeah. I know what you're thinking. Honestly. I'll be okay. I blanked out and only regained consciousness in here. The police have already spoken to me about potential intruders. I have a feeling you and I know differently, after that experience we witnessed with your headmaster but that's totally hush-hush, okay Charlie?'

Charlie nodded before his aunt and cousin joined him at his mother's side.

'Headmaster? Charlie in trouble, is he?' joked Kathleen, only catching half of the conversation.

His mum laughed and said, 'Noooo, just telling Charlie he must be on his best behaviour when he goes back to school and avoid the headmaster.'

His mum continued talking to her sister, and Louise was also listening, so Charlie decided that it would be the ideal moment to slip away discreetly. He knew that the time was ticking and that Sinistre would soon be hunting the book. He went to the toilet further along the corridor and locked himself in the cubicle. He took the book from his bag and opened it. The pages were all legible now, so he continued to read.

He discovered that the talisman he was wearing was freed from the book when all the challenges were completed. It was known as the Talisman of Enhancement. Whatever magic, power or thoughts the wearer has, the talisman enhances it tenfold.

He felt a coldness when he read about Sinistre's eyes always watching and that future readers of Charlie's story would see his evil piercing red eyes on the book cover. He briefly closed the book, holding his hand on the page he was on so as not to lose it and, sure enough, the red eyes were looking out from the cover. He shuddered, wondering if it was a warning and was unsure if they had been there before. He continued to read.

He discovered the significance of the design as it contained the four elementals. Fire in the flame. Air in the bright blue sky. Earth in the island with the campfire and the tree. Water in the ocean.

The completed parchments would show the location of the portal in the human world which leads to the elemental world. It was the only active two-way portal between the worlds and must be closed to prevent forthcoming chaos in the human world. That was more than enough for Charlie.

He closed the book, knowing what he had to do and where he had to do it.

He returned the book to his bag. He couldn't hear anyone in the bathroom so he spoke to Felina who was quietly perching on his shoulder.

'Felina, we need to get to that portal today and seal it, somehow.'

'We do, Charlie. Your human world will not stand a chance against the chaos.'

'Yeah, exactly. We are going there today because Sinistre isn't gonna lie around while this book exists. He has seen it now, which makes his hunger stronger.'

'You amaze me, Charlie, how you've picked up so much in such a short time. I'm so happy to be your guardian and will be loyal to the end. Let's do this.'

He nodded and they left the cubicle. A gentleman, holding his hands under a tap with no water running, stared in a peculiar way at Charlie as he passed.

They arrived back in the ward, where his mum and aunt were still nattering away and his cousin was looking a little bored, as she fiddled with a black dial at the end of the bed, next to a clipboard. They spoke for another half-hour and Charlie was getting a bit impatient. Aunt Kathleen and Louise finally said their goodbyes.

As they left, his mum said to him, 'Charlie, please be careful. Don't do anything reckless. I saw what that creature has in his head, and it's dark and hateful. I know that you're planning something, as you're just like your father. Just make sure you stay safe, okay?'

Charlie nodded and kissed his mum on her forehead.

'I'll see you later, Mum. Love you loads.'

'Love you too.'

She smiled proudly as Charlie left the ward to join his aunt and Louise. While they were heading along the corridor, Charlie stopped near the ward where Dennis was and turned to his aunt.

'Thanks for bringing me here. You two can head home as I'm going to see how Dennis is and stay a while with him. Griff or Dennis's parents will give me a lift to yours later.'

'As long as you're sure, Charlie. I'll come with you to check, just to be safe. A lot of peculiar things have been happening recently.'

His aunt followed him to the ward where Griff's and Dennis's parents were with Dennis, his mother, holding his hand. Aunt Kathleen checked with them if it was okay and offered her best wishes. Dennis's parents looked confused, but agreed to take Charlie to his aunt's once they left the hospital. His aunt was satisfied.

'I'll see you soon, Charlie. You can choose tea tonight.'

She smiled as he waved, and she left the hospital with Louise.

'Charlie, what're you up to?' Griff whispered.

'Griff, you're gonna have to cover for me, okay? Just tell Dennis's parents that it's okay and I've gone with my aunt instead.'

Griff gave Charlie a look saying, 'Okay, and don't be a putz. Just stay safe, okay? I wanna see you at school on Monday. Oh, how was your …?

Griff stopped in mid sentence seeing Charlie already rushing away. He made his way out of the hospital's other entrance, to be sure he wasn't seen. He found a secluded place by some large skips and said, 'Buckle up now, Felina. We're heading north for Scotland.'

He checked where the sun's position was to get his bearings for a northerly direction. He then meditated for a moment and managed to create a small tornado to surround them with boxes and dust. He started a jet stream below his shoes and lifted from the ground into flight, remaining hidden in the tornado disguise as they headed north.

Some passersby were fascinated by the dust tornado.

CHAPTER 31

THE POWER OF TEN

Sinistre had almost depleted his energy when he left Dennis in the woods of the human world. He clambered out of the portal back into his world, exhausted and almost transparent. The dark green and blackness of his rotting skin returned as he lay next to the portal pool.

He was back in his world by the Cave of the Dark, with Lezaragons Mount just a short distance away. As his energy returned he got up and, avoiding the mouth of the cave, headed straight for the mountain. He spread his arms and flames ignited under his claws as he rose to the top of it. He opened his arms wide to the storm cloud above.

'My children, come to me now. We have work to do,' he called with an evil hiss. It took a lot out of him as he almost lost his balance.

'Children, the time isssss almosssssst upon ussss.'

The red eyes of the demonuettes appeared randomly around the dark cloud. There were a lot fewer now as they flew down to meet their creator.

Sinistre walked among the crow-type creatures and tapped the red, razor-sharp beaks on ten of them. He waved his claw as the others flew back to the cloud, while his selected ten remained, flapping their wings. He held his side as he felt a stitch where he hadn't yet rejuvenated. To rebuild himself he would have to stay in his realm for at least twelve hours but it had only been about four. Above all, he wanted to destroy that book or the boy he despised.

A black cloud appeared as he waved his claws and, as he swirled them, he created a circular hoop of cloud. In its centre, a picture emerged of the Tallemseen Prophecy. He signalled to the demonuettes, 'Thissss book is to be +dessssstroyed.'

The demonuettes cawed in a frenzy as a signal that they understood. Sinistre closed the swirl and then reopened it revealing an image of a boy with dishevelled brown hair. They cawed wildly as they recognised him.

'Thissss isssss Charlie. You're to kill thissss boy on my command.'

The crow creatures cawed even louder, looking keen to get on with it and have it done.

'Come my babiesssssss, consssssider thisss as the ssstart of chaosss in the human world.'

Sinistre gave an evil cackle as he flew to ground level with the ten demonuettes following closely. They arrived next to the Cave of the Dark, but even the crow creatures avoided the mouth of the cave as they approached the portal pool.

Sinistre pointed to one of the demonuettes which came closer. He then pointed at the pool indicating it should go in but it wouldn't go near. Sinistre suddenly grabbed it, tightening his claws around it. The other nine manoeuvred back slightly as Sinistre threw the crow at the pool. It lost a few feathers in the process before going through in a flash. He then turned to the others to follow suit. They dived in unison, followed by Sinistre, becoming a mist of dark entity as he sank into the pool portal.

***

Charlie had to make a stop, not knowing exactly where he was but that he had been heading north for a couple of hours. He made sure that he didn't fly over the sea during his journey so that he wouldn't leave the United Kingdom.

He could make out a service station below and started to descend. Felina peeked from under Charlie's collar, accidentally tickling his neck which made him laugh and wobble slightly when he tried to land. He'd spied a copse next to the garage, landing there, managing to manoeuvre through the branches far enough away from the main entrance to the service station so as not to draw attention. After using the bathroom, he went into the newsagents, buying a ham and cheese sandwich, Irn-Bru which seemed prominent in the fridges and a packet of cheese and onion crisps.

He asked the lady at the till where he was, as well as directions to Loch Lomond. Her accent was recognisable and Charlie knew he must either be close or was already in Scotland. He didn't get many directions other than to follow the motorway northwards and that he would see signs for the loch. Charlie left and ate his snack, satisfied that he was travelling in the right direction. He set a droplet of Irn-bru on his fingertip to let Felina try it. She managed a tiny slurp before she burped loudly and held her mouth in embarrassment.

Charlie laughed and she burst out laughing too, having perked up with the taste of the drink. Charlie binned his packages and returned to the copse, making sure no one was looking. It would have been easier if he had a phone and could use GPS. His parents didn't want him to be involved with technology as it was corruptive, but they might consider it when he was eighteen, so there was a while to go.

He flew northward at speed and experimented with using another power by asking the breeze for directions as he once heard it speak to him. Making sure that he was travelling at a straight cruising altitude, he closed his eyes and whispered, 'Please guide me towards the Falls of Falloch and the northernmost part of Loch Lomond.'

He concentrated and even his whispers sounded like the breeze itself. Although he was cruising he had not realised he was slightly off course until he saw that motorway was not below him. He started to feel lost, but then he heard it.

A whistling voice in the breeze said, 'Veer sliiiiiightly left.'

Charlie felt confident as he obeyed and turned slightly left. It wasn't long before he spotted the motorway again and the breeze spoke in another whispery whistle, 'Staaaaay on this road, Charlie, for another fifty-two miles. You will then need a road they call the A82.'

He followed the instructions and kept a good direction as the wind hardly had to advise him. He passed over a lake and decided to take another quick break, so he landed in a woody area, again away from attention. He walked out and followed a winding path to an open area where there was a large aquarium, a few people playing the bagpipes in their kilt uniform and a shopping centre with cafés, and clothes shops, amongst others. There was a statue of a seal overlooking the water. Charlie popped into a café where he ordered a cup of tea and a piece of Scottish tablet that was on display at the counter. It was incredible, melt-in-the-mouth fudge, but much nicer than he had ever eaten. He quickly finished his tea and, as he left, he noticed the Loch Lomond fridge magnets, so he was very close to his destination. He went back to the wooded area, took off discreetly once more and continued over lots of high hills and a couple of smaller mountains. The loch seemed to give way to a large river with a very busy road on the left. He could see but a milky veil of mist covered everything.

Coincidentally, he spotted flashes of light on a tiny island in the large river that seemed to narrow further away from the loch. From above, he could look ahead and just make out the great waterfall that he thought must be his destination. He descended cautiously and landed safely in the woods near the island to get a closer look.

'Felina, are you able to get closer? I think something's going on there and I need to find out, as I can't see what those flashes are. It looks like that's where the portal is, so be extra cautious.'

Felina set off immediately, flying gently toward the island. As she left, Charlie decided to hide his bag. He removed his new wand which fitted well into a deep pocket of his jogging bottoms. He slid his bag, with the book and parchment, into the thick bushes, making sure to cover his tracks. He watched a few more flashes, maybe eight or nine in total, coming from the tree on the island. Then he saw another flash and could just make out a tiny shadow, no larger than a tennis ball, which flew from the tree. It was as Charlie suspected; the flashes were from the portal. He realised they were in danger and was about to call Felina to return, knowing terrible things were going to happen.

Charlie began to shiver, knowing something bad was about to happen. He saw another ball of black smoke pop out of the portal and hit Felina squarely, as her golden coat turned dark. She darted around erratically before dropping onto the ground. Charlie wanted to scream out but he couldn't open his mouth. He slipped his hand into his pocket and held the wand's handle, unsure of what to do with it as he was used to creating magic without a wand.

The flashes became larger by the tree as the portal opened fully in all its horrifying magnificence. A large dark manifestation with glowing red eyes entered through it. Charlie froze, staring up as Sinistre entered the human world. Charlie looked around, still confused about the ball that hit Felina. He heard a rustling to his right and saw a stag. At that moment, one of the black smoky balls struck the stag's head and it dropped to the grass, shaking erratically, roaring in pain.

Charlie could do nothing but concentrate on the scene in front of him, as an osprey dropped out of the sky and landed on the bank across the river. Sinistre flew along the river, away from Charlie, gaining speed as he went. Charlie used his enhanced vision to spy where Sinistre was heading. Two people were sitting in a small white fishing boat on the river. Sinistre aimed at one of them and entered their ear at speed, making the man stand up rigidly and drop his fishing rod into the water. He then began to shake violently and dropped into the boat. His boating partner looked to help as best he could but the boat was rocking so much, it made it difficult. But then, a huge wellington boot appeared from below the waterline and kicked him in the face. He fell into the water, taking his rod and satchel with him, while the man in the boat lay in a strange position.

Charlie was relieved to see the fisherman clamber up onto the bank, not far from the boat. However, being focussed on the fisherman, Charlie hadn't heard something approach him from behind. His concentration was broken when he felt a prod in his upper back. He turned slowly and noticed the end of a huge antler. Charlie looked to the ground where the stag had fallen but it was no longer there.

The antlers pushed at his back, budging him forward into the clearing. The man on the boat glared at Charlie, leaning his head to one side in interest. He raised his arms and the boat began to move of its own accord towards Charlie.

Charlie noted the busy road on the opposite bank and didn't want the people there to be involved. Without hesitation, he pulled the wand from his joggers and incanted a spell while swirling it in the air. He pointed it towards the road and the mist moved, becoming even thicker, eventually producing a long wall of thick pure white mist along the opposite bank. It hid the road from view and even the car lights beyond the mist were obscured. Charlie put the wand away and there was applause from the boat, as it neared the shore.

'What an amazing display, Charlie. Do you think that ssspell will protect you sssomehow? I think not.'

The man dismounted the boat and stepped onto the bank to join Charlie. He went nose-to-nose with him, sniffing the air and staring at Charlie with his big dark onyx eyes.

'I sssee you've become acquainted with one of my apprenticesss to the new human world, Charlie,' as he pointed behind him to the stag, which was still pushing its antlers hard against Charlie's back.

Sinistre continued, 'He'sss a beauty, isssn't he? Never realisssed your human world had sssuch ssstrange creaturesss. Why not meet my other friendsss? I believe you know one of them very well.'

He raised his arms and stepped back from Charlie with a huge grin allowing a plethora of animals and birds to climb and fly to the bank, joining him by his side. Charlie counted nine in total, including the stag; all with glowing red eyes.

CHAPTER 32

BATTLE AT THE PORTAL

'A m I meant to be impressed?' Charlie responded with a grin.

Sinistre smiled and stepped to the side. There was a black pixiedown hovering by his head; poised and ready to attack.

'Now then, Charlie. Where'ssssssss the book? Don't make me asssssk again.'

Charlie shrugged his shoulders and answered, 'Why'd I even tell you?'

'Becausssse of thissss.'

With that, Sinistre threw his hands towards Charlie. Two flames appeared from them, which shot forwards. Charlie didn't have time to react but he felt a warmth on his chest and the wand in his pocket reacted by creating a light arc around him which deflected the fireballs to the river which were extinguished by the water.

Charlie instantly leapt towards the loch. He flew with effortless grace across the surface, holding his arms apart using the gentle flight of air magic. It seemed as though the combination of the wand and talisman gave him more power. He felt the chill of danger but also the warmth of protection.

He heard a faint cry behind, 'Get him,' as he moved away from the island and the portal. He took the wand from his pocket as he moved along the bank, holding it out to thicken the mist and hide the scene from the road. He returned to where he had been and, out of nowhere, Felina smacked his face, causing him to lose his balance, landing hard against the edge of the bank and dropping his wand, which rolled into the river. He dived in after it just as Felina was about to hit his face again.

Initially, it was cold and dark but a small bright orange light pulsated from his chest. Another light came from the riverbed and started to float up towards him. Charlie realised that he could breathe, and the dark water was clearing. Just then, two fish with red glowing eyes torpedoed into his stomach, winding him. He curled himself up, holding his stomach, as he sank to the riverbed.

He tried to reach the wand but a large brown furry creature grabbed it and swam with an up-and-down wobble, propelled by a large paddle-like tail.

The two fish shot again towards Charlie like torpedoes and he barely dodged them as they went straight by where his face was. They were silver with a red stripe along the side of their bodies; rainbow trout but possessed. He decided to stay underwater and deal with these two, as he knew it would be harder to take on all the creatures at once.

He concentrated on where the furry animal went and, just as the fish darted back again, he shot forwards like a torpedo and they missed their mark. He soon caught up with the furry creature and saw that it was a beaver, with glowing red eyes. He shot a sonic wave towards it which caught its tail, throwing it off course, and it instantly dropped the wand. Charlie looked behind and saw the trout coming straight at him at full speed. He didn't want to hurt the creatures and looked around for some ideas.

By now, the beaver had regained control and was also heading towards Charlie. He managed to dive below as the three collided above him. The disruption caused a fountain on the surface of the water, attracting the attention of the other creatures on the land.

The beaver was winded in the collision and struggled to reach the surface. Charlie directed a sonic charge to help it reach the riverbank before it suffocated. It was almost catapulted from the water and stayed on the bank breathing rapidly.

The trout looked at Charlie with their glaring red eyes. He estimated they were almost forty inches long. Their jagged teeth were showing in a horrific grin. This took him by surprise as he had never studied fish and only imagined jaws to be on a shark.

He set his water-jet power in motion and returned to the island to see if there was something he could use from there. He kept close to the surface with the trout in pursuit.

From the bank, Sinistre stood, watching them return and he signalled the osprey to begin his hunt. The huge bird of prey circled, increasing its speed as it went higher into the sky, keeping its eyes on the target below the surface of the water.

Charlie suddenly became aware that he was in danger as not only did his body feel it but the talisman began to glow again in warning. He decided to speed up. The osprey had half-folded its wings, heading for the water. At the last moment, its talons snapped forwards to strike beneath the surface. Since Charlie increased his speed, so too had the trout. The bird's talons missed Charlie, but ripped through one of the fish and raised it from the water. As the osprey proceeded to eat the trout, its red eyes faded and the entity within diminished.

Sinistre went into a rage.

'You fool, you kill it if you kill its host. Have you not learnt anything?'

He raised his claws in the air and shot a flame bolt at the osprey. The bird's feathers smouldered, there was a final squawk, and it dropped dead on the bank.

'Now, let that be a lesssson to you other foolssssss. Forget the book, it's time for Charlie to die,' Sinistre cried out.

Charlie saw the spectacle and could hear what was happening through his enhanced hearing ability. The remaining trout also saw what happened and made no attempt to attack him.

The animals started to gather. They stamped their hooves, squawked and all the other noises animals would make in agreement. The trout turned to Charlie and the red glow in its eyes faded as a small dark smoky ball left through its eyes and the fish darted away. Charlie readied himself for impact, but the smoky entity moved slowly a short distance from him so that the edges of Charlie's shield turned a slight luminescent blue as it got close, but soon faded as it headed towards the island. There then seemed to be a camera flash and Charlie saw the small ball slip back through the portal unnoticed by anyone else.

Charlie looked over at Sinistre and the animals which were still making savage noises. He felt sorry that he was unable to help the osprey and the first trout, as he exited the water near the bank where he helped the beaver to shore. A warm breeze spun around him, drying him as he walked.

The beaver was still recovering, his eyes were faded and slightly red. Charlie spoke.

'I know you can hear me. You saw what your master did to your kind and, even though I know you're trying to kill me, I'm not gonna harm you. Every animal deserves a chance no matter what you were in that realm of the elementals. One of you that was in the fish has left through the portal. There may be a chance that you can do the same.'

The beaver shook a little as smoke escaped from its mouth, slightly faded, almost greyish black. The tiny entity moved slowly towards the island in the direction of Sinistre and the others but then shot into the woods. The beaver recovered and splashed into the water, swimming away from the commotion.

A fox with glowing red eyes appeared from the woods. Yapping in a high squeaky bark, it alerted the others to where he was. As they approached Charlie, he looked up, projecting himself into the air, using flame shoots. Two magpies with glowing eyes gave chase.

Charlie darted here and there before rising higher and flying over the treetops, evading the magpies' pecks. He was struggling to stay up, as fatigue began to set in. He remembered a movie where the hero had weaved in and out of trees and the pursuers were knocked from their floating bikes. He smiled to himself and weaved between the trees. The magpies followed relentlessly, with their eyes becoming fiercer as the red glow seemed on fire.

Charlie slowed until they were a few inches from his feet. Then he waved the wand at the branches ahead which made a pathway for him. When he went through, he flicked the wand and the branches snapped back into place, swatting one of the magpies into the tree opposite, knocking it out as it fell to the ground.

The remaining magpie avoided the tree by flying cautiously at a distance to one side. It continued pursuing Charlie as he weaved between the trees before lowering himself to the ground, at the foot of a huge tree. He was exhausted and thought he'd lost the magpie, but it had landed discreetly not too far away, watching him. He noticed the magpie as it slowly headed towards him, but he also saw something furry squatting behind it, moving stealthily closer. He realised it was a fox but wasn't sure if it was the one that had alerted the others.

Charlie called to the magpie to fly away but it raised its head, about to call out, when the fox leapt, sank its teeth into it and, with frantic flaps and loosening feathers, the bird's red eyes faded as the fox disappeared into the woods with its prize.

Charlie climbed a tree and settled in the large branches to rest for a moment, having safely popped the wand into his deep pocket. He thought he heard a rustle and saw a bug fly off. He relaxed, unaware that the bug was a little dark pixiedown watching his every move. It was now heading back to Sinistre to report what it saw, along with Charlie's location.

Charlie closed his eyes, meditating for a moment. He could hear the nature of the woods which made him feel better and his energy rose. He visualised the island and the area surrounding it, conjuring images in his mind as he began to formulate a plan to seal the portal. The hills and small rocky mountains were not far away but, unfortunately, it meant the tree would have to be in darkness. He would have to go through the thick mist, over the busy road and back. He was in a prime location and could do it, with a little magic.

It only took about five minutes but that was enough. Charlie opened his eyes to become fully aware of his location and whispered to himself, 'This is insane,' as he shook his head. The reality of his situation was starting to sink in.

He put his hands on his chest, holding the area where he could feel the talisman and leant his head back on the branch. Closing his eyes, he whispered with sincerity, 'Please help me through this and make it right.'

He pulled his hands away, opening his eyes. A momentary glow radiated from the talisman, which slowly went out. He patted the tree, whispering, 'Thank you.' He wasn't sure why but he wanted to thank it for allowing him to sit, and he climbed back down rather than use magic.

He became aware of rustling through the woods and the possessed man from the boat came through the bushes, along with some of the animals and the pixiedown floating by his head. The man had an awful smile on his face.

Charlie stood tall, showing no fear, as they formed a semi-circle around him, with the tree blocking his way behind.

CHAPTER 33

THE DARKEST HOUR

Charlie clenched his hands next to his pockets, not intending to use the wand. There were too many animals that could easily take it from him. The stench of Sinistre's breath became apparent as he approached, and, when he spoke, spittle hit Charlie's face.

'Charlieeee, it looks like thissss iss the end of the line for you. Any final requessstsssss?'

The animals jumped with excitement and Felina was content to sit on Sinistre's shoulder. At that moment, Charlie felt the warmth of his talisman as something solid clenched his arms tightly. He was lifted and placed in a position where he was free to run. The tree he stood by had somehow come alive, maybe from the magic of the talisman. The branches, that grabbed and rescued him, whipped back and thumped down, surrounding Sinistre and the animals with a wooden cage.

Charlie turned and ran. The dark Felina followed as she easily got through the bars of wood. Sinistre shouted out, 'Charlieee, you haven't got rid of me yet. I'll enjoy killing you sssslowly when I get my clawsss on you. I'll rip you to shredsssss.'

This unnerved Charlie a little as he ran towards the riverbank, which was closest to the island. Suddenly, he was struck on the back of the head. The pixiedown had caught up with him and sent an electrical ball while in pursuit. Charlie fell to the ground partially paralysed, with his head throbbing, as the dark pixiedown wavered about his eyes.

'Felina … this isn't you. Please hear me in there. I know you can fight the thing that's taken you. Please. It's me, Charlie.'

'Haha, Charlie. You think you can bring your little precious fairy back do you, with your begging? Got to admit, I'm enjoying watching you beg. My master will enjoy this.'

'Felina, come on, you got this. Listen to me.'

But the pixiedown laughed and proceeded to send electrical charges through his right arm, causing him to scream in pain. Fortunately, Charlie was left-handed and the wand was in his left pocket. He slipped his hand in, unnoticed, and grabbed the tip. He glanced at the portal of the tree with a plan whirling in his mind. He rolled suddenly towards his left, brought out the wand and pointed it directly at Felina.

'Sorry, Felina, and whatever has a hold over you. This is for your good. Honestly, for both of you.'

The dark pixiedown shot a huge electrical bolt towards him but it didn't hit the mark. The wand projected a luminescent blue light that captured the bolt in mid-flight, catapulting it back at Felina. It also held her in place. She felt the charge and tried her best to escape from the confines of the blue force.

'Oh, Charlie. I remember now. Oh, thank you. I'm back,' she cried.

The dark tone of her seedling cover proved that the entity possessing her was still active. Charlie was struggling with one arm as the wand felt like a fishing rod with its hook in the water and the tugging on the line was pulling it in all directions. He managed to grip it tightly but it was difficult to keep control. As his right arm began to get feeling back, he shook it and was able to grab the wand with both hands.

'No hard feelings,' Charlie mocked, as he rolled himself up from the ground, maintaining the hold over Felina, trapped in the luminescent beam. He thrust the wand backwards above his head and then forward towards the island, releasing the beam as it was about to hit the portal. Felina was hurled into the swirling sheen which flashed and she vanished.

Charlie heard loud cracks from the wood and realised that the animals and Sinistre had escaped. He looked towards the mist and knew he had to go through it to reach the rocks at the base of the hills, which he was planning to use to cover the tree and seal the portal within.

He went for it, with no time to lose. He set his flame jets on his shoes and sped through the mist on the other side of the lake, over the busy road, high enough that he was able to get over the traffic unseen. He spied three rocks that would fit around the tree perfectly. He closed his eyes as he imagined his hand lifting them and he opened his eyes to see them floating, and waiting for his next move.

He flew high again, heading back through the mist with the three huge long rocks and reached the island. With careful aim, he released one of the rocks and it embedded itself upright in the perfect spot, next to the tree. He dropped the second rock and it too landed exactly where he needed it.

Charlie looked up as he saw a magpie heading straight for him. It must have been the unconscious one from earlier. He managed to drop the last rock just before the magpie launched itself at his face. Fortunately, it also dropped exactly where needed, leaving the tree unharmed and surrounded by a triangular pattern of rocks. The rocks were tall enough above the tree that a rock on top would not damage it.

Charlie was almost done, but he still had the animals and Sinistre to contend with. He flew to the riverbank by the woods, aware that the magpie was still in pursuit. He landed, slightly wobbly, and felt a warmth flow down his cheek. Putting his hand up, he felt a thick wetness and pulled his hand away to see blood. The magpie had caught his cheek when it impacted his face.

He ducked at the last moment when he noticed the bird was almost on him again. It flew into the bush behind him and tangled its wings, giving him a chance to grab it with both hands, which prevented the bird from panicking or damaging its wings.

Charlie was about to launch himself at the tree to throw the magpie into the portal. He bent his knees in preparation but, suddenly, the magpie's head did a full turn, snapping its neck in the process. The glowing red eyes faded and Charlie held a lifeless body.

'How did you like that, Charlie? That'sss what I'm about to do to you, right at the end when you can't endure the pain any longer,' Sinistre gloated.

Charlie gritted his teeth in rage and turned to Sinistre as he appeared from the woods with an evil grin.

'Why did you have to kill it? It's never done you any harm.'

Charlie's eyes welled at the loss.

'Everything musssst die in the end, Charlie. Even thissss decrepit body I'm in will wither to dust, just like everybody elssse. I can ssstop that by taking thisss pathetic world and, actually, I might conssider giving you thisss one chance to live if you agree to join me.'

Charlie carefully placed the dead magpie down and slipped it under a bush. Sinistre stood gazing, waiting for an answer. There were four remaining animals, two on either side of Sinistre. A stag and an adder on one side, a wallaby and fox on the other. Each of their eyes glowed with that bright red colour, staring in Charlie's direction, perfectly still and waiting.

'We all know that isn't going to happen, don't we Sinistre?' cried out Charlie, unafraid of the consequences. Sinistre leaned his head to the right and his face turned from a grin to anger.

'I'm going to ignore that, Charlie. I know you ssseem to have a love for thessse pathetic creaturess of the human world.'

He pointed to each of the animals standing with him.

'And even for the human race filled with foolsss.'

He proceeded to point towards the mist. Charlie noticed a tiny flash and was confused until Sinistre continued.

'You think this veil of white ssmoke isssss enough to hide that human sssscum from me, as they travel in thossse mediocre contraptionsss?'

Sinistre waved his arm and the mist started to disperse, leaving a clear view of the road with flowing traffic.

'Thissss, Charlie, issss your abssssssolute final chance. They'll sssuffer in front of your eyessss before I desstroy you.'

With a wave of his arm, a grey car was forcefully tossed into the air. As Sinistre turned his hand and slammed it downwards, the car was thrown down on its roof into an oncoming car. He turned and used his other arm to hurl a force, knocking several cars and a van off the road into the cliffs next to them. One car had such an impact that it exploded.

'No, Sinistre. No more, please.'

Sinistre chose to ignore Charlie's pleas and, with a spin of his hand, tossed another vehicle in the air, which fell onto another that was already upside down with people trying to get out. The breeze picked up, which brought several phoenix downs along with it from the woods. Sinistre pointed his finger towards them and set them ablaze.

Charlie froze with terror at the sight, not sure what to do. Then he heard a whisper in his ear.

'I'm here, Charlie. Thanks for saving me when you threw me into the portal. The demonuette left me as we entered since we can't co-exist there and it became itself again. Anyway, Charlie, keep him fighting because he's losing energy the longer he's here. I'm going to try and enter his mouth because that is the only way I can lock him in that body. It might buy you some time. You'll see why. I haven't time to explain.'

Charlie turned to see Felina fly into the woods, undetected.

'Wait, Sinistre,' Charlie called out, raising his voice above the sounds of collisions and horns and screaming from the road. Sinistre stopped and gave Charlie his attention.

'What about a challenge?'

'A challenge? You intrigue me, Charlie.'

'Simple one. I will allow you to tie me up and you and your animals can attack me for five minutes. If I submit within that time, I'll join you. If not, then prepare for what's gonna come next but you have to leave those humans alone, either way.'

Sinistre only saw one sure way of this to conclude as they'd have him trapped either way. So he gave a smug response, 'I accccept, Charlie.'

Charlie stood his ground waiting for the animals to get close and surround him. Sinistre went into the woods and gathered pieces of branches which he threw towards Charlie. There were a lot of sirens and blue flashing lights approaching the mayhem on the road across the river. It seemed that no one had any idea the crashes were created on this side of the bank. After all, why would they?

Sinistre lifted his arms, the wood spun and started to build itself into a large complex cage around Charlie. While it was building, Charlie recited in his head all the magic he'd learned from the four elemental books. The animals stared at Charlie to make sure he didn't attempt to escape. The cage was built and the animals, along with Sinistre, entered.

Sinistre proceeded to tie the doors with a vine and, as he opened his mouth, Felina quickly threw herself in. Charlie spotted this as Sinistre began to cough and choke. The other animals were spooked.

'Are you okay, Sinistre? Do you want some help?' asked Charlie, showing concern.

Sinistre raised his hand, managing to compose himself.

'Jussst a bug or sssomething, although I'm flattered you offered to help, Charlie,' he grimaced.

By this time, the events were starting to get noticed from the other bank and Charlie was afraid. He knew that he had to summon his energy into a spell that he'd never done and he didn't want to put anyone in danger. At least being inside the cage he was shielded from view, the wooden bars tight enough that visibility was impossible from the other side of the river. He looked at the island and knew that he had to get one more rock for the monolith surrounding the tree.

'I've tied the exit, purely as a precaution, Charlie, you undersssstand. This is the cage where you'll either walk away alive with me, as partnersss, or where your rotting corpssse will be found. Now, time to take turns, my dark wings.'

It started with the stag charging straight into Charlie, pummelling him into the side of the cage and winding him as he dropped to the ground. As his hands touched the dirt and grass, the adder gripped hold of them in its jaws, secreting venom. Charlie cried out as a red mark began to inflame and he felt giddy. He felt a punch to his cheek as the wallaby thumped him with its tail. The final strike was when the fox bit down on his other hand, drawing blood.

'Had enough yet, Charlie?' Sinistre taunted, taking great pleasure from seeing him in pain.

As Charlie staggered to his feet, the stag caught him unawares and threw him in the air with its antlers. He hit the side of the cage, dropping to the ground when the snake struck again, biting the same wound, doubling the pain. Without using the wand, Charlie tried to go into a meditation state but unsuccessfully. The wallaby distracted him as he gave his leg an almighty whack with its tail and the fox followed through with a deep bite to his ankle.

CHAPTER 34

THE AFTERMATH

As Charlie lay helpless, Sinistre decided it was his turn. He smiled before pulling his foot back and booting Charlie's side with full force. Ribs cracked and Charlie screamed in agony. He couldn't handle any more torture, but then a breeze circled his ear and whispered, 'Cloooose your eyes and concentrate from your heaarrrt.' Then another breeze circled his other ear and whispered, 'Feeeeaaar noooo pain, feeeeaaar no moooore. Rememmmmmber the darkest hooooourrr.'

The stag grabbed Charlie's arm with its antlers but, this time, he didn't budge. The stag backed up a little and Charlie made his best effort to sit up. Groaning in agony, he painfully crossed his legs while holding his side and then he closed his eyes. Concentration showed on his face with tears trailing through the drying blood and dirt on his cheek. The snake came to bite again but couldn't get near as the ground began to vibrate. Charlie kept very still with his eyes closed, without any groaning, now, seemingly relaxed. The wallaby sent its tail thumping toward Charlie's head but it rebounded and hit the wallaby so hard that it spun in circles before landing awkwardly on the ground at the far end of the cage.

'What'sssss happening? Kill the boy now,' Sinistre roared.

Charlie opened his eyes wide and the animals backed away when they saw huge flames within them, burning brightly. He slowly looked up and stared, unblinking, into Sinistre's eyes. He stretched his arms outwards and began to gently float with his feet dangling as he rose towards the top of the cage, still staring at Sinistre.

Even Sinistre began to feel afraid as he stepped back towards the door of the cage and tried to unravel the knot he had tied. Charlie began to turn slowly and, as he did so, his chest where the talisman lay seemed to burst into flame, and began to spread over his body. His legs took on birdlike claws and a tail began to flow in flame. He curled his arms into his flaming body and started to spin faster, tilting his head back. As he spread out his arms, they turned into large wings of fire, which broke the cage into pieces and Sinistre collapsed to the ground.

A large bird's head with a flaming beak formed from Charlie's head. He let out a roaring shriek and stared at Sinistre. Flapping his flaming wings, he remained in position. The other animals ran away and they suddenly dropped as the black balls of smoke left their bodies and sped to the portal, in fear for their lives. They left through the portal and four lights flashed in acknowledgement.

Sinistre sat dumbstruck for a moment, before saying, 'What power isss thissss?'

Charlie had become a large ancient phoenix.

By now, all the drivers on the opposite side of the bank were out of their cars, staring at the spectacle. The phoenix dived at Sinistre, who held up his hands in fear, already weakened by the magic he had been using. But the phoenix flew above his head and away towards the vehicles, rising higher as he did so.

Sinistre squirmed and tried to abandon his host. He grabbed the tree and squeezed, trying to concentrate on leaving the body but he couldn't. He began to panic and went to the boat that was still lying against the bank. The oars had floated away so he used his hands as paddles to head towards the island as fast as he could.

From a distance, the sky was orange with the light of the flaming phoenix. It was a spectacular sight with trailing burning feathers, as the bird carried a large rock in its talons. He headed straight for Sinistre, holding the boulder out towards him and half-folding his wings as if going into a dive. Sinistre screamed and quickly dived from the boat into the water to avoid the rock.

The phoenix rose at the last moment and squawked a satisfied laugh as he flew above the island, landing gracefully on top of the three rocks. He placed the final rock on the top perfectly, then perched there for a moment, watching the water for signs of life.

He found what he was looking for. A little further up the bank, a man was climbing out of the river and lying on the bank. The phoenix flew and grabbed the man with his talons, taking him on a flight just over the trees away from the onlookers. He began his descent and released the man on the ground.

Charlie was starting to return to his body, as he landed, talons turned into feet. As he leaned forwards, the wings retracted, his hands steadied his fall. He was still flaming, but returned to the shape of a boy. The flames slowly extinguished as Charlie dropped with exhaustion, next to Sinistre.

'What wassss that?' Sinistre whispered, hardly able to speak or move.

'Some ancient power, apparently,' Charlie shrugged.

'I've never sssseen the like of thisss power. You truly sssurprissssse me, Charlie.'

'Well, aren't you going to kill me now?'

'It doesssn't matter now, Charlie. You did what the Chosssen One had to do. We'd lossssst already.'

Sinistre lay motionless and defeated.

'To wield a power of an elemental heart guardian wasss unheard of, until today.'

'I guess it'll never be heard of in your world now either.'

Sinistre tried to answer and coughed, trying to release whatever was stuck in his throat. Felina left discreetly through his open mouth and hid in the undergrowth of the woods.

Sinistre answered, 'I wouldn't be ssso sure. You had thosssse demonuettes flying ssscared and if you hadn't ssssealed me in thisss body, I'd have gone with them.'

Charlie managed to get up onto his knees. There was the sound of a helicopter that was getting closer. He felt pity for Sinistre and was saddened by his state. He stumbled towards him with tears building up, although he tried to look away and blink a few times so it would not show.

It was the first time they had ever properly looked into each other's eyes. Sinistre's eyes had turned a lighter shade than the blackness Charlie was used to seeing.

Sinistre could hardly speak and smiled, before saying, 'Funny. I never noticcccced until now that you have your father'ssss eyessss.'

'You knew him?'

'I know him,' Sinistre smiled and coughed. 'And it seemsss he'll now remain in the world of the elementsss.'

Charlie smiled.

'That's all I ever wanted to know. If he was still alive. That's reassuring. I know he'll be okay.'

Sinistre chuckled and his last breath escaped as the man's eyes became hazel, although bloodshot, before he closed them and collapsed as a dark mist escaped from his lips and dispersed into nothing.

Charlie let his tears flow. He was happy with the knowledge that his dad was alive. But he felt a strange sorrow for Sinistre who seemed relieved to give up the fight.

Charlie began to feel dizzy and sick, with his hand still in pain from the snakebite. He crawled slowly towards the woods and Felina flew alongside him, remaining silent. He tugged at his backpack which was hidden under the bush, before clumsily putting it over one shoulder while balancing on his knees.

He crawled from the woods and raised his voice over the sound of propellors which was drowning the car horns on the road opposite.

'Thank you, Felina. Please don't leave me.'

He smiled tearfully and heard a whisper in his ear before he collapsed, 'I won't leave you, Charlie. And thank you too.'

He heard a radio getting closer and voices shouting, 'I've found a boy, get the stretcher.'

Then the sounds faded.

***

Charlie woke to the sound of beeps and footsteps in a busy room with curtains around him. A nurse was finishing writing something before replacing a clipboard.

'Nice to see you're awake, Master Wafe,' she smiled. 'We don't get many admitted with snakebites as bad as yours in the UK, and it looks like you've been dragged through a few fields.'

Charlie smiled as the nurse pulled back the curtains and, in the bed next to him, was a sight he did not expect. It was his mum. She was overjoyed to see him awake.

'My baby boy,' she cried as she pulled herself out of bed.

His mum was healing well. Charlie had a few tubes around him that made him feel like a string puppet.

His mum continued, 'Charlie, I love you so much, my son. What on earth happened to you?'

She hugged him and he winced a bit as it was still painful.

'How come they brought you up here, Mum?'

'Up here?' his mum laughed. 'I've not moved anywhere, my love. I've been here all the time. They flew you down here from some hospital in Scotland.'

'Wait? I'm confused. How did they find me?'

'Well, that's the strange thing Char. There was condensation on one of the hospital windows and a nurse called out for Charlie as it was your name that had been written on the window, with 'Vale of Leven' written next to it. I just said, 'That's my boy's name,' and they thought it was too much of a coincidence. They knew that hospital in Scotland and, when they called, you were there. They had you transferred. So how come you were up in Scotland then?'

Charlie explained as much as he could remember and his mum was impressed as well as concerned. She was relieved to know that it was all over regarding Sinistre.

***

A few days later, they were allowed to leave the hospital. Charlie's wounds and fever healed miraculously fast. Felina pointed out that the power of the phoenix also has the power to heal. It just took a little longer than normal being Charlie's first time. Aunt Kathleen had their home ready to return to after the police had given it the all-clear.

Amongst the mail on the table was the parachute charity event for Charlie. There were also a couple of newspapers and one of them caught Charlie's attention showing his headmaster. Mr Grimauld had been cleared of charges and admitted for therapy. Another headline mentioned the fake sightings of a large firebird at Loch Lomond, a hoax phoenix apparently, although the large stone monolith on the island couldn't be explained and had become a tourist attraction.

Charlie took his bag upstairs and placed the wand from his pocket into it. There was hardly any furniture in his room as everything had been taken away in the skip, so he tucked the bag under the bed.

'Are you there, Felina?'

The little pixiedown came out from under the bed.

'I was relaxing in your bag for a minute.'

Charlie laughed.

'Would you mind …?'

'… looking after the bag?' Felina finished for him. 'Of course, I don't mind.'

'Awww thanks, Felina. As always.'

'Well, I try my best, Charlie.'

'I think it's time I reassured Mum with the good news that we know Dad is alive.'

'Do you feel you should?' asked Felina.

'Yep, never been so sure in all my life. I think she needs to hear it.'

And with that, he got up excitedly and ran downstairs, calling to his mum.

***

ACKNOWLEDGEMENTS

I have so many people to thank big time for their help throughout this journey, to bring Charlie to you. Too numerous to mention everyone, but you know who you are - I'm truly grateful for the wonderful love and support I've received.

First and foremost starting with you, the reader, for joining and sharing Charlie's great adventure. Thank you for acquiring this book, it really means the world to me.

My family, Barbara and Roger Underwood (Mum and Dad), brothers Steven & Robert and my sister Caroline. Thanks for your patience, support and believing in me; love you loads.

Lynda Nash, a wonderful Welsh author and my incredible tutor while I was on a creative writing course where Charlie was born.

To Michael Heppell and his incredibly brilliant Write That Book Masterclass, bringing sparks of energy and inspiration back into my life, and for giving me the magic and motivation to continue Charlie's story.

Through taking part in the Masterclass, I've way too many to thank but honestly, you're all outstanding and I love and appreciate all the support you give. Special mentions to Matthew Bird for assisting me with the wonderful cover design and typesetting this book. To my wonderful editor Christine Beech who gave so much support and helped to bring the words to life. My amazing web designer Rob Townsend who did a magical job getting my website together. Rebecca Farrell for her creative art in the pictures she'd kindly designed for each chapter along with my phoenix logo, and her friend Nadia in her continuing support and for recommending Becca. Sarah McGeough and her wonderful support, advice and fabulous coaching.

My accountability teams who supported and pushed each other through the challenging *author-coaster* journey. Starting with 'The Write Club' with Marilyn, Carolyne, Helen, Sharon, Michelle and Alex. Followed by 'Higgledy-Piggledy', with Jackie, Stefanie, Lisa, Emma, Kath, Rosalyn and Michelle. And finally 'Positively Magical' with John, Carolyne, Sandra, Rosee, Christine, Sally, Alison, Jean, Juliet and Richard.

Special mentions to the London Writers Salon where their 8am writers' hour was superb in helping me stay on track with writing time every day.

My first book coaching community; Max, Ben and Anna with fantastic coaching through each important segment and bonus training in Write Your First Novel public group.

Hay House Writers training support programme with the fabulous duo Reid and Kelly. TJ Bren for his outstanding feedback and editing assistance for which I'm truly grateful. I must mention a huge thanks to John and Nicole McCallum at the really lovely Bus Stop Coffee Shop in Alexandria who kindly provided me a place and encouragement for my book launch.

My lovely Neigbours Colin and Ann who supported me throughout, helping me so much with transport and the most delicious homemade food while I was busy tapping away at the keyboard. I really could go on but I have to stop somewhere; thanks to all my friends for their awesome support, JohnJo, Fiona, Nurse Anna, Tadas, Rachel, Tricia, Gillian (get your grandpas story out, we need to hear it), Jill, Jeannie, Karl, Roger, Victoria, Eleanor, Andrea… and infinitely more. Thank You!

ABOUT THE AUTHOR

Paul Underwood is a professional magician, creative writer and author of the upcoming trilogy "The Elemental Chronicles."

Paul has spent the last decade creating and performing magic which gives his fantasy and adventure books for young adults a unique and creative air of mystery and illusion. His first novel *A Storm Incoming* from the *Elemental Chronicles* was published on 2nd May 2023, Paul's birthday.

He has performed magic on stage at the Raglan Festival in Wales and has table hopped with his magic in many UK restaurants and bars. Paul completed Creative Writing with Welsh author Lynda Nash, The Writers Bureau Online Course and the Write That Book Masterclass with Sunday Times No.1 best selling author Michael Heppell.

Paul resides in the stunning and mystical location of Loch Lomond in Scotland. He genuinely works from the cupboard under his stairs where he continues to create more books and magic.